The gulls came at them again, and Trevor pulled the three boys down with him, curling his body over them for protection. The birds dove at him, squawking furiously. Trevor could hear Markie crying and the wounded boy whimpering softly.

"In here! Quick!" The ship's captain held open the door to the bridge, not ten feet away.

Trevor had scooped Markie into his arms and started to rise when he felt a sharp blow to the back of his head and heard a triumphant caw. The sudden pain in his head made him dizzy, and he staggered.

The captain dragged Trevor and the boys into the bridge, then shoved the door shut, just as the gulls attacked. The lead gull smashed into the door's glass window with a thud.

Trevor could feel himself slipping into unconsciousness. His last thought was: It's a goddamn Alfred Hitchcock movie.

Then everything went black.

William Relling Jr.
BRUJO

A TOM DOHERTY ASSOCIATES BOOK

This is a work of fiction. All the characters and events portrayed in this book are fictional, and any resemblance to real people or incidents is purely coincidental.

BRUJO

Copyright © 1986 by William Relling Jr.

The author has quoted from the following copyrighted material:

"Start All Over Again," written by Casey Harrison, copyright © 1980, 1984 by Kingfish Music, Inc.

The diaries of Fr. Antonio de la Ascensión are in the public domain. The excerpts used were taken from *Los Angeles: Biography of a City,* edited by John and LaRee Caughey, copyright © 1976 by the Regents of the University of California.

All rights reserved, including the right to reproduce this book or portions thereof in any form.

First printing: December 1986

A TOR Book

Published by Tom Doherty Associates, Inc.
49 West 24 Street
New York, N.Y. 10010

ISBN: 0-812-52510-8
CAN. ED.: 0-812-52511-6

Printed in the United States

0 9 8 7 6 5 4 3 2 1

For Ann

AUTHOR'S NOTE

Brujo is a work of fiction. The characters in the novel exist only in the author's imagination, and any resemblance between them and people who live in the real world is coincidental and unintended.

However, the places described herein are real places, though visitors to and residents of Santa Catalina Island will recognize that I have changed some of these places to suit the needs of the story. As a famous someone once wrote, this is a monstrous impertinence and as good a definition of the word "novel" as any.

I'd like to thank the following people for their friendship and advice, without which this book would probably not exist: my instructors in the Professional Writing Program at the University of Southern California, specifically Mr. Paul Gillette, Mr. Ben Pesta, and the late Mr. William Goyen; Ms. Patricia Romano; and Mr. Marston Smith, who gave me the idea for *Brujo* in the first place.

I would also like to give special thanks to my friend Dr. John V. Richardson of the UCLA School of Library and Information Science for all of his help in researching this book. It couldn't have been done without him.

W.R.

But now ask the beasts,
And they shall teach thee;
And the fowls of the air,
And they shall tell thee:

Or speak to the earth,
And it shall teach thee;
And the fishes of the sea shall declare unto thee.

    Job 12:7–8

Prologue

George Shatto and A. C. Sumner were the first men to conceive of Santa Catalina Island as a resort, and in 1887 they purchased the entire island for $200,000. Shatto and Sumner were also responsible for designing the city of Avalon; late in 1887 they built the first hotel in the city—the Metropole—on a barren, flat tract of land fronting what the Santa Catalina Indians used to call the Bay of the Seven Moons. When the hotel's foundation was laid, workmen found hundreds of artifacts buried in the blackened, fish-oil-soaked ground, indicating that the site had been one of many places that were important to the extinct tribe which had once inhabited the island.

For four years George Shatto and A. C. Sumner worked hard at trying to establish Avalon as a fishing resort. Shatto hired surveyors to lay out the city's streets, auctioned off parcels of land to prospective homeowners, and arranged for a steamship to make biweekly crossings of the San Pedro Channel from the mainland. Unfortunately their efforts were mainly futile, and in 1892 they found themselves unable to meet their mortgage payments. Catalina was taken away from George Shatto and his partner in a sheriff's sale.

The island was bought by Joseph, William, and Hancock Banning—three brothers who, like George Shatto, envisioned Avalon as a resort town. In 1894 the Bannings formed the Santa Catalina Island Company, a family corporation devoted to the development of Catalina into a fisherman's paradise.

However, the Bannings also ran into trouble. In the early 1900s competing transportation interests who controlled cross-channel passenger boat service to Avalon began a bloody waterfront war that lasted for better than nine years. The Bannings helped form the Avalon Freeholders Improvement Association in 1909 to enforce law and order, but the waterfront fights continued. It wasn't until 1913, when Avalon was incorporated as a city, that things settled down.

But only for a while. Two years later, in November 1915, a mysterious fire broke out early one morning on the wharf. The fire was a disaster, as it not only destroyed the greater part of the city but dealt a crippling blow to the Bannings' financial fortune as well. Losses from the fire totaled more than a million dollars.

In February 1919 a syndicate that included William Wrigley, Jr., the chewing-gum magnate and millionaire sportsman from Chicago, bought a portion of the stock of the Santa Catalina Company. In October of that year Wrigley acquired a majority interest in the company, and a new era of development began.

At that time only a few people, who had bought lots from George Shatto thirty years before, owned property on the island—the rest of the land was held by the Santa Catalina Company. Most of the summertime vacationers held one-year leases on twenty-square-foot lots, for which they paid twenty-five dollars a year and on which they erected tents or built flimsy cottages. When William Wrigley took control of the Santa Catalina Company, he announced that all lessees could buy their property outright, and soon most of the land in Avalon was privately owned. This helped to establish the first permanent island population since the days of the Indians.

When William Wrigley died in 1932, his son Philip took control of the Santa Catalina Island Company, and for years he worked to transform Catalina to match *his* vision of what California should be. Philip Wrigley had thousands of plants barged over from the mainland, including huge, ancient palm trees which were planted along Avalon's beachfront. He also shipped in tons of fine sand, which were used to cover the city's rocky beach, and erected a low, curving wall along the front of Avalon Bay. Everything was paid for by the company. The entire town was given a face-lift as well, and businesses backed by company money built new façades on many of Avalon's buildings. Soon Catalina became a favorite vacation spot for many wealthy southern Californians.

World War II interrupted Catalina's growth cycle, and after the war—for better than twenty years—the island's tourist business fell off. The tiny wooden-frame houses that dotted the hillsides around Avalon Bay were repainted year after year, and the number of permanent island residents remained relatively constant, but few visitors from the mainland came across the channel. Tourists seemed to prefer the burgeoning Hawaiian resorts and the glittering Orange County amusement parks to the relaxed pace of Avalon. Except for the sport fishermen, who had always been attracted to the island, Catalina lay quiet and isolated.

In the early 1970s, however, Catalina was rediscovered, mostly by southern Californians seeking a quiet week or weekend. It was about that time, in 1972, that the Santa Catalina Island Conservancy was formed to preserve Catalina in its natural state. In 1975 the Conservancy received from the Wrigley family a $16-million gift of sixty-six square miles of land—approximately 86 percent of the entire island—including fifty-four miles of coastline. The Conservancy dedicated its huge portion of land to many uses, but particularly as a sanctuary for the many forms of plant and animal life that flourished on the island.

By 1975 Catalina was once more one of the most popular areas on the Pacific Coast, and since then more than 500,000 visitors have come to the island each year. The 42,000 acres owned and operated by the Santa Catalina Island Conservancy are technically open to the public, but the land's use is severely restricted. As a result, most of the visitors to Catalina must stay in the island's only open port—Avalon.

The city is slightly more than one square mile in area, and the year-round population is usually between 1,400 and 2,200. During the summer, though, there are as many as 10,000 visitors to Avalon in a day, an influx that often creates problems for the city's government and maintenance facilities. Consequently the best time to visit Catalina may be in the late winter or early spring, when it is off-season for tourists and there are comparatively few visitors from the mainland. Many of the islanders themselves are away as well—those who live there only during the summer and whose houses will be boarded up for several more weeks. Although a number of Avalon's restaurants and shops are closed at that time of year, the hotels remain open, and it is easy to find somewhere to stay. It is often during this time that Santa Catalina Island is one of the most beautiful and peaceful vacation spots on the face of the earth.

Friday

The Brujo awoke.

He awoke from a sleep that was not sleep. He awoke and felt the earth and sand covering him, felt the things that crawled in the sand and fed on his flesh.

He drew a breath and opened his eyes.

Darkness. Darkness unchanged from when he had been buried alive so long ago. The Brujo was not aware that he was blind, that the creeping things had eaten out his eyes more than a hundred years before.

He had been awakened by a disturbance, an odd vibration, an unusual sensation.

A voice.

They have returned, the voice whispered to him. *They violate the sacred place.*

Then it was gone.

The Brujo did not know how long he had slept. All he knew was that he had been awakened and that *they* had returned.

Now he would have his revenge.

One

Grace Mitchum's favorite time of the day was before the sun came up, when the only sounds she could hear were the noises of the night animals or the crash of the ocean on the shore. She always worked better in the early morning. It was a habit she had gotten into during her undergraduate days as a journalism major at Northwestern University in the 1950s. She had loved living near the water in Evanston, having grown up on a land-locked farm in western Nebraska, but living next to Lake Michigan had nothing on living next to the Pacific Ocean.

William Relling Jr.

Grace had been in Avalon, on Santa Catalina Island, for—now, how long was it? she wondered. It wasn't long after she had come west for the first time, after a movie studio had bought the rights to her second—no—her *third* novel, which had ended up as a dreadful television miniseries. That would be 1970, when people had often mentioned Grace's name in the same breath as Jacqueline Susann. The memory still caused Grace to shudder unpleasantly.

She had tried living on the southern California mainland for months, but found Los Angeles distasteful. Mostly it was the people, whom Grace saw right through—even the wealthy ones and the ones who were supposed to be "artists," from whom she expected better. They all fawned over Grace, and she was a constant guest at parties and film screenings and art exhibitions and benefits. But she soon became bored with LA, then angry, then merely impatient to leave.

Grace had been making plans to move back east when her lover, Celia, suggested a weekend trip to Catalina, just as a lark. Grace fell in love with the island at first sight.

She spied the "House for Sale" sign the second day of their visit, as she and Celia were bicycling back to their hotel from the botanical gardens in Avalon Canyon. That same afternoon Grace gave a check for the down payment to the real-estate agent whose name was on the sign.

That Celia hadn't wanted to move from the mainland genuinely surprised Grace. Hadn't Celia been the one to suggest that they visit Catalina in the first place? But she didn't feel about Los Angeles the way that Grace did, nor did she relish the quiet, slackened pace at which life on Catalina seemed to proceed. Celia issued an ultimatum—either come back to the mainland or forget the relationship—which had also been unexpected. But there was something so appealing about the island that Grace Mitchum simply couldn't not live here. She was *meant* to be here.

That was more than a dozen years ago, and clichéd as it sounded, everything had worked out for the best. Grace was easily accepted by the other islanders. She became politically and socially active in the community and was a familiar figure pedaling around Avalon with Bridey, her Scotch terrier, perched in her bicycle basket.

Never in her life before coming to Catalina had Grace felt so content, had such a sense of belonging. It was reflected in her work. She had written a half-dozen books during her years in Avalon, and all of them had done quite well.

She was working on a new novel, one that excited her tremendously. It was a love story set in the Far East in the late 1930s. She had become fascinated with the tales she had been told by another islander, a woman who had been living in Shanghai at the time of the Japanese invasion of China. As was usually the case when Grace was in the grip of a new project, she awoke each morning before dawn, tingling with anticipation, eager to be at work.

William Relling Jr.

When the clock radio next to Grace's bed buzzed at 5:15 on Friday morning, she was already up and dressed. It was still dark—the sun wouldn't rise for at least another hour—but already, in mid-March, it was getting light earlier in the day.

Grace switched off the alarm and wondered why her dog hadn't come springing into the bedroom. Bridey did that every morning when she heard the radio go off.

Grace called, "Bridey?" She listened for a moment, but couldn't hear the dog anywhere in the house.

Grace went into the kitchen, filled a teakettle with fresh water, and put it on the stove to boil. She stepped over to the refrigerator and pulled out half a grapefruit, set the grapefruit on her dinette table, then moved to a cabinet near the kitchen door and found a mug and tea bag. Grace paused by the back door and toed the little doggie slot at its base to be sure it wasn't stuck. Then she opened the door, poked her head outside, and called again. "Bridey!"

There was no answer save the distant rush of the surf. "Come on, Bridey!" Grace invited. "Come here, girl!"

But there was no sign of the dog.

Grace switched on the outdoor light and stepped from the house onto her backyard patio. It was very foggy and chilly—typical for the time of year—and Grace immediately wished that she had put on a sweater. She wrapped her arms around herself, shivering. There was a slight breeze, but except for the faraway roar of the ocean, all was quiet.

Which was odd. There were always animals about—usually birds like the sea gulls and ravens. Occasionally, too, other animals worked up enough nerve to come close to civilization. More than once Grace had shooed wild pigs or goats off her property, and one time she had frightened a mule deer from her backyard. The birds were *always* there. They would caw and chatter, sometimes making a terrible racket.

But this morning there were no birds. There was only the remote sound of the ocean.

The hairs on the back of Grace's neck started to tickle. She hugged herself more tightly. She was suddenly afraid for Bridey.

Grace turned back into the house. She came out again moments later, dressed in a heavy wool pullover and carrying a flash lantern. Grace moved away from the patio apprehensively, calling for her dog again.

The light from the lantern wavered ahead of her as Grace stepped cautiously, trying to force her imagination to calm itself. She remembered what Mr. Barker, her real-estate agent, had once told her. There were still a few bald eagles on the island who built their nests on the sheer cliffs that overhung the sea. The birds were rarely seen, but there were stories of an occasional eagle swooping out of the sky to snatch some small animal—a lizard or a field mouse or some such thing. Mr. Barker had told Grace about the eagles because one of his other clients had reported losing an Angora kitten that way.

Grace frowned. Bridey was a small dog, and there were any number of wild animals loose, literally in her own backyard. Eagles and pigs and goats and even rattlesnakes . . .

There. Something was ahead of her. Two tiny, glowing spots in the grass reflected the lantern's beam. Grace paused, then she stepped forward hesitantly, till she was right on top of the spots and could see clearly what they were.

Grace drew in her breath sharply and whispered, "Oh, my God."

Bridey lay at her feet. The light from the lantern glinted off the dog's open, dead eyes. Grace knelt down and examined Bridey carefully and had to clench her jaw to keep from becoming ill.

Bridey was on her back, all four paws splayed out awkwardly. Her head lolled to one side, her tongue sagged from her mouth. Some . . . *thing* had sliced open the dog's body from neck to belly. Bridey's heart and lungs, stomach and intestines, had been pulled out and lay bloody and glistening in the light, as if someone had begun an abrupt, crude dissection, then had just as abruptly stopped. Part of what horrified Grace was that she doubted that it had been done by an animal. It looked more like some kind of sadistic prank.

A noise overhead startled her. She pointed the lantern upward, but the light could not pierce the fog. She heard the noise again, the flapping of a bird's wings. Grace thought she spied a shadow, for an instant, as it moved across the sky.

She climbed to her feet quickly and took a step back toward her house to call the police. But before she could take a second step, Grace heard something else.

A whimper.

Grace turned to look back at her dog, and her eyes grew large. She cried to herself, *This isn't happening*!

Grace told herself that she had to be imagining that she saw Bridey's body shaking, as if it were being jolted by an electrical shock. She had to be imagining that she saw the dog turn her head and look up at her mistress with dead, black eyes.

She had to be imagining that Bridey snarled.

Two

The dog yelped outside the bedroom window.

Trevor Baldwin opened one eye and remembered that he had left the window open the night before to let the ocean breeze blow in unobstructed. The window curtains flapped lazily.

The dog barked again. Trevor threw off the sheet and blanket covering him and walked naked to the window. He noticed that, as often happened along the southern California mainland coast, the early morning low clouds had turned the sea and sky to gray. A breeze fluttered through and Trevor shivered. The dog let out another yelp, and Trevor pressed his face to the window screen. "Shut up, Burt!" he yelled.

On the other side of Trevor's bed, a blond head poked from under the covers. Trevor turned to look at the bed. He grinned.

A hand crawled from under and pulled the covers back over the head. "That goddamn dog of yours," came a soft, muffled voice.

Trevor climbed onto the bed on his hands and knees, sliding one hand under the covers. "C'mon, Valerie," he cooed. "Time to get up."

Suddenly Trevor goosed her, and Valerie Heath whooped, flipping off the sheet and blanket. She glared at Trevor sleepily. "When are you gonna shoot that goddamn dog, Trev?" she asked.

"We could always sleep at your place." Trevor rolled back under the covers, pulling them up to his shoulders.

"Good idea," Valerie said. "Then my neighbors'll see you, and they'll all wonder how I can be so low class as to be sleeping with a hard hat."

A smile turned up the corners of Trevor's lips. "So that's what you really think of me," he said. "A hard hat."

He had begun to play both of his hands over Valerie's body and she giggled. She pushed him away and tried to force a mock scowl.

"I knew it would come out sooner or later," Trevor said. "You only wanted me 'cause you knew I was good with my *hands*!"

Trevor had his fingers on both sides of Valerie's rib cage and he tickled her hard. She squealed and tried to pull free to tickle him back. "Stop it! Stop it!" Valerie cried, laughing.

She grabbed Trevor's ribs and he jumped back. Valerie was on him in an instant, pinning his shoulders to the bed with her hands.

"C'mon," she challenged him. "C'mon, tough guy."

Trevor's eyelids closed halfway.

"Oh, no, you don't," Valerie said. "Don't give me that bedroom-eyes bit."

Trevor reached with his right hand to caress Valerie's bare belly. Then, slowly, he moved to the insides of her thighs.

"It's not that easy, buster," Valerie said.

Trevor gave her a wink. "Oh, yes, it is."

By the time Valerie had taken a shower, dressed, and sat down at the small oak table in the breakfast nook off Trevor's tiny kitchen, he had already prepared a plate for her and was standing at the stove, turning sizzling pieces of bacon for himself. He wore only a towel that he had tied around his waist as an apron.

Valerie came into the kitchen and patted him playfully on his bare backside. "I love how you dress for breakfast," she said.

Trevor swatted at her hand with the spatula. "I read someplace that you should always fry bacon in the nude," he said. "That way you keep the fire turned down and it doesn't burn."

The bacon spat at Trevor, spraying his bare chest, and he howled.

Valerie was still giggling when Trevor sat down with his own plate in the chair opposite her. While they ate, he and Valerie talked over what they were planning to do for the weekend. Trevor had told her the night before that they were unexpectedly going to be a threesome, that his ex-wife, Claudia, was dropping off Trevor's son, Markie, later in the afternoon. The junior high school where Valerie taught let out at four o'clock, so she agreed to meet Trevor and his son at El Cholo, Mark Baldwin's favorite Mexican restaurant, for dinner at seven. After that, Valerie said, they could just play it by ear.

Valerie chewed a piece of bacon. "You didn't tell me how come you're getting Markie today," she said. "I thought he wasn't yours again till next weekend."

Trevor shrugged and poked at his plate with a fork. "Claudia and her boyfriend are going skiing, up to his place at Mammoth. Last good snow of the season."

"Ray the gynecologist?"

"Yeah." Trevor leaned back in his chair. "He's really not a bad guy, y'know. I'd love to have his job. Poking around in ladies' hoo-hoos all day long and getting paid for it? What a racket."

"You'd get bored in a week," Valerie said. "They all look alike."

Trevor eyed her evilly. "And just how would you know that, Miss Heath?" he asked.

Valerie threw her napkin at him.

* * *

BRUJO

After breakfast, Trevor walked Valerie to her car. He was still dressed only in his towel, and he flipped it at her as she pulled her little Austin-Healy out of his driveway. He held the towel in front of him as he watched Valerie make a left turn at the stop sign at the end of the street. The car sped up the hill toward Pacific Coast Highway, away from the beach.

Trevor turned back to the house, stepping along a flagstone path that led to a wrought-iron gate set in a high stone wall, not at all concerned that any of his neighbors might be upset by his bare ass. This is California, Trevor said to himself. Naked man on the street? Happens every day.

Trevor pushed through the gate into the patio area around the swimming pool behind his house. The thought struck him—not for the first time—that many of the houses along the beach in California were built backward. This part of his house—the garage, stone wall, pool, and patio—was the rear, but the gate that he had come through was the only way to get onto his property. The front of the house, the address side, was a sloping hill covered with vegetation, mostly the green and purple ice plants that grew like crazy everywhere from Santa Barbara to San Diego, but especially around LA. Trevor had done the landscaping for his house and had built the redwood deck that was his front porch. The only problem was there was no way to enter the front of the house from the street on that side. Weird.

Trevor had bought the house fourteen years

before, a little more than a year after he started his contracting business. He and Claudia had been married for three years, and he'd been only twenty-four years old. When he bought the house, its cost—even for Laguna Beach—was comparatively cheap, barely a fifth of what it was worth now. Today the price would be several hundred thousand dollars—and Trevor could still afford to pay it.

Trevor shut the gate behind him. Burt, his golden retriever, loped up to him happily and followed Trevor to the deep end of the pool. The man dropped his towel on the concrete edge, poised for a moment, then dived into the chilly water.

Trevor swam mechanically. He kept himself in good shape, and he could let his body do the work while his mind detached.

Like everything else in their relationship, buying the house had been Claudia's idea. As had been their marriage, Markie, and, finally, their divorce. What had shocked Trevor most at the time was that he had been so stupid for so long.

By the time Trevor was twenty-seven he had a beautiful wife and owned a beach home and a successful business. He loved them all, so it had seemed to him an even trade-off.

Claudia hadn't thought so. Trevor's workdays ran ten, twelve, fourteen hours long—partly because he didn't trust many people to supervise jobs on-site and partly because he enjoyed his work. At that time there was more than enough business for a building contractor in Orange County,

California. The area grew incredibly in the 1970s and '80s.

So Trevor was simply unaware that his wife was unhappy because he spent so much time at work. Claudia got pregnant with Markie, she told him, because she figured that a child would keep Trevor at home more. Which had happened. But Markie also kept Claudia at home, and as it turned out, that wasn't what she wanted, either.

Trevor boosted himself out of the pool and sat on the edge. His toes dangled in the water. If it wasn't for the house, he said to himself, I'd have gone crackers. It was the only thing in his life that didn't change, the only thing that was stable.

And now he had Valerie . . .

They had met only two and a half months before, at a New Year's Eve party, but by the end of January both Trevor and Valerie knew that they were serious about each other. Valerie was twenty-eight—ten years younger than Trevor—and had never been married. She told Trevor on their first date that she had all but given up on meeting someone whom she could love and still enjoy being around. At the time Trevor didn't know what Valerie meant, but now he believed that he was beginning to understand her. Valerie is an amazing woman, he thought. She's beautiful, intelligent, funny. And best of all, she can put up with me.

Trevor grabbed his towel and climbed to his feet. He padded through the glass patio doors into the house and on into the bathroom. He glanced at the digital clock on the shelf near the sink and

William Relling Jr.

smiled to himself. It was 8:35. At least he had cured his workaholism. Trevor hadn't been in before 8:00 A.M. in over two years.

He heard the phone ringing as he turned off the water in the shower. Trevor couldn't remember whether he had switched on the answering machine, and he trotted, still dripping, from the bathroom.

The machine was on, and Trevor picked up the phone receiver in time to hear Bradley Cusimano asking Trevor to call him as soon as possible. Brad was a real-estate developer for whom Trevor had worked on occasion. Among other jobs, Trevor had contracted Brad's ranch house in Mission Viejo.

"Bradley," Trevor said into the phone. "What's up?"

Brad greeted Trevor warmly, then told him that he was calling from a hotel in Avalon on Santa Catalina Island. Brad asked what Trevor was doing for the weekend.

Trevor was a bit surprised, because he and Brad weren't close friends. Then Brad explained that he had picked up some property on Catalina, and he wanted Trevor to be his guest on the island while they discussed business.

"I'd love to, Brad," Trevor said. "But I've got my kid this weekend."

"What the hell," Brad said. "Bring him along."

Trevor answered, "I'm also supposed to be doing something with my girlfriend—"

"Jesus Christ, Trev. If you don't wanna come, say so."

Trevor smiled as he pictured Cusimano's exasperated expression.

"Okay," Brad said finally. "I'm inviting all three of you. But you can pay for your own goddamn transportation."

Trevor accepted.

A half hour later he was tooling to his office in the BMW that he had bought the end of the past year. This is great, Trevor said to himself. Catalina was a place that Markie had never seen. Trevor would have to get in touch with Valerie at school and tell her about the change in plans, but he didn't think that it would be difficult to talk her into going.

Trevor smiled. Even if Valerie couldn't make it, and even if Claudia might scold him later for spoiling Markie, the trip would be worth it.

The darkness was still there, but the Brujo could feel the sand and earth that covered him grow warmer. He knew now that the voice that had awakened him from his long sleep had been *Chinigchinich*. The sun. His god was with him.

William Relling Jr.

The Brujo's mind *reached* out, seeking his spirit-brother, the raven. The raven would help him to remember.

His first spirit-vision had come to him when the Brujo was only a boy. The sun had spoken to him, introducing him to the raven, who was to be his protector and guide. It was the will of *Chinigchinich* that the Brujo become a shaman of the Pimugnan, his people.

He had been named "Brujo" by the white priests, whom he distrusted, even though they had settled on the mainland long before he was born and had befriended the Pimugnan. The priests told him that in their language the word meant "sorcerer."

The Brujo remembered the priests. He remembered trying to convince his people that the priests were Evil Ones, as were all of those who came to invade their island, Pimu. But too many of his people refused to believe him, until it was too late.

The Evil Ones destroyed his people. The hate darkened his memory.

He felt stronger now, and it was easy for him to search for the raven. At last the Brujo found the bird, resting on the side of a cliff.

The raven shook itself and allowed the Brujo to come inside. The Brujo felt that he was much stronger now than when he first awoke.

The raven opened its eyes, and the Brujo *saw*.

Three

Eric Walker trudged up the fire trail twenty paces behind his "guide," Robert Cruz. Eric was struggling to keep up because he wasn't yet wide awake. He had only been asleep a couple of hours when Robert had rousted him out of bed, got him dressed, hauled him into the kitchen, fed him coffee and a bran muffin, and rolled him out the door.

But Robert had barely said a word to Eric the entire time, and since they had hit the trail, Robert had been playing mountain goat. He stayed just far enough ahead to let Eric know that he was being snubbed.

Eric was pretty sure he knew why. No doubt Robert had guessed that the reason Eric hadn't gotten in till well after three in the morning was that he had been on the beach balling Sandy Laham, the most gorgeous of the female students at the University of Southern California's Marine Science Center. Robert Cruz had been unsuccessfully trying to nail her since last September, and Eric hadn't even been on Catalina a week before he had charmed his way into Sandy's pants.

Eric smiled to himself, remembering Sandy. He said out loud to Robert, softly, "I know what'cher thinkin' . . ." Eric's smile broadened. Clint Eastwood.

Robert turned around. "Say something?"

Eric shook his head no. "Nothing. But wait up for me a second, okay?"

Robert stopped and looked down at Eric, who was scrambling to catch up. Eric noticed the expression on Robert's face. He's not happy, Eric said to himself.

"You're the one who wanted to see the reservoir," Robert said. "I've been there."

Eric caught up with Robert, who immediately turned away and started up the trail again. Eric was out of breath, and he grabbed for the sleeve of Robert's khaki jacket. "Wait a second," he panted.

Robert spun around and eyed Eric impatiently.

Eric let go of the other young man, then unslung the canteen he was carrying on his shoulder. "Gimme a break," he said. He took a long swallow of water.

"You're the one—"

"Yeah, I know," Eric said, cutting Robert off. "I'm the one who wanted to see the reservoir. You told me that already. I'd just like to know who it was put the bug up your ass. You haven't said shit to me all morning." Eric paused to take another drink. "Yesterday everything was fine."

"Nothing's wrong with me."

"You can't fool me, Cruz," Eric said. "I've known you way too long."

Robert glared at him, not saying anything.

Finally Eric asked, "Are you mad about Sandy?"

Robert's face darkened.

Oh-oh, Eric thought. Struck a nerve. "Look," he began, "you told me that you and Sandy—"

"Forget it," Robert said abruptly. He started back up the trail.

Eric trotted after him. "Hey, Robert, wait a minute. You said yourself that she wasn't getting it on with anybody here, right? Especially not you. So what's the big deal?"

Robert whirled around. "The big deal is *you*, man," he said angrily. "Mister Frat Boy Preppy Shit. Mister Charm. Fuck anything that walks."

"What the hell are you talking about?"

"It's always been that way with you, man," Robert said. "Chicks just fall at your feet."

Eric looked at Robert incredulously. Then he burst out laughing, and it took him several seconds to get control of himself. "I don't believe it," he sputtered. "I don't fucking believe it. You're jealous."

"Fuck you," Robert said.

Eric wiped tears from his eyes. "No, man, I'm sorry. I didn't know you were keeping this inside all these years." He started chuckling again. "Y'know, Robert, I always wondered why you wouldn't ever introduce me to your little sister. I knew Mexicans were supposed to be hot-blooded, but this . . ."

Robert Cruz stood in front of Eric, fists clenched at his sides. Eric had fallen onto his knees, convulsed. He was holding his sides, still laughing.

"You're a prick, Walker," Robert said at last. Then he stepped past Eric and started down the trail that led back down toward the ocean and the Marine Center.

"Hey, wait!" Eric called to Robert's back. "Aren't you afraid I'll get lost?" He laughed again. "C'mon back, Robert! You didn't give me a chance to tell you what happened with Sandy last night! If I'd've known you were this hot for her, I would've had you come along!"

Eric watched as Robert climbed down the dirt trail, the way they had come, and was soon out of sight. "I thought he'd at least give me the finger," Eric muttered.

Sometimes Robert can be a real asshole, Eric said to himself. After all, it had been Robert's idea that Eric visit Catalina in the first place. Robert was the one trying to convince Eric not to transfer from USC. They had known each other for two and a half years, ever since they had been paired as freshman roommates, and both had gone into marine biology. Now Eric was thinking about finishing his degree at the Scripps Institute in La Jolla, which was much closer to his San Diego home than USC was. Eric was checking out USC's Catalina facility because Robert had practically begged him to come.

Eric looked past where Robert had disappeared, to the Marine Center and the blue-green ocean beyond. Robert was certainly right about one thing, Eric thought. It was beautiful here, especially now that nearly all of the morning's low clouds had broken up.

A little to his left Eric could see the edge of Blue Cavern Point, a sheer rock ledge that jutted from the shore. He could also make out the ship rock light that was just off shore. He was only about two miles from the Isthmus Cove side of Two Harbors—which was midisland—on the north side, facing the mainland. Sandy Laham had taken him to Isthmus Cove last night.

Eric reached for his canteen and took another drink. Then he came to his feet and looked back up the tiny fire trail. It was a steady, steep climb to the top of the ridge that led to the reservoir, and he had another half mile or so to go till he got to the summit. He wished that he had decided to use the main road and taken a bicycle, which had been Robert's first suggestion. But no, Eric had to be Daniel Boone.

He shrugged, took a deep breath, and started

up the trail. Sandy wanted to go to a hotel in Avalon that night, and he had promised that he would be back early enough in the afternoon so that she could also take him snorkeling off the point before they went to town.

Eric had gone about fifty yards up the trail when he heard something rustling in the underbrush behind him. He stopped and stood still, listening. His heart beat faster. He turned around.

There was nothing there.

He looked to both sides of the trail and was about to resume his hike when the shrub growth below him and to his left shivered. Eric heard a loud grunt. He backed up a step, bent down slowly, and picked up a clod of dirt that was lying near his feet.

The brush shook violently, and the filthy, bristled snout of a wild pig poked its way out. The pig sniffed.

Eric's shoulders sagged. "You scared the piss out of me," he said to the pig, and chucked the dirt clod at the beast. The dirt struck the pig just above the snout, and the thing grunted, annoyed, then hunkered back into the brush.

"My first wild boar," Eric said out loud, feeling pleased with himself. He had heard about the pigs on Catalina and that you shouldn't mess with them if you could help it. They had notoriously bad tempers. Eric was a bit surprised that this one hadn't been too tough to scare off.

He had taken about a dozen steps up the trail before the rustling in the underbrush stopped him again. Eric spoke as he turned around, "Hey, look, fella—"

Eric caught himself. There were three of them this time. Three grubby, brown and black boars—all of them full grown, as far as Eric could tell. The beasts easily weighed several hundred pounds each. Eric could smell them, though they were still a good thirty yards away from him.

But what chilled the young man was that the pigs were obviously staring at him. With three sets of tiny, black, hate-filled eyes.

The pigs clambered from the brush, and Eric backed away from them instinctively. He knew that he didn't dare turn his back to them, and he held one hand behind him to catch himself in case he stumbled on the trail.

He heard something behind him. Eric spun around too quickly and lost his balance, falling to the ground.

Two more pigs had appeared higher up on the trail, blocking his way.

Eric looked around frantically, trying to spot an escape route or find some weapon with which he could defend himself—a rock, a stick—anything. He scrambled to his feet, constantly turning from side to side, trying to keep an eye on the beasts that stalked him.

Eric didn't know which way to run. He would never make it through the brush—God only knew what else might be there, but for sure he would fall and knock himself unconscious or break a leg or something.

William Relling Jr.

A loud cry from overhead startled him. Eric's head jerked up, and he saw, outlined against the blue morning sky, a black winged shape circling directly above him.

Eric's frightened mind flashed: It's a vulture! It knows I'm gonna die—

The bird *skreeked* at him, and the young man felt momentarily relieved. It was only a raven. No big deal . . .

He looked back at the pigs. They were much closer to him now, circling him.

Eric Walker screamed, *"Robert!!!"*

As the animals charged.

Four

Casey Harrison awoke with a start, shot up in bed, and screamed out loud.

His hands tightly grasped the blanket that covered him. His hair hung down in his face and was soaked with sweat.

Casey held on to the covers for several seconds. Then, gradually, his body became less rigid, his chest heaved, and he began to breathe easier. Casey loosened his grip, held himself up with one hand, and pushed back his damp hair with the other.

Jesus, he said to himself. Crazy fucking dream.

William Relling Jr.

Casey threw off the covers and swung his legs over the edge of the bed. He was still wearing his jeans—the same pair that he had been wearing for the past six days straight, though nobody had complained yet. His feet were bare. It amazed him that he had remembered to take off his shoes.

He pushed himself up off the bed too fast, and a bright, jagged shot of pain exploded behind his eyes. Casey groaned and sat back down very hard. He buried his face in his hands.

He moaned aloud softly. "No more. I swear to God, no more toot and cheap wine. Not together." Casey shook his head gently. "Never again."

Casey lifted his eyes and looked across the room at his reflection in the mirror that hung on the wall above his dresser. He shuddered. "Ohh," he groaned to the mirror. "You look damn near as bad as I feel."

He wondered whether there was any aspirin left in the medicine cabinet. Probably not, though he couldn't be absolutely sure. It was getting harder all the time to trust his memory. Last night— Thursday, wasn't it? The latest in a string of bad nights. Casey had hoped that he had left them all behind once he split from the band. That was what the gig in Avalon was all about.

It had been real nice at first, when he started the job at the end of February. Playing the hotel lounge was steady, if not very demanding, work. He stayed clean for the first week and dried out, which was probably a good thing.

Casey was very happy to be away from the LA

grind, which was driving him insane—what with the endless nighttime gigs and showcases for record-company execs (which paid shit money, if any) and the day jobs that all the guys in the band had to work to support themselves (which didn't pay much better). And the drugs. He was glad to be out of all that, no doubt about it.

But he hadn't expected Catalina to bore him out of his skull.

Casey remembered how surprised and pleased he had been the day Crissy Bendyk, the band's manager, told him that she had set up a "working vacation" for him at the El Capitan Hotel on Catalina. He had gone to her office expecting the worst, because the night before—at the band's St. Valentine's Day gig at Club Lingerie in Hollywood—Casey had gotten into a fight with some asshole customer in the middle of their set, and it had nearly turned into a riot.

What hadn't surprised him, though, was that the entire band had been in on the deal. They were worried that Casey Harrison, twenty-six-year-old ace keyboardist, cofounder, and chief songwriter of LA's soon-to-break-into-the-big-time group Fat Chance, was having a nervous breakdown. Thereby terminally fucking any shot the band might have. They saw it coming—too much pressure, too little rest, too much cocaine and booze and pills.

So by mutual agreement the band went into a two-month hiatus, and while Crissy Bendyk hit record execs with demo tapes, Casey was supposed to take it easy. All he had to do was stay in shape and be no more than an hour or so from LA, in case something should break.

Casey took the gig: 9:00 P.M. to 1:00 A.M., Wednesday through Saturday, for eight weeks till the end of April. His name and an eight-by-ten publicity still appeared on a sandwich board outside the Crow's Nest Lounge of the El Capitan Hotel, which also provided Casey with room and board and $275 a week. All considered, the deal wasn't too shabby.

It was an easy gig, because except for the week before Easter, early spring was the hotel's slack season. The bar didn't handle many customers—there were few tourists and fewer locals dropping in during the week. But business was healthy enough on Fridays and Saturdays to pay for Casey's services and those of Gus and Wes, the bartenders who alternated weeknights singly and worked together on weekends. It wasn't very tough, either, for Casey to work up enough lounge piano standards—which he sprinkled with a number of his own tunes—to get him through a night.

Casey kicked back during his first few days on the island, playing the lounge at night, sleeping past noon, and then playing tourist himself during the day. Casey got to Catalina on a Monday, settled in on Tuesday, rehearsed and played his first gig Wednesday. By the end of his first week there, he had taken the three-and-a-half-hour Inland Motor Tour twice; had hiked and camped overnight near the Wrigley Ranch; had bought a bicycle and gone up and down every street in Avalon; and had even taken a ride in a glass-bottomed boat his second Monday afternoon there—though the boat didn't make it back to the harbor in time to keep Casey from getting drenched in a sudden, unexpected thundershower. By then he had exhausted what diversion Catalina had to offer, and Casey was beginning to think that his "vacation" wasn't such a hot idea after all.

He telephoned Gerry Gray, the band's bass player and his closest friend, and invited him to Catalina for a visit. Gerry had come the week before on Wednesday, and that night he went to work with Casey, sitting in on bass and guitar for one set. After the bar closed they went up to Casey's room, and Gerry pulled out the two grams of Peruvian Flake he had brought with him from LA. Casey had also picked up a quart of Jack Daniel's, and that night he got pleasantly loaded for the first time in two weeks.

It wasn't the last. Gerry put him onto a painter he knew who lived in Avalon and dealt drugs a little on the side, and Casey began to visit the guy regularly. Casey also started drinking again, mostly because he didn't have much else to do.

He managed to convince himself that everything was cool because he was resting. The only reason that he got fucked up was to stave off the boredom. Casey never missed a night at work, but he spent most of his waking hours in a stupor. He was used to that.

But he had never had nightmares before.

Casey lay back gently on the bed, resting his

head on the pillow, staring at the ceiling. Just thinking about the dream scared him a little.

He shivered. Then he closed his eyes.

And he dreamed.

Casey was alone on a beach, lying on the sand. He could hear the ocean crashing on the shore.

Suddenly he was surrounded by people who were howling at him and laughing. They gathered around him, but Casey couldn't see their faces.

They grabbed him. He tried to fight, tried to pull away. He tried to scream at them, but no sound came from his mouth.

They dragged him along the beach. One of them had dug a pit in the sand, and they dragged Casey toward the pit. He kept trying to scream for help, but it did no good.

For a moment they let go of him. But he could not move. It was as if his arms and legs were paralyzed, and Casey could neither move nor make a sound.

They threw him into the pit.

As he fell, Casey told himself that he would wake up when he hit bottom. It was just a dream, and he knew that when you fell in a dream you woke up when you hit, or you were dead. It didn't keep him from being frightened, but he knew that he was going to wake up. It was only a dream.

Except that Casey didn't wake up.

He crashed to the bottom of the pit. The wind was knocked out of him, but he wasn't really hurt. Strangely he didn't feel any pain.

Casey tried to force himself to calm down and

figure out what had happened to him. He looked around and decided that the pit was too steep to climb, even if he could get his arms and legs to move. The walls were sheer, smooth earth and sand. He tried, but he couldn't make his hands reach out and touch the walls.

He looked up and saw their shadow-faces circling the rim of the pit.

Then he heard something. It was an odd sound, a kind of tapping. It was very faint and far away.

Casey felt something brush against his cheek. Then again. Then it was falling all over him, falling from above. Casey looked up again.

They were filling in the pit.

Casey twisted furiously, trying to get to his feet. It still did no good. The pit began to fill with sand and earth, up to Casey's thighs, his waist, his chest. Faster and faster, till he was buried up to his chin. The sand and dirt spilled into Casey's mouth, and at last he could hear himself scream—

Casey's eyes snapped open.

He could feel his heart hammering inside his chest, and his breaths came short and quick. He exhaled deeply. Slow down, he told himself. Slow down.

Casey sat up on the edge of the bed. He paused there, trying to pull himself together, trying to think about something other than the dream. He looked around and noticed for the first time that his room was still semidark. It had to be late in the morning, but Casey had long ago gotten into the habit of closing off his bedroom to daylight. He smiled grimly. I'm just like a vampire, he said to himself.

His headache had returned, stronger than before.

Casey eased himself from the bed and shuffled toward the bathroom. He stepped through the doorway, reaching for the light switch by habit. The fluorescent tube clicked on, and the light stung Casey's eyes. He rubbed his forehead with one hand and opened the medicine cabinet above the sink with the other.

"Son of a bitch," Casey grumbled. No aspirin. Nothing except his razor, a toothbrush, and a can of shaving cream. He shook his head, then shrugged.

Casey bent to the sink and turned on the cold-water tap. He cupped his hands beneath the spray, then, bracing himself, splashed the water on his face. He turned off the water and took a step toward the toilet.

Tap-tap-tap-tap.

Casey froze.

The sound had come from the bedroom, very softly. Casey stood still, not completely sure that he had even heard it. Unconsciously he held his breath. Waiting.

Then: *ta-ta-tap.*

Casey looked up at his reflection in the mirror on the door of the medicine cabinet. His face had grown pale. A knot of fear tightened in his stomach. His headache had vanished.

Tap-tap-tap-tap.

Casey moved stiffly away from the mirror. He switched off the bathroom light as he stepped through the doorway into the bedroom. He looked around the room, at the same time wanting and not wanting to see—

Ta-tap.

The sound came from the window next to Casey's bed. A line of sunlight speared through a slit where the pair of drapes covering the window came together. Something was there, behind the drapes. A shadow.

Casey hesitated for a moment, then got up his nerve and stepped to the window. He threw open the drapes.

Casey cried out, startled. He wet his pants as he stumbled back from the window and fell against the bed. He collapsed to the floor.

On the ledge outside the window, its red eyes glaring at Casey, was a huge raven.

The Brujo was satisfied. Not only had the first of the Evil Ones suffered his vengeance for despoiling the sacred worship ground of the Pimugnan but the Brujo had also made contact via the raven with one who, he was certain, could serve him.

The Brujo had only been testing his power. He had guided beasts that were stupid and brutish. They were easy for him to control.

That there was more than one of them had not made it any more difficult. It was not the same as *reaching* the raven, who was the Brujo's spirit-brother. But they were fellow beasts, and they could carry out the Brujo's will.

The sensation that he had felt as he led the beasts was pleasure, an emotion the Brujo had not felt since he was a boy, so long ago. Along with the pleasure, he felt satisfaction.

It was not merely the satisfaction of revenge. The Brujo was also satisfied that he could control the power.

And with that power, he *reached*.

Five

Markie Baldwin raced up the metal steps to the top deck of the triple-level, red and white passenger boat, looking for his father among the half-dozen people there. Trevor was leaning on the starboard rail, gazing past his son toward the rocks that lined both sides of the Long Beach jetty.

Markie trotted to his father's side. "I found out the name of our boat, Dad," the boy said. "It's the *Long Beach King.*"

"That makes sense," Trevor smiled. "But did you find out how long it's gonna be till we shove off?"

William Relling Jr.

Markie made a show of pulling up the sleeve of his California Angels jacket and holding up his wrist. He was wearing the Spider-Man watch that Trevor had given him for Christmas. "One o'clock," Markie said. "Any minute now."

Trevor eyed him. "When did you learn to tell time?"

"I been workin' on it, Dad. Honest."

Trevor gave his son a look of "Oh, yeah?" Markie smiled sheepishly and said, "I asked the guy who took our suitcases downstairs."

"You're pretty shrewd for a six-year-old," Trevor said.

"Six and a half," Markie corrected him.

Trevor laughed. "Sorry, sport, I forgot. Six and a half."

The boat's rear engines had been idling since Trevor and Markie came on board, but now the engines began to rumble more loudly. The *King* backed out of its slip into the small man-made inlet where the Long Beach/Catalina Cruises boats were docked.

Markie pointed to another pair of passenger boats, identical to the *Long Beach King*, that were still moored at the dock. The boats were unattended, and Markie asked his father why those weren't going, too. Trevor told the boy that the extra boats were only used in the summertime, that not enough people went to Catalina this time of year to fill them.

While his father was speaking, Markie spotted

something off the *King*'s bow. The boy yelled out in amazement, "Holy crap!"

Trevor's eyes widened in surprise. Markie noticed. "Uhhhh . . . look there, Dad," he sputtered.

A quarter of a mile ahead of them in the channel, to the starboard side of the *King*, lay a huge ocean liner that was resting gently aside the rock jetty.

"*Queen Mary*, right, Dad?" Markie asked.

Trevor had narrowed his eyes in mock displeasure. "Holy crap?"

Markie punched his father's arm playfully. "It slipped out. Sorry. I didn't mean it. But that's the *Queen Mary*, right?"

"That's her."

The passenger boat cruised easily past the liner's bow. The huge ocean-going ship dwarfed the smaller boats in the channel, including the *Long Beach King*, as well as the cars and trucks that were parked along the wharf next to her. Markie started to count the portholes on the *Queen*, but the boat glided by too quickly for him to get past twenty.

A loudspeaker suddenly crackled to life atop the *King*'s bridge. A man's voice, distorted by the speaker, introduced itself as Captain Peters and welcomed the passengers aboard. "In just a few minutes," the voice said, "we'll reach our cruising speed of twelve knots. That should put us into Avalon harbor in an hour and fifty minutes."

The loudspeaker droned on. "We're anticipating

a fairly strong southwest swell, so I'd especially like to remind you youngsters that there's no running on the decks. If you have any questions about anything at all, feel free to talk to any of the crew. We hope you have a pleasant trip and that you enjoy your visit to Catalina."

Markie dug into the pocket of his jeans and fished out a handful of change. "Is it okay if I get a Coke, Dad? I got my own money."

"Sure, sport."

"I'm gonna go back and talk to the guy with the suitcases again, too," Markie said. "Will you be okay by yourself?"

Trevor grinned. "I'm fine, Mark. I'll wait right here for you, but you come back and let me know if you find out anything important."

Markie nodded, then he turned away and headed back down the steps that led to the two lower decks, one hand holding on to the guardrail that was nearly as tall as he.

Trevor watched the boy's head bob out of sight. Then he turned to look out at the ocean, smiling to himself.

There was something about Markie that always made him feel good, and Trevor often caught himself wondering how he and Claudia could have produced such a kid. Markie wasn't really very much like either one of them. The boy was bright and quick-witted—in fact, much too old for his age. Markie had a dry sense of humor, though most of the time he seemed very serious and wise. Valerie

Heath had once accused the boy of being sage, and Markie had said it was better than being parsley. Trevor had no idea how his son had been able to come up with that.

Trevor also sometimes wondered why Markie didn't seem to mind shuttling back and forth between the homes of his divorced parents. The boy liked both of them, and he appeared to understand that Trevor and Claudia could not live together. If Markie felt bad about his parents' breakup, he certainly never let it show. At least not to Trevor.

Trevor thought it was too bad that the only thing he and Claudia had in common anymore was their son, and it was fortunate that they were usually able to work things out amiably when it came to Markie. Trevor had few complaints about the way Claudia raised the boy, and she always contacted him when a major decision regarding Markie's well-being needed to be made. Claudia would occasionally chide Trevor when she thought he was spoiling Markie. He was always taking the boy to restaurants and movies and ball games, and it made her look like a heavy, Claudia said, when Markie came home and she had to sometimes tell him no.

It had surprised Trevor a little, then, that Claudia thought the trip to Catalina was a great idea. She made arrangements for Markie to be let out of school early for the day. As long as Trevor was willing to drive to west LA and pick the boy up,

William Relling Jr.

instead of Claudia's having to run Markie down to Laguna, it was fine with her.

Trevor was looking forward to playing tourist with Valerie and Markie over the weekend. I'm sorry we couldn't all go together, Trevor thought. Markie liked Valerie a lot. But when Trevor called her at school earlier that morning, Valerie told him that she had talked to her mother, who lived in Corona del Mar, and had promised to visit before she went on to meet Trevor and Markie at the restaurant, as they had originally planned. That made even a late afternoon boat from Long Beach out of the question—it was too short a notice. So Trevor arranged for Valerie to fly to Catalina Island early Saturday afternoon. He would take care of his business with Brad Cusimano on Friday night, so they would still have most of the weekend together.

Without warning, the boat began to tilt far to port. Trevor had to clutch the rail with both hands to keep from tumbling to the metal benches that were bolted to the deck behind him. The boat lifted thirty degrees to the left, settled itself, then tilted the other way.

The loudspeaker atop the bridge came on again, and the captain's voice advised the passengers that they had indeed caught the swell. "If you are prone to motion sickness," the captain's voice said, "please don't go into one of the inside bathrooms. If you close yourself in, you'll only feel worse. Stay outside on deck and have someone get you one of the white bags from our concession counters—"

"Hey! Dad!"

Trevor turned to see Markie lurching up the steps like a drunk. The boy was wearing a wide grin, and as the boat teetered from side to side, Markie held out both arms, trying to keep his balance. The boy finally made it to the rail and grabbed his father.

Trevor was chuckling. "Nice ride, eh, sport?"

Markie laughed. "It's just like Disneyland. I saw some lady downstairs who looked kinda green."

"She's probably not the only one," Trevor said. He steered Markie away from the rail to a bench and they sat down. Markie imitated Trevor and held on to the underside of the bench with both hands.

Markie asked, "Is it gonna be like this the whole way?"

"Let's hope not. That's more ride than we paid for."

The boy laughed again, then turned to gaze out toward the ocean. Far ahead of the boat loomed a dark green and brown shape, partially covered by clouds.

Markie lifted one hand to tug at his father's sleeve. "Is that Catalina?" he asked.

"That's it."

"It doesn't look so big from here," Markie said. "I can see all of it."

"We're still better than fifteen miles away," Trevor told him. "It's big enough."

"How big?"

William Relling Jr.

Trevor told the boy what he knew about Catalina. They were going to stay in Avalon, the island's only city. Trevor knew about the Wrigley Ranch and the airport that had been built on top of two mountains, and that the island was inhabited by all sorts of animals—pigs and wild goats and even herds of buffalo. A movie company making a western in the 1920s had brought the buffalo over originally, and now the herds were protected by law. Anyone who killed a buffalo had to pay a heavy fine and, somehow, come up with a replacement.

Trevor said, "That's what's most fun about Catalina, that it's like a giant zoo. Everything's out in the open, and all the animals just run around."

"Do we get to *see* 'em?" Markie asked excitedly.

Trevor smiled. "Sure we can. There's a tour that goes all around Catalina. You can see everything."

The swells had calmed and the boat was running more smoothly once again. Trevor and Markie watched two teenage boys in jeans and ski vests leaning over the starboard rail near the bridge. The boys were pointing toward the water off the bow, yelling to each other happily. Markie jumped up from the bench and ran to the boys.

Trevor saw the taller of the two teenagers bend down to tell Markie something. Then Markie stretched over the top of the rail, staring in the direction the older boys had been pointing.

Markie turned away from the rail and ran back

BRUJO

to his father. "Seals, Dad!" he cried. "There's a whole bunch of seals out in the water!"

Trevor followed his son back to the rail. Off the *King*'s starboard bow, about three hundred yards ahead of them, a half-dozen sleek brown shapes were gliding through the water. Occasionally one of the shapes would leap into the air, dive underwater, then poke its head above the surface moments later.

"See, Dad," Markie said. "Seals."

The tall boy turned to Markie and said, "They're not seals. They're sea lions."

"I didn't know there was a difference," Trevor said.

"Sea lions are a little bigger," the boy told him. "But we were really hopin' to see a whale."

Markie's eyes grew large. "A *whale*?"

"This time of year a lot of 'em swim north from Mexico," the boy answered. "They go right through this channel. You can see gray whales all the time."

The sea lions had moved off out of sight, and Markie clung to the top of the rail and waved. "See you later, lions," he called.

"Keep an eye out for dolphins, too," the tall boy told Markie. "We might see a couple of them."

Markie's face lit up. He turned to his father and said, "This is great, Dad. This is the best boat ride."

A trio of sea gulls that had been pacing the sea lions swung around in a lazy circle toward the boat. The other teenage boy, who hadn't spoken while they were watching the sea lions, reached into the pocket of his vest. He pulled out an open bag of Fritos corn chips and said, "Watch this."

The boy held one corn chip in the air, extending his arm over the rail. The three gulls had come around to match pace with the boat, and the largest of the three—a mottled gray and white bird—beat its wings hard till it was close enough to swoop down and snatch the chip from the boy's fingers.

Markie squealed with delight. "Try it," the boy said to him, and he held out the bag.

Markie reached for a corn chip and held it out as the other boy had done. The two smaller gulls sailed toward him in tandem. The first came in too quickly, misjudging its dive, and missed, but the second was able to nip the Frito from Markie's hand before he could jerk it away.

Trevor Baldwin noticed that eight or ten more gulls had appeared around the boat and had fallen in with the first three. Markie reached for the bag of Fritos that the teenager held out for him, and raised another corn chip for the birds. A pair of newcomers separated from the rest, and they came swooping toward the boys and man standing at the deck rail.

At that instant Trevor's mind flashed: Something's wrong! He reached for his son and called sharply, "Mark!"

The boy turned to look at his father just as the first gull snatched the corn chip that Markie was holding. The bird snapped, catching both the Frito and the tip of Markie's finger. Markie howled in pain and surprise.

The second gull abruptly changed its course upward, then, just as abruptly, came diving at the two older boys. They didn't notice because their attention was on Markie. But Trevor, who was kneeling beside his son, happened to look up and spot it.

Trevor cried, "Watch out!"

The taller of the boys dodged, but the gull cannily shifted its attack. It struck the other boy full in the face. The boy screamed and grabbed at his eyes, and a thin line of blood trickled down his left cheek.

Suddenly the dozen sea gulls that were pacing the *King* were attacking the passengers who were out in the open, on the top deck and the rear of the second deck. Trevor could hear people below him running and screaming. Fortunately there weren't many passengers on board, and most were already inside, within the enclosed parts of the two lower decks.

The gulls came at them again, and Trevor pulled the three boys down with him, curling his body over them for protection. The birds dove at him, squawking furiously, and Trevor scrunched down further, jamming the boys hard against the deck rail. He could hear Markie crying—more in fright than in pain—and the other boy whom the gull had struck was whimpering softly. The taller boy was trying to cover up his friend as best he could.

Trevor heard a voice calling to him, "In here! Quick!"

He looked up cautiously. A heavyset man in a white uniform shirt and dark trousers was holding open the door to the bridge, not ten feet away. Trevor nudged the boy next to him. The boy nodded, then crouched and slipped an arm around his injured friend.

Trevor had scooped Markie in his arms and started to rise when he felt a sharp blow to the back of his head and heard a triumphant caw. Trevor grunted, staggering.

"C'mon!" called the man in the doorway. "Now!"

Trevor struggled to regain his feet, though the pain in his head made him dizzy. The two teenagers were up with him, and Trevor pushed them ahead of him toward the door. He hunched down behind the boys and ran as fast as he could, but Markie weighed him down.

From the corner of his eye Trevor saw the pair of gulls diving at him again.

He had ducked, shutting his eyes, anticipating another blow, when he felt a strong hand on his forearm. The hand dragged him through the doorway. Trevor opened his eyes in time to see the heavyset man push the door shut, just as it was reached by the gull in the lead. The bird hadn't time to change direction, and it smashed into the door's glass window with a thud, then fell to the deck outside.

The pain and dizziness in Trevor's head were suddenly much worse. He barely heard the heavyset man speaking to him: "Give me the boy, mister, and let's check you out."

Trevor could feel himself slipping into unconsciousness. His last thought was: It's a goddamn Alfred Hitchcock movie.

Then everything went black.

Six

Drs. Glen Matlock and Jacqueline Berke left Oxnard Marina at 7:30 Friday morning aboard Matlock's forty-two-foot Ranger. Their course was south-southeast for Santa Catalina Island. They took their time sailing the channel and dropped anchor off Kelp Point, on Catalina's ocean side, a little after one that afternoon.

The weekend was to be a treat for both of them. Jackie Berke hadn't taken more than a few days off since the previous July, when she had begun her psychiatric residency at the state hospital in Camarillo. From the beginning of her residency she had cultivated an image as an icy, emotionless workaholic—deliberately, because it kept at bay her more lecherous colleagues on the hospital's medical staff.

Except for Glen Matlock.

Matlock was a forty-one-year-old psychiatrist who had been on staff at the hospital for eight years when Jackie Berke started there. Dr. Matlock also maintained a small, private practice in Port Hueneme, where he had an apartment. Like Jackie Berke, Matlock had a reputation as a workaholic—a bachelor recluse who devoted most of his free time to the beautiful sailboat that he kept at the marina in nearby Oxnard. Some of his colleagues suspected that Dr. Matlock was gay. Jackie discovered otherwise following the staff Christmas party, when she had agreed to visit Matlock's sailboat and ended up spending the night with him.

The two of them worked very hard for the next couple of months to keep their relationship a secret from most of their professional acquaintances. That was why Jackie had been reluctant to agree to a four-day weekend sail. She was afraid that it would look suspicious if she and Matlock took the same days off. She had finally given in, though, after Matlock had said that anybody who got suspicious could attempt aerial fornication with the moon.

Matlock was in the galley, bent to a small refrigerator next to the propane stove. He pulled out two bottles of Heineken dark beer and set them on a tray next to the sandwiches he had made. He lifted the tray and carried it up the steps that led from the cabin to the deck above. "Lunch, Jackie," he called ahead of him.

Matlock emerged from the cabin into the afternoon sunshine. Jackie Berke stood on the deck, toweling herself dry. She was dressed in a bright yellow one-piece swimsuit, and Matlock noticed admiringly that it flattered her. The suit set off Jackie's light, freckled skin and auburn hair. She looked terrific.

Dr. Glen's personal prescription for overworked psych residents, Matlock thought to himself. Four days away from it all, and nobody knowing where you are.

He set the tray on a small table between two deck chairs and said, "Here we are, Dr. Berke."

Jackie Berke smiled at him. "You are such a romantic sap, Matlock," she said. She leaned forward and kissed him lightly.

Matlock put his arms around her, pulling her close. "You gotta admit," he said, "I know my business."

They kissed again, more passionately.

Jackie pulled away from him. Shivering, she wrapped her towel around herself and sat down at the table. Matlock sat down opposite her and reached for his beer. "You should be cold," he said after taking a long swallow. "That ocean is probably all of fifty degrees. Invigorating, ain't it?"

"Feels good," Jackie said. One hand poked from the folds of her towel and picked up a sandwich. "How come you native Californians never go in the water?" she asked.

"Only in a wet suit," Matlock told her. "That's how you can tell the natives from the tourists—the tourists are blue. Natives know the ocean is too goddamn cold."

"I don't know how you can be such a great sailor when you don't like the water."

Matlock smiled. "I like being *on* the water. Not in it."

The sailboat rocked gently, and the two of them sat without speaking for some minutes, simply enjoying each other's company while they finished their lunch.

Until a shadow passed over their boat, moving quickly. Glen Matlock looked up and pointed. "Look at that," he said.

Jackie looked toward the island and saw a huge black bird riding the air currents, wings spread magnificently. "What is it?" she asked.

"A raven. They're all over Catalina. A lot of 'em nest on the cliffs."

Matlock finished his sandwich, leaned back in his chair, and lit a cigarette. "There's something a lot of people don't know about this island," he said. "The Indians that used to live here—before the white men came—were all animal worshipers. Especially the birds. Ravens, gulls, eagles . . ."

"No kidding," Jackie said blandly.

Matlock eyed her. "I can tell you're interested."

"I'm sorry," Jackie apologized. "Really. I didn't know there were any Indians here."

"There aren't anymore," said Matlock. He told her about the Pimu tribe that had once inhabited

Catalina. The tribe had lived on the island for centuries, but the last Pimu Indians had died in the early 1800s on the California mainland, where they had been transported by Spanish mission priests.

Matlock rested his cigarette in an ashtray beside his empty plate. "It's really kind of sad," he said, finishing his story. "There aren't any descendants of the Catalina Indians around anywhere. They—"

Matlock was interrupted by a strange, savage cry overhead. The raven they had seen before had returned with three newcomers, a trio of sea gulls. The gulls were diving hard and fast at the boat. The raven simply hovered, perhaps fifty feet above the deck.

Glen Matlock said, "What in the hell is this?"

He barely had time to cover up when the first gull struck a glancing blow to the side of his head, knocking him out of his chair.

A second gull came in behind the first, and the two birds flapped about Matlock's head, squawking and jabbing at him with razor-sharp beaks. The third gull zeroed in on Jackie. She screamed as it chased her down the steps into the boat's cabin.

Matlock drew himself to his knees and cried out, "Jackie!" He grabbed one of the birds by a wing and hurled it away violently. The gull crashed into the side of the boat, fell to the deck, then lay still.

Matlock reached for the second bird, but it swung around behind him and attacked viciously between his shoulder blades. The pain was excruciating, and it sent the man to the deck once more.

The third gull had cornered Jackie in the cabin's galley. She tried to turn away from the bird as it flailed about her head and shoulders. She was looking for a weapon, and at last she spotted a counter drawer where she knew Glen Matlock kept kitchen utensils. Jackie yanked the drawer open, and everything in it clattered to the floor.

She found what she was looking for. Jackie bent and picked up a long carving knife, then spun around and lunged at the bird. She missed and went crashing into the propane stove, breaking it loose from the metal lines that connected the stove to the tanks that supplied its gas.

The gull came at her again while Jackie was off-balance. She tried to sidestep, but stumbled on the cutlery she had dropped before. As she tumbled to the floor, the knife she was holding twisted in her hand. She fell onto the knife, driving the blade deep into her belly.

Outside, Glen Matlock had climbed to his feet and lurched to the cabin. He paused in the doorway and saw Jackie Berke lying on her back atop the pile of kitchen utensils. The handle of the carving knife jutted from her stomach. Jackie's eyes were open and staring.

As the sight registered, he was attacked again by the gull.

The bird attached itself to Matlock's neck, and the man roared in agony and rage. He grabbed at the gull, ripping it from him. The bird struggled futilely as Matlock snapped its neck. He dropped it, still fluttering, from his hands.

Matlock had just reached the bottom of the cabin steps when the third gull rushed him from inside, hitting him full force in the chest. Matlock stumbled backward, losing his balance, and fell, cracking the back of his head on the steps. He blacked out.

An odor brought him to a few minutes later.

Propane!

The psychiatrist's mind raced. Propane—heavier than air. It'll settle on the deck—

There was a noise behind him. Matlock rolled over painfully, and he saw a gull standing on the deck table outside, next to an empty beer bottle it had knocked over. Next to Matlock's ashtray.

My cigarette, Matlock thought.

It has to be out. It has to be.

The gull nudged the ashtray to the edge of the table with its beak. Matlock cried to himself, How can it know?

The gull knocked the ashtray off the table just as Glen Matlock opened his mouth to scream.

His scream was lost in the sound of the explosion.

Seven

Dad? Hey, Dad?

The words were printed in luminous green on the insides of Trevor Baldwin's eyelids. His head ached. He thought, Am I dreaming?

Then he could hear his son's voice, muted and far away. "Hey, Dad?" Markie asked. "You okay?"

A pungent odor struck Trevor's nostrils and he jerked away. *Too fast*. Nausea swept over him; Trevor groaned.

He opened his eyes.

Before him was Markie, standing beside the heavyset man who had pulled them into the bridge.

Both of them looked worried. The man was holding a bottle of smelling salts.

Trevor tried to smile at his son. "Okay, sport."

"Are you all right, Mr. Baldwin?" asked the heavyset man.

Trevor nodded painfully. He touched the back of his head, and a sharp twinge made him wince. His hair was wet. He looked at his fingertips; they were tinged with red. "How long was I out?" Trevor asked.

"Not long," the man told him. "But you've got a pretty good gash."

Trevor nodded slowly, acknowledging. "Captain Peters?" he asked.

"That's right," the man answered. "We've radioed ahead, and there'll be somebody to take you to the hospital. You and your friend over there both need stitches." The captain gestured at the injured boy, who was holding a wet paper towel to his forehead.

"He's gonna be all right," the captain said. "But an inch lower and he'd have lost an eye."

Captain Peters frowned. "You two are the only ones who got badly hurt, Mr. Baldwin. Everybody below is okay. Scared, but okay." The man's eyes narrowed. "You mind telling me what happened out there?"

Markie exclaimed, "The sea gulls!"

"I saw the gulls," said Captain Peters. "I'd just like to know what made 'em come at you like they did."

BRUJO

Trevor shrugged. "The boys were feeding them Fritos."

"Nothing wrong with that," the captain said.

"One of 'em *bit* me," said Markie.

The captain rubbed his jaw. "That happens, too."

Trevor cut in. "Yeah, but the next thing we knew, the goddamn birds were dive-bombing us." He paused and looked at Captain Peters pointedly. "I thought maybe you'd know what made 'em do that."

The captain shook his head. "I've never seen anything like it in my life."

He turned to gaze out the window of the bridge. Santa Catalina Island was not far ahead, and the boats in Avalon harbor and the houses on the hillsides surrounding the cove were visible. "Less than a half hour till we dock," Captain Peters said. "We'll have to report this." He took a deep breath. "I just don't know what we're gonna report."

The captain moved away from Trevor and Markie to check on the boy. He was still shaking his head. Markie peered up at his father. "You sure you're okay, Dad?" he asked.

"I'm fine, Mark," Trevor lied. He couldn't bring himself to say anything to his son about an indistinct feeling that was gnawing at him, something that he couldn't put his finger on.

Markie was still looking worried. Trevor mussed the boy's hair. "I'm okay. Really."

Markie nodded.

"What happened to the birds?" Trevor asked.

Markie's expression changed, and he looked at

Trevor oddly, as if he were regarding his father from very far away. "They disappeared, Dad," he said quietly. "That one smacked into the door and . . ." Markie's voice trailed off.

Markie shuddered, and Trevor sensed that whatever it was that bothered him was affecting his son as well.

"They just disappeared," Markie whispered.

Twenty minutes later the *Long Beach King* pulled into the Catalina Cruises dock at the southeast end of Avalon Bay. Trevor, Markie, and the two teenagers who had been with them on the bridge were led off the boat by a crew member, a young woman who took them ahead of the other passengers who were crowded on the first deck.

Waiting at the top of the gangplank were three Avalon policemen in khaki uniforms. With the policemen was a tanned, curly-haired man who was dressed in a knit Ralph Lauren Polo shirt, cotton slacks, and Topsiders. The man stepped around the policemen at the top of the ramp and said, "Trevor, what the hell *is* this?"

Trevor replied, "Hi, Brad."

One of the officers moved down the gangplank past Trevor and the boys. The other policemen took charge of the casualties and led them to a pair of open Jeep CJs marked "Avalon Police" that waited on the road at the end of the dock. Bradley Cusimano fell in with the group.

Brad took Trevor's arm. "What's going on, Trev?" he asked impatiently. "I drive over to pick you up

BRUJO

and find out that half the town's police force is here to haul you away."

Trevor smiled wanly. "I got bit by a sea gull."

Brad looked at him dumbfounded as the taller of the two policemen loaded Trevor and Markie in the lead Jeep, while the policeman's partner took the two teenagers with him in the other vehicle. Brad asked where the policemen were taking the Baldwins.

"Hospital," the policeman grunted to Brad. He switched on the ignition and the Jeep lurched forward, heading into town. The second police vehicle rolled away immediately behind the first.

Brad trotted to an electric cart that was parked near a bicycle rack at the end of the dock. He hopped into the cart, flipped the starter switch, and sped up the narrow road that encircled Avalon's beachfront, following the two Jeeps.

He was several hundred yards behind the policemen as the Jeeps passed two front blocks of storefront shops and restaurants that faced Avalon Bay. They made a sharp left turn onto Avalon Canyon Road, then went another eighth of a mile up the narrow, slightly inclined road that lay between small, variously colored, wood-frame houses, many of which had been boarded up for the winter.

At the top of the incline a triangular patch of green parkland lay between the branches of the road. The Jeeps took the right fork, then cut an immediate left turn into the driveway of a long, low-slung, warehouselike building. A sign in front of the building read "Avalon Community Hospital."

William Relling Jr.

The police vehicles slid to a stop on either side of a third Jeep that was parked in the driveway, a hardtop CJ on whose doors was lettered "City of Avalon—Chief of Police." Trevor and Markie were helped out by the tall policeman, who then guided them up a concrete walkway toward the hospital's emergency entrance.

A man and three women were standing together just inside the Emergency Entrance's glass doors. Two of the women worked for the hospital. One of them was dressed in nurse's whites, and the other was a small Asian woman who wore slacks and a lab coat. A stethoscope was hung around the Asian woman's neck.

The third woman was older than the other two—she looked to Trevor Baldwin to be in her early fifties—and she was neatly, if casually, dressed in jeans and a wool pullover. Her attention was focused on the dark-haired man beside her. He was about ten years younger than she, Trevor guessed, and he wore the same uniform khakis as the two policemen who were leading the boys and Trevor up the walk.

The doors slid open, and Trevor could hear the man talking to the older woman. The man's voice sounded tired. "We've done everything we can, Grace," the man was saying. "I've been telling you that all morning . . ."

The man paused to glance over at the two policemen, who had moved Trevor and the boys inside the door. "Where d'ya want 'em, Chief?" the tall policeman asked.

The woman in the lab coat spoke up. "With me."

She and the nurse broke from their group and took Trevor and the injured teenager from the officers. Both of the policemen looked to the dark-haired man.

"They're Dr. Wong's patients," the man said simply. "All we want is to ask 'em some questions."

The older woman reached for the man's sleeve and said, "Ray, I—"

The man turned on her unexpectedly, cutting her off. "Dammit, Grace, will you *wait*—"

The man caught himself. The woman's face was flushed with sudden anger, and she looked as if she were about to snap back at him.

"I'm sorry, Grace," the man apologized. "But let me take care of this first, all right?"

The doctor was leading Trevor away toward an examination room off the hospital's main corridor. The dark-haired man called to her, "Dr. Wong, how long before I can talk to him?"

"Give me thirty minutes, Chief," the doctor called back. Then she led Trevor into the exam room and pushed the door shut behind them.

The top of Trevor's head was numb, and it was difficult for him to keep from touching it. His fingers gingerly probed the area of shaved scalp and the tiny bumps that were his dozen stitches, but he could barely sense the pressure of his fingertips.

"The anesthetic will wear off in a few hours,"

William Relling Jr.

Dr. Wong told him. "Since your X rays were negative, you're free to go anytime you want. Or as soon as the chief is through with you."

She went to the door and gestured to someone in the hallway. The dark-haired man and Markie walked into the room.

Trevor sat on the edge of an examination table in the center of the room, propping himself with his hands. Markie looked at his father with the same worried expression he had had earlier, when Trevor had come to on the bridge of the passenger boat.

"He'll be just fine," Dr. Wong said, smiling at Markie. Then she stepped out into the hallway and let the door close behind her.

Markie was still frowning slightly. Trevor grinned at his son and said, "You heard the doctor, sport." He patted the exam table. Markie moved away from the dark-haired man, and Trevor hoisted the boy onto the table beside him.

The dark-haired man leaned against a washbasin that was next to the door. "Your boy gave me a pretty good account of what happened on the boat, Mr. Baldwin," the man said. "Now I'd like to hear what you have to say about it."

"I don't know what more I can tell you, Chief—"

"Buckler. Ray Buckler. Actually, the more information we can get, the better. We'd appreciate your help."

Trevor took his time recounting the story of the bird attack aboard the *Long Beach King*. He was a bit bothered at first when he thought the chief was only half listening to what he said. But when Buckler interrupted him twice, asking him to clarify a couple of points in his story, Trevor realized that the man was in fact listening to him intently, that it was only Buckler's attitude that made him seem disinterested. But Trevor also noticed that both times the chief interrupted his story, Markie had looked at Ray Buckler with a dark expression. *Now, what in the hell is that for?* Trevor wondered to himself.

"After the captain pulled you into the bridge," the chief said, "then what?"

Trevor shrugged. "Not much. I passed out for a couple of minutes, and when I came to, the birds were gone. A half hour later the boat docked, and we got off. Your men brought us up here."

Chief Buckler seemed to consider Trevor's story for a moment. Then he nodded slowly and said, "Uh-huh. That's pretty much what your son told us, Mr. Baldwin." Buckler gave Markie a friendly smile, and Trevor noticed that Markie did not smile back. The chief looked to Trevor again and said, "I want to thank both of you for talking to me. This probably wasn't the best start to your weekend."

Trevor was surprised. "That's it?"

"That's it. What else is there?" Buckler stretched, then stepped over to the door and held it open. Trevor hopped down from the examination table, then lifted Markie to the floor. They followed the chief into the hallway.

William Relling Jr.

Trevor checked out at the emergency desk. The woman in the pullover was no longer around. Chief Buckler escorted him and Markie outside, to where Brad Cusimano was waiting for them in his cart.

"At least everything *looks* copacetic," Brad said, smiling.

Buckler gave Brad a weary smile in return. "As far as your friends are concerned," the chief said, "the doctor's given Mr. Baldwin a clean bill—"

"*Chief!*"

The three men and Markie turned to look at the policeman who had driven the second Jeep to the hospital. He was jogging toward the four of them from the emergency entrance.

"Just a second, Dave," Buckler called.

The policeman drew up alongside the chief. "Andy's on the radio from the reservoir," he said, out of breath. "They're just about to bag that kid's body they scraped off the trail—"

Buckler's glare cut the policeman off. The chief motioned to the Baldwins and Brad Cusimano, and said angrily to the young officer, "You mind waiting till I get back inside?"

The policeman looked sheepishly from the people in the cart to Ray Buckler.

"Tell Andy I'm on my way," the chief said. The policeman nodded to him, then turned and trotted back toward the hospital.

Buckler shook his head sadly and muttered under his breath, "Dumb shit." He looked up. "Sorry," he said.

Trevor forced a smile. "Guess this just isn't your day, Chief," he said.

"Tell me about it," Ray Buckler grumbled.

Hours earlier, the Brujo had watched with raven's eyes the fire that had consumed the sailboat below him. He had taken vengeance.

The satisfaction that he had felt earlier had given way to new emotions as he tested the limits of his power. He had felt frustration at the failure of his winged brothers' earlier attack upon the invaders at sea. His brothers were still too few in number, and the Brujo's power was not yet strong enough for him to enlist the aid of the beasts of the sea.

With the Brujo's frustration had come rage.

He directed that rage toward the two Evil Ones on the smaller ship. The Brujo felt the agony his brother creatures suffered at the hands of the white man on the burning craft below. The birds' deaths had saddened and infuriated him.

The strong emotions fueled the Brujo's power, and he was able to *reach* the unconscious mind of the white man. It was much the same as when he had touched the mind of the woman whose dog the raven had killed, causing her to see the dog come back to life.

In the man's mind the Brujo had discovered the means of destroying him. With fire.

Afterward, he had withdrawn from the raven, exhausted. The power was growing, but slowly. It was difficult to *reach* human beings unless their minds were somehow weakened already or, like the one whom the Brujo had chosen to serve him, they were as easily led as the beasts. The Brujo needed to have the power fully under his control.

But while he rested, he suddenly felt his spirit touched by a new presence. He came alert and *reached*, but whatever it was that had touched him for a fleeting instant had passed by and was gone. The sensation remained: He had been touched by one like him, a special one, one who had not been on the island when the Brujo awoke but who was here now. One in whom the power lay dormant but very strong.

The Brujo felt his excitement growing. *I must find him*, he whispered to himself. He prayed.

Chinigchinich, help me. Chinigchinich . . .

But there was only the darkness.

Suddenly the Brujo felt doubt. The Evil Ones had returned, of that the Brujo was certain. And *Chinigchinich* had awakened him, had allowed another with the power to touch him . . .

But for what purpose?

Darkness.

For what purpose, if not vengeance? Why give

him the power? *Chinigchinich* must want vengeance, as the Brujo himself wanted vengeance . . .

Darkness.

Chinigchinich must remember what the Evil Ones had done to his people, as the Brujo himself remembered . . .

Darkness.

The Brujo's power surged. He *reached*.

The darkness had driven him insane.

Eight

Casey Harrison was alone in the dark.

He sat cross-legged on his bed, his bare back and shoulders against the wall at the head of the bed. He stared blankly at the door opposite him.

Casey was not aware that he had been in that same position for nearly seven hours, nor was he aware that the sun had set two hours before.

He knew that the room was dark, and a chilliness had spread from the crotch of his jeans and turned his skin to gooseflesh.

Casey was aware of the darkness, and the chill, and the *nightmare*.

William Relling Jr.

It was as if a part of his consciousness had detached. A portion of his mind could observe what was happening to him but couldn't motivate any action. That part was aware of Casey's physical conditions—the chilliness and the dark—as well as the nightmare that had been replaying itself in his mind continuously for the past several hours.

Ever since Casey saw the raven.

The way that the dream ran over and over reminded the detached part of Casey's consciousness of a moviola, a machine that ran the same film loop endlessly on the projection screen of Casey's mind. All Casey could do was watch.

It was the same dream he had been having for the past several nights, the dream in which Casey saw himself buried alive. Now, however, he was wide awake. He could see himself in the pit, struggling, unable to move—until that last moment when the sand and earth pouring into the pit spilled into his mouth and nostrils, choking him, and it was too late . . .

The dream repeated itself for hours—it would finish a loop then immediately begin again. Casey Harrison sat quietly on his bed, hypnotized by the nightmare images in his mind's eye.

But, strangely, the dream didn't frighten him anymore.

At first, the detached portion of Casey's consciousness simply did not accept the dream's reality. Like a man looking at an onrushing tidal wave or a descending avalanche who makes no attempt to escape, he was unable to believe that what his senses were showing was actually happening to him. Casey told himself that what happened in the dream was happening to somebody else.

Somebody else . . .

But as the hours passed and Casey watched the nightmare unreel in his mind again and again, the feeling of detachment changed. Each time the scene started over, each time Casey saw himself captured and bound and dragged to the pit, a new feeling grew stronger.

Casey wanted *revenge*.

Neither Casey-in-the-dream nor Casey-observing-the-dream was afraid of the Evil Ones who tortured him. Casey could only feel his hatred for them and a need to repay them for what they did, for what they were doing, for what they *would* do to him, as long as the dream recurred.

But I don't know who they are.

Casey forced himself to concentrate on their faces, but he couldn't see them clearly, couldn't bring them into focus. They were shadows.

Who are you?

Casey watched the dream a dozen more times. He still could not identify them, could not see the faces of his killers.

Who are you?

The frustration fired Casey's rage.

Who are you!

Brrrrrrrinnnng . . .

Casey twisted furiously, trying to get to his feet.

Whoareyouwhoareyouwhoareyouwho!!!!!

Brrrrriiinnnng . . . brrrriiiinnnngg . . .

William Relling Jr.

Casey struck reflexively at the telephone on the nightstand next to his bed. The phone crashed to the floor, jangling the receiver off the hook.

A tiny, distant voice floated up to him. "Casey? Hey, Casey, you there?"

Casey shook himself, feeling as if someone had thrown ice water in his face. A switch had closed in his brain, and he could move again. It took several seconds for him to realize where he was.

The tiny voice said, "Hey, man, you there?"

Casey reached for the receiver. He looked at it oddly for a moment, then held it to his ear.

"Casey—"

"Who are you?" Casey's voice was a dry croak.

"It's Wes, man," the voice answered. "You okay?"

"Wes?"

"Yeah. You know, from the bar." The voice paused. "You don't sound so good, man. You sure you're okay?"

Remember, Casey told himself.

"I'm fine," he said into the phone. "What d'ya want?"

"You said you were gonna stop by and see your friend today. Remember?"

Casey had gotten up from the bed to step to the window. He pushed aside the drapes. He frowned at the night outside, puzzled. "What time is it?" he asked.

The voice chuckled at him. "It's almost eight o'clock, man. You musta got some excellent stuff, 'cause you really sound *wasted*." Then the voice said more softly, "Boss lady just cruised in. I gotta go. You're on in an hour. You're gonna be here, right?"

"I'll be there."

Casey hung up and replaced the telephone on the nightstand. He sat down on the edge of the bed.

The room was dark.

I'll be there, Casey told himself. I'll be there.

Because he knew that *they* would be there, too.

Nine

Trevor Baldwin was trying to figure out when his day had gotten away from him.

It started off fine, he thought. Markie had been ready to go when Trevor arrived at his ex-wife's apartment, and Valerie Heath's plane reservations had been easily taken care of. Everything had gone smoothly until Trevor and the boy got on the *Long Beach King*.

Not that I mind a little adventure once in a while, Trevor said to himself, but this is ridiculous. First the bird attack, then the hospital—and the doctor had been right about the anesthetic wearing off. Trevor's stitches had begun to itch late in the afternoon, and it had been damn near impossible for him to keep from scratching. It wasn't long before the itch had shifted to a dull soreness that was even more annoying.

So. The boat, the hospital, then Brad . . .

Trevor frowned. Brad had made kind of a pain in the ass of himself after they left the hospital. Granted, he had been good about taking care of the Baldwins' hotel reservations, had seen that their luggage was delivered from the boat, and had kept an eye on Markie while Trevor was being stitched up. But when they had pulled away from the hospital, Trevor asked Brad to take them to the hotel so he could rest a little. It was already past four o'clock, Brad had argued, and it would be light only for another couple of hours at the most, and the property Brad wanted to look at was not that far away.

Only after Trevor had insisted adamantly had Brad given in and driven the Baldwins to the hotel. Trevor could tell that Brad was unhappy about it, but there wasn't much Brad could do if he wanted Trevor to come to work on his project. Grudgingly he agreed that the trip to the site could wait until Saturday morning.

He offered to treat Trevor and Markie to dinner, after they unpacked and had a chance to relax for a couple hours, and Trevor accepted. Shortly after 7:30, he and Markie were ushered into the El Capitan Hotel's restaurant, just off the lobby, next to the hotel bar.

Brujo

* * *

At a few minutes past nine o'clock, Trevor was sipping a cup of coffee while Markie finished a chocolate sundae. Brad Cusimano had gone to the rest room, leaving them alone.

Trevor was looking at his son thoughtfully. Thank God for small favors, he said to himself. Markie hadn't acted in the least unhappy or bored since they left the hospital, had asked questions about what few sights of Catalina Island they had seen while driving, and seemed to be having a good time. Unlike his father.

Trevor was trying to think of an excuse to call it a night. He looked down at his watch, then back to his son. "Past your bedtime, sport," Trevor said.

Markie swallowed a spoonful of ice cream. "Mom lets me stay up late on Fridays."

"I'm not your mom, Mark."

"I know." The boy looked up at Trevor, questioning his father with his eyes. "How come you don't like Mr. Cusimano, Dad?" Markie asked.

Trevor was taken aback. "Who says I don't like Mr. Cusimano?"

Markie shrugged. "You don't talk much to him. He talks all the time."

"I like him fine, Mark," Trevor said. "I just . . ."

He paused. His son was looking at him with an odd, knowing expression, as if to say, Who are you trying to kid? Markie looked at his father for a moment, then turned back to his ice cream.

You're still pretty goddamn shrewd for a six-year-old, Trevor said to himself.

"Tell you what," Trevor said. "You finish your dessert, and I'll take you back up to our room, and you can stay up and watch TV till I finish with Mr. Cusimano. How's that?"

"Okay with me," Markie said.

"Me, too," said Brad as he sat back down at the table. "I was hoping to get a chance tonight to show you the preliminary sketches I brought, Trev. If you want, you can stop by my room on your way up."

Trevor shook his head no, then smiled apologetically. "The least I owe you is a nightcap," he said. "Why don't you pick up the sketches and meet me in the bar?"

"You sure you're not too tired?" Brad asked. "It won't take more than a half hour."

"I'm starting to feel a whole lot better," Trevor said.

While Brad paid the check, Trevor walked Markie up to their room on the hotel's third floor. Trevor watched his son change into pajamas, brush his teeth, and climb into bed.

Trevor tucked Markie in, then sat down on the edge of his bed. "Listen, Mark," he began.

Markie looked at his father curiously. Trevor wasn't at all sure how to bring up what was on his mind.

"You mind if I ask you a personal question?"

Markie shrugged. "Sure, Dad."

Trevor looked at his son, hoping that he didn't appear to be too serious. "How come you didn't like that cop?" he asked.

Markie's face darkened. "What cop?"

"You know who," Trevor said. "Chief Buckler."

"Oh. Him."

"Yeah. Him."

Markie pressed his lips together.

"Did he say something to you?" Trevor asked. "Something you didn't like?"

Markie shook his head. "Huh-uh. Nothin' like that."

"Then what?"

Markie's jaw clenched.

"C'mon, Mark." Trevor urged. "I let you ask me about Mr. Cusimano."

"His name is Ray, Dad," Markie blurted.

"Ray?"

Markie was looking hard at his father, waiting for him to understand.

Then it came to Trevor. Ray was the name of Claudia's boyfriend. Ray the gynecologist.

Trevor nodded slowly as the realization came to him, thinking that perhaps he didn't know his son as well as he thought. "You're not mad at me, are you, Dad?" Markie asked.

Trevor managed a smile. "No, sport," he said. "I'm not mad." He pulled the covers up to Markie's chest, kissed him good night, and left him watching an umpteenth rerun of *It's a Mad, Mad, Mad, Mad World*, promising to be back before the movie was over at eleven.

William Relling Jr.

* * *

Trevor walked into the Crow's Nest Lounge at a little after ten o'clock. Brad wasn't there yet, so Trevor ordered a bottle of Henry Weinhardt's and found an empty table near a picture window that overlooked Avalon Bay.

The El Capitan Hotel was part of a small, Spanish-style, crafts-oriented shopping area called El Encanto. The hotel itself stood on a slight rise above Crescent Avenue, the street that encircled Avalon's beachfront.

Trevor had a fine view, lit by a pale full moon. To his left, on the northeast point of Avalon Bay, stood the round, twelve-story Avalon Casino, the famous ballroom and movie palace that was one of the island's prime tourist attractions. Below the casino the moonlight glinted darkly off Avalon Bay, which was dotted with two dozen or so private yachts moored there. Only a handful of boats weren't tarped or tied down or both, a sure sign that it was off-season for vacationers.

The relatively small number of people in the Crow's Nest Lounge was another sign. Counting the two bartenders, the long-haired guy playing the piano, and himself, Trevor figured there were maybe twenty-five people, making the room barely half full. Still, Trevor didn't doubt that the bar did good business in the summer. The El Capitan was a new hotel and had a great location, and the bar would get lots of spillover business from the restaurant.

Trevor motioned to Brad Cusimano, who had

stepped through the entrance to the bar and was looking around the room. Brad stopped at the bar and ordered a drink, then walked over to where Trevor was sitting. Brad drew a second table alongside Trevor's and spread on it a sheaf of architect's sketches.

They went over the sketches for several minutes. In his mind, Trevor began to outline the costs of what Brad wanted done. Brad wanted Trevor to handle the skeletal and exterior work for ten condominiums, which would take advantage of the natural lay of the land on which they were to be built. Brad was hoping to begin construction as soon as possible, in order to be finished with the exterior by New Year's, thereby avoiding southern California's rainy winter season which ran from January through March. Trevor told him that there shouldn't be any problem making the deadline, assuming that Brad's description of the land was accurate. Then, after some coaxing, Trevor gave Brad the rough figure that he had calculated for the cost of the job.

Brad leaned back in his chair, thinking. Then, slowly, he smiled.

"Sounds good, Trev," he said. "Sounds real good. I don't think we'll have any trouble working something out." They shook hands, and Brad signaled the bartenders for another round.

Trevor was surprised with himself, but pleased. He hadn't really been expecting to make any kind of potential business deal at all, much less one that had been so easy and painless. One of the bartenders—whose name, Wes, was on a plastic badge pinned to his shirt—brought their drinks, and Trevor gave him a ten-dollar bill. "Keep it," Trevor said as the guy reached into a pocket for change. The bartender nodded thanks, and as he left their table, Brad and Trevor toasted to success.

Trevor settled back in his seat, and for the first time he paid attention to the pianist-singer who was performing on a tiny raised stage next to the bar. Trevor had noticed the guy's name on a board in the hotel lobby: Casey Harrison.

He was singing:

> "It's night time again
> Can't say where I've been
> You start all over again
> Start all over again"

The guy's not bad, Trevor thought. He's got a nice, smooth voice—maybe a little boozy, but smooth.

Casey Harrison's voice didn't match his appearance. He was young—maybe twenty-five or so—and he looked as if he had stepped out of a time machine from the year 1969. He had scraggly, shoulder-length hair, a couple days' growth of beard, and was wearing worn jeans, a T-shirt, and sneakers. And the guy moved like he was fucked up. His upper body was swaying, just a little, like it was hard for him to sit up.

He looks like he came in here to get warm, Trevor thought.

Brad Cusimano must have been thinking the same thing. He leaned over to Trevor and whispered, "Spare change?" Trevor chuckled.

Casey Harrison began another song, an upbeat rock and roll tune that surprised Trevor because he recognized it, a Billy Joel song called "You May Be Right." Trevor listened to the singer, until all of a sudden he realized that the long day was catching up with him. Trevor felt very tired, and he leaned his chair back against the window behind him and yawned.

"Whatsamatter?" Brad said, grinning. "You don't like rock and roll?"

Trevor stifled another yawn and grinned back. "I'm an old man, Bradley," he said. "This night life's too much for—"

Whump!

Something outside had smacked into the glass behind Trevor's head. Startled, he pitched forward and caught the table in front of him with both hands.

Trevor heard Brad cry out, "Jesus Christ!"

Brad was looking out the window past Trevor, his eyes wide with disbelief. As Trevor began to turn around, it struck him that the entire room had become silent. The singer had stopped in the middle of his song, no one was talking. It was as if all sound and movement in the bar had been frozen—until whatever it was *whumped* into the glass again, and someone in the bar screamed.

Everything began to happen in fast motion. Trevor spun around, and he saw at least a dozen dark, winged shapes silhouetted against the moonlit sky. They were flying right at him from the other side of the glass.

Trevor cringed reflexively. *Not those goddamn birds again!*

Trevor watched one of the shapes smash into the window head-on. It smeared the glass with blood as it fluttered and fell. The window shuddered, and light sparkled off tiny cracks in the glass that had been caused by the creature's impact. Trevor had gotten a good look at the thing, at its furry, rat-shaped head and its wings, covered with leathery skin rather than feathers.

In a single instant the rest of the creatures crashed through the weakened window, exploding the shattered glass inward, and the Crow's Nest Lounge was filled with bats.

Trevor hit the floor as the creatures burst into the room. Brad Cusimano had already taken cover beneath their two tables.

From under their shield Trevor and Brad watched the lounge degenerate into a scene of panic. About half of the customers had managed to escape the room right away, but many of those who hadn't were shrieking in terror of the creatures that flittered maddeningly around them. Trevor saw a middle-aged woman fall to the floor near the entrance to the bar, with two of the beasts tangled in her hair. The bartender named Wes was trying to pull the creatures off her while a third bat flapped in his face, nipping at his eyes. The other bartender had gotten a broom and was swatting at the rest of the bats, trying to divert their attention from the people fleeing the room.

Suddenly Trevor's gaze was drawn to Casey Harrison.

The young musician was standing at the edge of the stage, not moving. He was watching what was happening, but he seemed not interested, as if what he was watching weren't real. Even more strange was that the bats seemed just as uninterested in him, as if he weren't even there.

Trevor saw Casey Harrison shiver violently. Then, slowly, the young man raised his hands into the air, as if in supplication.

And he screamed.

Trevor wasn't certain, but it sounded to him as if Casey Harrison was actually shrieking *words*, though in a language that Trevor couldn't understand. The young man held his hands high over his head, priestlike, and screamed the words over and over.

Then, abruptly, he stopped. He lowered his arms and spread them open, as if to embrace the bats.

Brad whispered, "What the hell is this?"

The bats had flown into a circle above the young musician, forming a weird, living halo over his head. Casey Harrison closed his eyes and looked as if he was praying.

Then his eyes snapped open and he leaped from the stage, running full-out, directly at Trevor and Brad.

They cringed and ducked, but instead of crashing into them, the musician vaulted over the tables, jumped through the shattered window, and was off into the night.

Trevor looked up cautiously and saw the bats join into a dark cloud and fly out the window after Casey Harrison.

Stunned, Trevor stared in disbelief at the broken window. Something touched his arm, and he yelped, startled.

"Christ, Trev!" Brad said, jerking back his hand.

Trevor sighed. He swallowed hard. "It's okay," he said. "My fault."

Brad shook his head. "No, man, I'm sorry," he apologized. "I didn't mean to scare—"

Brad caught himself. Then he looked at Trevor strangely and said, "I wish you could tell me what it is with you and these fucking animals."

Trevor's voice was hushed. "I wish I knew myself," he said, staring out the window once more. "I swear to God, I wish I knew."

Saturday

For the first time in nearly two centuries, the Brujo felt strong.

He was relishing his power. Never before had it been so strong. It is the will of *Chinigchinich*, the Brujo told himself. He was to be his god's instrument of vengeance. Of that the Brujo no longer had any doubt.

Still, the Brujo had not felt truly alive until that moment when he *reached* the mind of the one whom he had chosen, The-One-Who-Would-Serve. Only then, when he guided The-One and sent him into the night with his brother creatures, when with The-One the Brujo could feel the sting of the night air on his flesh, could feel the blood coursing through his veins, could feel the sights and smells and sensations of a world the Brujo had not known for almost two hundred years. Only then . . .

Alive.

The Brujo guided The-One-Who-Would-Serve into the hills, away from the city. He lead The-One to shelter near a strange, metal pond, not far from where his brothers had attacked the young white man who had been the first to suffer the Brujo's vengeance.

The-One-Who-Would-Serve remained there while the Brujo read his thoughts. The Brujo needed to learn more about those whom *Chinigchinich* would have him destroy.

After a time, he allowed The-One to sleep. Then the Brujo searched once more, briefly, for the spirit that had touched him earlier, the spirit who knew the power. The-One-Who-Would-Serve was a mere vessel, simply another beast who could be bent to the Brujo's will. But this spirit, The-Other . . .

He is near, the Brujo told himself. But the Brujo could not find him. He was hidden in darkness.

Then, as the night sky began to lighten to gray, the Brujo awakened The-One and brought him to his feet. At the same time, the Brujo *reached* the raven, instructing the bird to accompany The-One-Who-Would-Serve. The Brujo realized that, because he could *reach* both his spirit-brother and The-One together at the same time, the power was at last fully under his control . . .

Ten

At 5:30 on Saturday morning Ray Buckler lay in bed wide awake. Not because he was an early riser—Buckler had abandoned that habit when he was promoted from patrolman to sergeant of the Los Angeles Police Department fifteen years before. He was awake simply because he had scarcely slept the entire night. He had come home dog-tired, shortly after 1:00 A.M., and had immediately undressed and fallen into bed. He must have dozed for an hour or so, because he remembered looking at his wristwatch that he had set on the nightstand next to the bed, and the numbers had read 2:35.

Ray Buckler had been awake ever since.

He lay with his arms folded behind his head, resting them on his pillow. What was it that guy Baldwin said? Buckler was thinking. "Guess it wasn't your day, Chief." Buckler smiled to himself ruefully. Brother, you don't know the half of it.

The sea gull attack aboard the *Long Beach King* was only the beginning. There had also been the case of Grace Mitchum's dog—and Grace had made a royal pain in the ass of herself all Friday morning, till the chief had snapped at her in the hallway of the Avalon Community Hospital.

After that, Buckler had had to go look at the kid whose body had been discovered near the West Summit Reservoir. What a colossal fucking mess *that* had been . . .

I feel sorry for that friend of his who found him, Buckler thought. He wondered what could have gone through Robert Cruz's mind when he found his friend ripped to pieces, whole hunks of his flesh torn away, his insides mashed and chewed. Or when he stumbled across Walker's dismembered head in the bushes, ten yards from the rest of him.

Ray Buckler shuddered a little, recalling the sight. It was as bad as anything he had seen while he was with the LAPD. But the dumb son of a bitch shouldn't have been screwing around with those wild pigs, Buckler told himself. That had to be what happened. The chief's men had found the animals' prints in spatters of the dead kid's blood.

Buckler shuddered again. Christ, there must have been a half dozen of the goddamn things.

Right after he had spoken to Eric Walker's parents on the phone, informing them of their son's death, Ray Buckler had gotten the report of the wrecked sailboat anchored in a cove between Kelp Point and Cape Cortez on the island's ocean side. Two day hikers had spotted the burning wreck late in the afternoon, and when they first saw it, they said, smoke was still pouring from the boat's deck. By the time the police and the Coast Guard got to the boat it was after dark and the fire was nearly out. All that was left for Chief Buckler to do was to arrange for the transportation to the mainland of two more bodies.

At 10:45 Friday night, as Buckler was finally slipping into his jacket to go home, there came the call from the night manager of the El Capitan Hotel. The end to a perfect day, Buckler thought.

The chief had ended up staying at the hotel for an hour while he helped a pair of his officers get statements from the witnesses in the Crow's Nest Lounge, including Trevor Baldwin and Brad Cusimano. Then he had arranged for the eight people who had actually been bitten by the bats to be taken to the hospital for treatment. Buckler was grateful that none of them had been badly injured. Then he would never have gotten home.

As it was, it had taken another hour back at his office to run a check on Casey Harrison and to get hold of Harrison's "To Be Notified in Case of Emergency," a woman named Bendyk who lived

William Relling Jr.

in LA. At last somebody tracked her down, and she called the chief at 12:30 from a rock and roll club in Santa Monica. Their phone connection was terrible, and what with the noise in the club blaring behind her, Buckler was barely able to hear the woman. Finally she agreed to call the chief back Saturday morning, but at least he had been able to get out of her that Harrison was "undergoing psychiatric counseling." Whatever the hell that meant. The chief would find out when he talked to Ms. Bendyk again, in a few hours.

A few hours. Buckler sighed.

This job wasn't supposed to be that tough, Buckler thought. That was the main reason he had taken it four years before, because two years before that—when he was forty-two and had just been promoted to lieutenant—he had suffered a coronary thrombosis that had hit him one Sunday afternoon while he was jogging around the track of Van Nuys High School near his San Fernando Valley home. Buckler probably would have died had not his jogging partner been the high school's varsity football coach, who had with him his keys to the school. The coach was able to get to a phone quickly and call an ambulance.

Ray Buckler had undergone open-heart surgery to correct an arterial blockage. Nine months later he was back on limited duty with the LAPD's Special Investigative Division, but his health had effectively curtailed any further upward movement in the department's ranks.

However, Buckler's wife, Jeanne, was a cousin

of one of Los Angeles County's supervisors, and when the chief of Avalon's Police Department retired, the supervisor recommended Lieutenant Ray Buckler for the chief's position. That recommendation—plus those of Buckler's superiors in the LAPD, plus his solid if not particularly distinguished service record—made him more than qualified. Avalon's City Council offered him the job.

Ray Buckler and his wife settled comfortably in Avalon, and the job turned out to be pretty much what he had expected. Things got a little hairy in the summer months, when boatloads of tourists arrived continuously during the daylight hours from Memorial Day through mid-September, but usually Chief Buckler and his men dealt with no more serious criminals than out-of-towners who got a bit too drunk and disorderly.

Not that people didn't occasionally die on Catalina from one thing or another. Not a summer went by without at least one fatality, but most often it was a swimmer who had been caught in a riptide and drowned or a hiker who had taken a tumble from a cliff. The deaths were always from something that was easy to understand and explain.

That was what bothered Chief Buckler most right now. There didn't seem to be a real explanation for all that had happened on Friday. He had three people dead—three people and a dog—and another handful of people injured. On the surface there didn't seem to be much of a connection between anything that had happened, except that three of the cases—and probably that of Grace Mitchum's dog, too—involved animal attacks.

Buckler had tried to come up with explanations. Grace's dog? It could have been a hungry eagle. Grace might have scared it off before it had finished eating Bridey. Eric Walker? He did something that bothered the pigs, and they came after him. The *Long Beach King*? Everybody knows that sea gulls are nasty and unpredictable. The sailboat? Something on board exploded, for whatever reason. The bats? One of the chief's men had guessed that they were red bats that had been attracted by the lights and movement behind the window of the bar. Casey Harrison? He's a looney tune.

Buckler frowned. It wasn't that there weren't explanations. On the contrary, he had at least one explanation for each separate incident. The problem was that twenty-odd years as a cop had made Ray Buckler very distrustful of coincidences—especially bad ones—and this morning he had about three coincidences too many to account for.

Buckler was grateful that his wife was away for the weekend. Jeanne Buckler was visiting their only child—their daughter, Carole, who was a graduate student at the University of San Francisco. The chief was considering whether it was too early to give them a call when the telephone next to his bed rang. Buckler glanced at his watch as he reached for the receiver. It was 6:05.

On the line was Sergeant Carl Ritter, the desk officer for the graveyard shift. Ritter apologized for waking the chief, then told him that an emergency call had just come in from El Rancho Escondido, the Wrigley Ranch in the middle of Santa Catalina Island. Ritter had sent Jim Medina, one of the two patrolmen working the night shift, to answer the call.

"But I thought I should call you, Chief," Ritter said. "That girl Katy was the one who phoned. You know, the one who helps Cap Willison with the horses sometimes? But . . ." Ritter paused.

"But what?" Buckler asked.

"We got cut off, Chief. And when I was talking to Katy, she sounded scared shitless. She couldn't hardly talk at all."

The chief instructed Ritter to wake another two patrolmen and send them as backup for the first man. Fifteen minutes later Ray Buckler was in his Jeep, heading for his office in the Avalon Civic Building.

The tiny streets of Avalon were quiet and deserted. The headlights of Ray Buckler's Jeep cut the low fog very little, and the chief drove carefully. Nearly half the houses he passed, it seemed, were boarded up and empty.

Buckler shivered involuntarily. It's a goddamn ghost town, he thought.

Eleven

Officer Jim Medina couldn't decide whether he was more angry with Carl Ritter for radioing him an hour before Medina was to go off duty or with himself for answering the goddamn call. Like all policemen, Officer Medina dreaded any end-of-shift disturbance that would keep him overtime, most of which time would be spent writing reports.

Medina frowned. Too late to worry about it now, he thought.

He tried to forget how comfortable he had been in his Jeep, parked in the lot of Catalina's airport. Early in his three-year career with the Avalon

William Relling Jr.

Police Department, Jim Medina had learned that the airport was one of the best spots on the island from which to watch the sun rise over the mainland. Sergeant Ritter's radio call had roused him from a pleasant half sleep, and Medina was still a bit groggy as he maneuvered the Jeep down the narrow blacktop road that covered the four miles from the Airport-in-the-Sky to El Rancho Escondido.

Medina wondered what could possibly be wrong at the Wrigley Ranch, which was what most people called El Rancho Escondido. He had only been to the property a couple of times himself, most recently when his brother and sister-in-law had come to Catalina for a weekend several months before, and Medina had taken them on the Inland Motor Tour that showed them the entire island. The tour bus had stopped for about forty-five minutes at Rancho Escondido.

There wasn't a whole lot to the place, Medina recalled. The tourists got off the bus and were greeted by an old guy who called himself "Cap" and who, Medina found out later, was the ranch's only real full-time resident. The Wrigley family rarely used the ranch property anymore, except for an occasional vacation, but Cap Willison still took care of the prize-winning Arabian horses owned and bred there by the Wrigleys.

During his tourist spiel Cap had said that he had been employed by the Wrigley family for thirty-five years, ever since he had retired, and before that he'd been one of the top stuntmen/

wranglers in Hollywood in the 1940s. Jim Medina had no problem believing that the old guy was exactly who he said he was, because Cap gave Medina and his fellow bus riders a demonstration of his horsemanship. Cap had to be sixty-five years old if he was a day, but the old guy handled a horse as well as any cowboy Medina had ever seen on television or in the movies.

So what could be wrong? Medina doubted that it was a burglar or a trespasser—the ranch was too isolated and inaccessible for a thief—and Cap Willison wouldn't have any trouble dealing with stray overnighters on his own. Maybe Cap had gotten hurt—had broken a bone or something—and was calling for a ride to Avalon because he couldn't drive himself.

The Jeep came to the crest of the ridge overlooking the ranch. Officer Medina braked the vehicle and paused to look down on the property, trying to peer through the gray, predawn mist that enshrouded the ranch buildings and corrals. Medina was about to start down the hill when an odd thought struck him. He sat back in the driver's seat.

El Rancho Escondido. Spanish for "the hidden ranch."

Medina grunted to himself, feeling a bit silly about his momentary apprehension. Hidden Ranch. Good name for the place, Medina told himself.

He shrugged, pushed the Jeep into gear, and started down the incline that led to the ranch's main gate. Medina made his way slowly. The fog reduced his visibility to barely fifty feet, and he had no intention of rolling into the huge metal gate that marked the entrance to the ranch. He could imagine trying to explain to Chief Buckler that he had damaged both city and private property. Much better just to take it easy.

Medina peered through the windshield, looking for the gate, till the beams from the Jeep's headlights reflected from something metallic. He slowed down until he felt the vehicle's front wheels rumble over some sort of grate. Cattle guard. Medina brought the Jeep to a quick stop, set the emergency brake, switched off the ignition and removed the keys, but left the Jeep's headlights on. Then he reached under the seat for a flashlight and climbed out of the vehicle, shutting the door behind him as quietly as he could.

The gate was bolted and chained, and it didn't appear to have been recently disturbed. Medina gave it a strong push, to make sure, and the gate held securely.

The policeman took a step backward and rubbed his jaw, thinking. Then he strapped the flashlight to his Sam Browne belt and vaulted over the metal barricade and onto the ranch property.

Medina unsheathed his flashlight and flipped it on. The gray fog had lightened only a little since he arrived at the ranch, and it was still difficult to see. Medina's boots crunched loudly on the gravel drive that led from the gate to the ranch's outbuildings. Something about the sound disturbed him.

Medina stopped, realizing that that was the only sound he could hear. He stood still for several seconds, listening intently. There was no sound—no breeze, no animals or insects, nothing except the soft exhale of his own breath.

He shuddered slightly, then caught himself. "You're a cop, goddammit," he muttered aloud. The sound of his own voice reassured him a little.

Why can't I hear the horses?

The policeman started moving again, shining his flashlight beam over the empty corrals and misty outbuildings he passed on his way to the squat, barnlike main stable at the end of the gravel drive. Medina stepped cautiously, trying to make as little sound as possible.

A dozen paces brought him close enough to make out the tall wooden doors that opened into the stable, and Medina could at last hear something other than the sound of his own footfalls. The stable doors were hanging open, and their hinges creaked softly as Medina approached. It seemed to him that the doors were beckoning him into the gloom.

Medina paused once more, just outside the stable. He was suddenly aware of a chill that danced along his spine. His skin felt clammy.

Something's in there, he told himself. Something—

The policeman forced a deep breath. *Stop being a fucking baby.*

Medina pushed aside one of the twin stable doors and stepped into the building, holding his flashlight as steadily as he could. Dawn had just begun to brighten the cracks in the wooden slats that made up the stable's walls and ceiling, and it took several moments for Medina's eyes to adjust to the eerie, gray half-light that surrounded him.

The stable was deserted.

Medina moved slowly along the straw-covered dirt floor, unable to shake the odd, unsettling chill he still felt. Something should be in here, he thought. At least the horses—

Medina froze.

All of the walls of the individual stalls—half a dozen along each side of him—had been smashed, splintered into pieces, as if a miniature tornado had whipped through the inside of the building, leaving only the exterior walls and ceiling intact. Medina bent down and picked up a piece of a shattered two-by-four that had once been part of a stall gate.

And he saw the blood.

One side of the piece of wood in Medina's hand was sprinkled with dark droplets that glistened in the beam of his flashlight. He dropped the broken board to the floor and noticed that everything around him—the straw, the chunks of splintered wood, the dirt floor itself—was spattered with blood. Medina was standing in the middle of a trail that began a little behind him in a sticky pile of matted straw, then ran ahead of him and led into the last stall on his left.

Medina closed his eyes for a moment, steeling himself. Then he crouched and moved toward the stall, trying hard not to imagine what might be there. When he glimpsed a bloodied pair of human feet poking from the legs of tattered pajamas, Jim Medina's stomach heaved violently. He dropped the flashlight, breaking it, then fell to all fours, vomiting.

It was some minutes before Officer Medina felt strong enough to examine the body in the stall, and another few minutes before he staggered from the stable, on his way back to the Jeep. He was halfway down the drive, trying to compose in his mind what he would say to Carl Ritter over the radio, when from the ranch bunkhouse to his right Medina heard someone—or something—whimpering.

His policeman's instincts took over, and Jim Medina dashed to the bunkhouse porch, his .38 caliber service revolver cocked and ready in his hand. The door to the bunkhouse was bolted from the inside, so the policeman leaned back and smashed a booted foot through a door panel. Medina reached inside and was able to unlatch the door and let himself in.

The shades had been drawn over the bunkhouse windows, and it was even darker than it had been in the stable, though the morning outside had grown brighter. Medina cursed himself for breaking his flashlight, and he crossed the threshold into the bunkhouse warily.

A girl's voice shrieked, "Don't touch me!"

Medina dropped into a crouch and peered into the shadowy gloom. The dark shapes of single bunks lined the walls on both sides of him, and he spotted the girl huddled in a far corner, behind the last bunk to Medina's right. He took a step into the room, and the girl shrieked again.

"I'm a policeman, goddamn it!" Medina yelled.

The girl screamed, "Stay away from me!"

"I said I'm a policeman!" Medina took another few steps forward, then stopped abruptly when he saw that the girl wasn't looking at him. Instead, she was staring, wide-eyed with terror, at something on the floor not far from her. He couldn't see what.

The girl began to whimper. "Cap . . . Cap . . . I'm so sorry . . ."

Medina took another step, and the girl turned to look at him. He could see her face clearly now, and her expression shifted from terror to puzzlement.

"Please," she said. "Don't."

"I'm a policeman," Medina said, moving closer to her. "Tell me what happened. What happened to Cap?"

The girl looked at him oddly. "The horses," she said, as if she were talking to a child. "The horses got scared. Cap got in their way."

Medina eased himself another few feet forward. "I'm gonna help—"

Chikka-chikka-chikka-chikka.

Jim Medina felt his heart tighten. He was near enough to the girl to see what she had been screaming at when he first came in.

Coiled on the floor near the end of the bunk, a

few feet from where the girl huddled in the corner, was a rattlesnake. Its horned tail was vibrating rapidly, and the snake's head was wavering from side to side, as if trying to determine which of the human shapes demanded its attention.

Jim Medina felt chill fingers playing over his skin. Slowly he shifted, trying to bring both hands to his revolver.

"Poor Cap . . ." the girl whispered. "Poor horses." She looked at Medina. "Horses are scared of snakes," she said, her voice far away.

"Just sit still," Medina whispered back. He was sighting on the snake's head when he heard behind him on the floor a soft scraping that raised hackles on his neck.

Medina whirled around, but not fast enough to sidestep a second rattlesnake. The snake struck a lightning-quick blow to the man's left calf, and Medina cried out at the sharp, burning pain. He tried to swat the reptile with his pistol, but the snake hung on to his leg, clinging by its fangs.

Medina tumbled away, losing his balance, and fell to the bunkhouse floor within a few feet of the first rattler. The policeman raised an arm to fight it off, but the snake was too swift. Its strike caught the man in the throat, just below his chin.

He grabbed at the reptile, but the snake evaded his grasp and slid back into its position near the girl. The other snake had let go of his leg as well, and Medina watched it slide away from him, toward the open bunkhouse door.

The man gingerly touched his throat and was

surprised that he didn't feel any pain. Dimly he was aware that his arms and legs had grown numb. He tried to drag himself toward the girl, but his body wouldn't respond. He shivered once, then lay still.

Jim Medina watched the snake near the girl raise its head and peer at him, as if trying to decide whether to attack again. Then it settled back down, almost at the same instant that Officer Jim Medina realized that his breathing had stopped, and closed his eyes.

The snake whispered to the raven, and the bird passed on the snake's words to his spirit-brother. The snake had freed the beasts who were the prisoners of the Evil Ones, and two more of the Evil Ones had died.

The beasts' imprisonment had angered the Brujo. At first he had tried to *reach* the strange and beautiful creatures himself, but they could not hear the Brujo speaking to them. For too long had they been prisoners.

So the Brujo had commanded the raven to speak

BRUJO

to the snake, and the snake had done as the Brujo wished.

The Brujo was pleased.

He had the raven return to The-One-Who-Would-Serve and guide The-One to a high place, a place from which the Brujo could watch with The-One's eyes the coming of his god *Chinigchinich*, the sun.

Twelve

The music slipped in softly, over the edge of Trevor Baldwin's consciousness. It was just loud enough for him to make out the words to the theme song of *The Flintstones*.

Trevor smiled to himself, rolled over in his bed, and opened his eyelids partway, enough so that he could see Markie sitting on the floor in front of the TV set.

The telephone on the nightstand between their two beds rang. Markie sprang from the floor and snatched the receiver before it could jangle a second time. "H'lo?" he said softly.

William Relling Jr.

Trevor had closed his eyes, playing possum. He heard Markie say into the phone, "He's still sleepin', Mr. Cusimano." There was a few seconds' pause, then Markie whispered, "Okay. Bye."

Markie gently replaced the telephone receiver on its cradle, then padded back to his spot on the floor. Trevor waited for a bit, then he began to moan in a low voice.

Markie kept his eyes glued to the television. Trevor groaned louder.

Markie still gave no sign that he heard his father, and Trevor had to force himself to keep from chuckling out loud as he slid out from under the covers of his bed. His bare feet touched the floor, and Trevor cooed, "Ooooooooooooh, Chase Monster. *Chase* Monster . . ."

Markie spun around. The boy squealed in fear and delight as Trevor made a grab for him. Markie leaped up from the floor, still squealing, and scrambled for his bed.

Trevor was on him in an instant, and Markie yanked the bedcovers up over his head. The covers muffled the boy's screams as his father rolled him from side to side. All the while Trevor groaned, "Chase Monster! Chaaaaaaaaaaaaase Monster!"

Then Trevor let go and slid off the boy-sized lump of bedclothes. He scooted to the top of the bed and sat cross-legged against the headboard. Trevor was grinning broadly as he leaned over to pat Markie on the rump. "Good morning, son," Trevor said cheerfully.

* * *

Brujo

After Trevor and Markie had showered and dressed, they left their hotel to meet Brad Cusimano for breakfast in a little coffee shop halfway down the block from the El Encanto shopping plaza. Trevor stopped at the hotel desk on their way out and telephoned the Catalina airport to confirm the time of arrival of Valerie Heath's flight. The plane was due at noon, which meant that they needed to be on their way out of Avalon no later than 10:30 if Trevor was going to get a look at Brad Cusimano's condominium site and still get to the airport in time to meet Valerie.

Brad was waiting for Trevor and Markie in a window booth that afforded a fine view of Avalon Bay. By ten o'clock the early morning low clouds had burned off, and everything was bathed in bright sunshine. Crescent Avenue, Avalon's main street, was relatively uncrowded for a Saturday morning, and Trevor guessed that it was because many prospective island visitors had been put off by reports of a storm that was heading northeast from Hawaii, a storm that was supposed to have materialized sometime between midnight Friday and 6:00 A.M. Saturday. Trevor was pleased that the storm hadn't come, and it looked as if it was going to be a beautiful, clear day.

From their booth they could also see the corner of the El Capitan Hotel, about a quarter of a mile up Crescent Avenue from where they sat. Markie pointed to a pair of workmen who had lowered a scaffold from the hotel's roof and were replacing the lounge's shattered window with a piece of plywood.

Brad and Trevor took turns telling Markie an abridged version of why the men were putting a board over a hole where a window used to be, and both of them were surprised to discover that they hadn't been very disturbed by what had happened in the lounge the night before. Once they were let go by the police, both Trevor and Brad had gone to their rooms and slept like babies, unlike Markie, who had been awakened by a strange nightmare a little before dawn. The boy had no memory at all of the dream's content and seemed to be just fine now.

"You should have seen that singer, Mark," Brad was saying. "Weirdest thing I ever saw. The guy was just standing there, screaming at everybody, but nobody could understand what the heck he was saying."

Markie took a swallow of milk, set down his glass, and wiped the white mustache from his upper lip with the back of his hand. "Ching-ching-itch," he burped.

Trevor paused with a forkful of scrambled eggs halfway between the plate and his mouth. He and Brad exchanged puzzled expressions, then turned to look at the boy. "What did you say, Mark?" Trevor asked.

The boy was chewing a piece of cinnamon toast. "Ching-ching-itch," Markie repeated. "That's what he was saying."

Trevor felt an odd tickle along the back of his neck. "Mark, how did you know—"

"Excuse me."

Trevor turned to face a tall, sandy-haired, heavyset man who had suddenly appeared beside him.

"I don't mean to interrupt your breakfast," the man went on, "but I couldn't help overhearing. You were in the El Capitan bar last night?"

Trevor nodded. The man slid into the booth next to Brad Cusimano, who was looking at the newcomer with obvious distaste. The man didn't seem to notice Brad at all. "I've been hearing about it all morning," the man said to Trevor. "Craziest goddamn thing."

Trevor frowned. "Look, mister—" he began.

"Jesus, I'm sorry." The man stuck out a large hand. "Doyle. Alex Doyle."

Trevor introduced himself, Markie, and Brad. Alex Doyle's eyes widened when he turned to the man next to him. "Cusimano," Alex said. "I didn't recognize you at first."

"You know each other?" Trevor asked.

"We've met before," Brad said, not happily.

Alex Doyle ignored him and turned back to Trevor. "This really happened last night?" he asked. "The bats and everything?"

Trevor nodded again. But before he could say anything, Brad cut in and said to the man beside him, "Doyle, what the hell do you want?"

Alex Doyle directed his explanation to Trevor and Markie. He said that he was the head librarian—in fact, the only librarian—for Avalon's branch of the Los Angeles County Public Library. Which didn't have anything to do with why he had come over to their table, he said. But he had heard Markie say something that had caught his attention.

Alex Doyle looked at the boy. "You said *Chinigchinich*?"

Markie nodded. "That's what the guy was saying last night. Ching-ching-itch."

Alex Doyle looked at the boy in wonderment. "It's amazing that you'd understand it," he said.

"More amazing than you know," Trevor said. "Markie wasn't even there. And neither of us told him."

The heavyset man's eyebrows went up. "Do you know what *Chinigchinich* is, Mark?" he asked.

Markie shook his head no.

"How about that," Alex Doyle chuckled. Then he began to scratch his forehead, thinking.

None of them spoke for several moments till, at last, Brad Cusimano said impatiently, "Well?"

Alex Doyle spoke absently, not really focusing his attention on any of them. "It's kind of a hobby of mine," he said. "Indians used to inhabit Catalina, hundreds of years before any white men came here. Their name for Catalina was 'Pimu.' And the name of their god—their main god, the sun god—was *Chinigchinich*."

"No shit," Brad muttered.

Alex Doyle paid no mind to the man sitting beside him. "It's not exactly common knowledge," he said to Trevor. "That's why I tuned in when I heard the boy say it."

Brad tapped his watch. "This is all real interesting, Mr. Doyle, but we've got another appointment . . ."

The librarian apologized again for bothering them and climbed from the seat to let them out. While Brad paid for their meal, Alex Doyle followed Markie and Trevor outside. They paused in front of the door to the coffee shop, and the heavyset man spoke to Trevor softly, so that no one else could hear him. "Mr. Baldwin, would you mind dropping by the library this afternoon if you get a chance?" he asked. "You and Mark? I'd really like to talk to you some more."

Almost without thinking, Trevor nodded. Doyle gave him a thin smile in return, then walked away. As Trevor watched the man disappear around a corner, he felt the same gnawing at the pit of his stomach that he had felt the day before on the bridge of the *Long Beach King*.

Brad emerged from the coffee shop to join the Baldwins on the sidewalk. As they started up the street toward the hotel, Trevor said to Brad, "That guy Doyle. Where do you know him from?"

Brad made a face, then told Trevor that Alex Doyle was one of the "irate citizens" of Avalon who had been fighting Brad's condominium project. "And then he's got the nerve to come over and spoil my breakfast," Brad grunted. "Jeez, Trev, could you believe that guy? What an asshole."

Trevor smiled to himself. He'd begun to suspect that Brad hadn't quite told the truth about his property being nearby when Brad drove the electric cart to a rental office and exchanged it for a small Jeep. Brad drove them north out of Avalon, heading for the island's interior. Trevor listened to Brad describe his plans in greater detail as the Jeep bumped over the narrow asphalt road that led to Two Harbors, at the opposite end of the island from Avalon.

Thirty minutes later they arrived at the barren property where Brad Cusimano and his partners were planning to build. The property was a small natural amphitheater that lay on the other side of several hills that blocked the land from Two Harbors proper, where there was a marina and a small Coast Guard installation. Brad explained to Trevor that he had spent five years negotiating with the Santa Catalina Island Conservancy and the Avalon City Council, first trying to acquire the land and then trying to get permission to build on it. Brad had also fought with several islanders who wanted to maintain strict control of Catalina's population, something that a condominium project would certainly disrupt.

Brad showed Trevor and Markie around the site, guiding them between wooden markers that indicated the boundaries of his property. The markers had been placed on Thursday, Brad explained, when he and his partners and some officials from Avalon had held a groundbreaking ceremony. Brad told Trevor that the property was virgin land and had never been developed, that before Thursday afternoon's clearing and groundbreaking, this particular piece of Santa Catalina Island had never been touched.

They left the site at 11:15. Brad drove back toward the island's interior, along a different road that rose gradually along a ridge that Trevor guessed was the spine of the island. At several points along the way, they could see the ocean on both sides of them.

The Jeep arrived at Catalina's Airport-in-the-Sky at 11:30. The only other vehicle in the parking lot was an airport shuttle bus from one of the hotels, an old Dodge van, newly painted white, with the hotel's logo in red and blue on its side. The driver was a young Mexican who looked to Trevor to be about nineteen years old, and he had only two passengers, an elderly couple. Clearly they were on their way back to the mainland; Brad and Trevor watched the driver unload their luggage from a small storage area behind the driver's seat.

Brad joked to Trevor that the couple's leaving was a bad sign for any hotel after what had happened Friday night in the El Capitan. Having two guests move out early this time of year no doubt reduced any lodging's population by a good 25 percent.

Since Valerie's plane wasn't due for another half hour, Trevor, Markie, and Brad decided to spend a little time exploring. There wasn't much to see. The airport, such as it was, stood on two acres of plateau at one of the island's highest points of elevation, at sixteen hundred feet above sea level.

William Relling Jr.

There was a single runway, a strip of asphalt barely three quarters of a mile long that ended abruptly at one edge of a cliff overhanging a drop of several hundred feet. There were few outbuildings: a cluster of aluminum and steel hangars that lay along the northwestern edge of the plateau, and in front of which sat rows of private planes that sparkled in the late morning sun, and a long, low, wood and brick structure. Picnic benches were spread near the parking lot. The long building served as a combination snack bar/waiting room/control tower, and it was there that Markie found someone to answer his questions.

Mr. Carr was the airport's weekend air traffic controller. Markie had spotted him through a doorway beyond the snack bar. The boy had managed to slip around a bored-looking teenage girl behind the snack bar's counter, and the controller invited Markie to watch him guide in the plane on which Valerie was a passenger. Markie accepted the invitation gleefully.

Trevor and Brad had been outside, and by the time they found Markie, the boy had gotten Mr. Carr's encapsulated history of the Airport-in-the-Sky. In 1946 the Santa Catalina Island Company hired a construction crew to shear the tops off a pair of mountain peaks, level the land, and lay a runway. Before then, Mr. Carr told Markie, the only aircraft allowed to fly to Catalina were seaplanes. The passengers had to get on and off the planes via a floating walkway that extended well into Avalon Bay.

Markie could hardly wait to repeat the story to his father and Brad, but before he could begin, the air controller's shortwave radio crackled loudly. Carr reached for his headset and said into the microphone, "Go 'head, seven-three."

"Roger, skyport," came a voice from the shortwave's speaker. "We got—"

The voice was suddenly cut off by a violent hiss of static. Then, for only a moment, it returned: "—skyport . . . *Jesus Christ!*"

The air controller barked into the microphone, "Seven-three, do you copy? Do you have a Mayday?"

He was answered by another blast of static from the radio. The controller repeated his request harshly, but there was no response from the plane.

The man tore off his headset, leaped from his seat, and bolted from the room.

Trevor and Brad were on the man's heels. They ran outside to the dirt parking lot between the building and the edge of the runway strip. Carr stopped there and looked off toward the horizon to the east. As Trevor came up behind him, he heard the air controller whispering, "Please pull up. Dear God, please let him pull up . . ."

Trevor looked in the direction that Carr was facing and spotted the tiny airplane shape, outlined against the clean blue sky. The shape grew larger, second by second, and as it approached, Trevor could feel the gnawing fear return to the pit of his stomach.

The plane was tilting crazily from side to side,

as if a giant stick ran along its underbelly, and the hand that held that stick kept twisting it back and forth, back and forth. Trevor could see that the plane's landing gear had not come down.

But what was most frightening was the ominous dark cloud that seemed to envelop the nose of the craft. As the plane continued its lunatic approach, Trevor's stomach heaved. "My God," he choked. "Valerie . . ."

Trevor heard the air controller beside him whisper, "Please . . . please . . ." as the plane began to drop.

Thirteen

Valerie Heath spent Friday night in the pleasant company of her mother and stepfather, Dorrie and Bill Kruetzemann, in their apartment a few miles north of Laguna Beach in Corona del Mar. Valerie's mother prepared lobster Mornay for supper from the *New Larousse Gastronomique* that Valerie had given her on her birthday two weeks before. Dorrie had recently taken up gourmet cooking as a hobby, and her husband had passed on the word to his stepdaughter that her mother had made a specific request for the cookbook that "both James Beard and Julia Child said if they could have only one, that would be the book they'd want."

William Relling Jr.

After supper they went up to the apartment's roof deck to watch the night fog roll in from the ocean. The fog slowly blanketed the stars and the inky, blue-black night with a deep, misty, charcoal gray. They talked for hours, sipping the hot buttered rum that Bill carried up after he had cleared the supper table.

While they talked, Valerie occasionally glanced surreptitiously at her mother and stepfather, catching the two of them as they nuzzled each other lovingly. Their behavior rarely failed to make Valerie smile, even though she had seen them sneak squeezes often in the five years that Bill and her mother had been married. They reminded Valerie of her seventh- and eighth-grade students in the throes of puppy love. An amazing thing, Valerie thought. Both Dorrie and Bill had lost a spouse some fourteen years before, and both of them were on the far side of sixty years old—yet more often than not, Dorrie and Bill treated each other with more genuine, and public, tenderness than any other couple that Valerie knew. Certainly much more than she and Trevor did.

That thought didn't occur to Valerie until hours later, when she lay in bed alone, in her apartment in South Laguna. She was thinking about her coming weekend with Trevor and his son. Valerie told herself that she was looking forward to the weekend, of course, and that she enjoyed the times when Markie Baldwin came along with his father. So there really wasn't any problem . . .

Or was there? Valerie knew that she was in love

with Trevor, whatever that meant, just as she knew that Trevor was in love with her. She had more or less made up her mind that she would marry Trevor if they were still together six months from now. Trevor was all for marriage—in fact, at least once every other week for the past two months he had asked Valerie to marry him.

So what's the problem? Valerie asked herself.

Ah, she answered, that is the Question.

Valerie lay on the bed in her darkened bedroom, arms folded behind her head, staring at the ceiling. How many times have I had this conversation with myself? she asked rhetorically. And why at some point did it always boil down to the same Question?

So what's the problem?

The Question had appeared in each of the three previous serious relationships in Valerie's life, and in each case Valerie had an easy, if painful, answer. The last man she had been involved with, for example, was one of her colleagues at school. He was also married, and not about to leave his wife. The affair had disintegrated badly and had left Valerie in a role she had sworn she would never play: the other woman. She spent too many nights alone, asking herself the Question over and over, and always she had come up with the same simple, obvious answer.

Which brings us to Trevor Baldwin, Valerie thought.

She and Trevor seemed to fit together so well that Valerie could hardly believe they had only known each other for less than three months. She remembered the New Year's Eve dinner party where they met, at the Irvine home of one of her stepfather's friends, a man who turned out to be one of Trevor's silent partners. At first Valerie had been miffed when she discovered that her meeting Trevor had all been arranged by her mother and Bill: she and Trevor were the only two people invited to the party who did not come with a "significant other," and they had been conveniently placed next to each other at the dinner table by Dorrie herself. Not that Valerie minded the man himself—Trevor was certainly attractive, tall and good-looking in a dark, Tom Selleck kind of way—but the whole idea of blind dates had soured long ago. She would have told her mother so in no uncertain terms, except that she and Trevor got along from the moment they were introduced, when Valerie found out that he was even more uncomfortable at being set up with somebody than she was.

The following weekend they went out on their first real date. Trevor took her to dinner at Villa Nova in Newport Beach, which by coincidence was one of Valerie's favorite restaurants, then to a revival of *Major Barbara* at the South Coast Repertory Theater.

On Wednesday of the following week, Valerie went to dinner at Trevor's house in Laguna, a dinner that he prepared himself, all Chinese—egg rolls, fried rice, egg fu yung, beef with broccoli, moo shu pork, steamed rice, almond cookies, Tsing Tao beer. Valerie taught him how to eat with chopsticks, an art that Trevor had never been able to master.

Afterward they sat on the deck at the front of Trevor's house, Valerie bundled in the bulky fisherman's sweater that he had lent to her, snuggling together in the chilly evening air, looking out at the black ocean. She knew that Trevor wanted her to stay the night, but that he was wrestling with himself, not knowing what to say or how to say it. It was refreshing and warm to be with a man who possessed a little sensitivity and didn't come on to her like the usual macho shitheads she encountered all too often. Valerie smiled at him as he pulled her close, and she said, "You don't have to ask me anything." Then she kissed him, and that was that.

On the weekend after that first night they spent together, Valerie met Trevor's little boy. She immediately fell in love with Markie; he was simply a great kid. After the weekend was over, when she and Trevor were driving down to Orange County after having taken Markie home to Trevor's ex-wife's place in west LA, Valerie began to take stock of what it was she was getting into. They drove in silence, not having to speak to each other, enjoying the drive, and occasionally Trevor would look over at her and she could see the light in his eyes and the small smile that she soon learned meant that they didn't have to be doing anything, that he just liked to be with her. She decided then that she liked to be with him, too.

Not that he was without his faults, she told

herself. His work often interfered with their plans, like the Valentine's Day trip to San Francisco that had to be canceled at the last minute because of some building permit snafu that forced Trevor to run up to Anaheim and spend all day and night straightening it out. Neither was Trevor very much on public displays of affection. She thought that it embarrassed him to hold hands or put his arm around her or even tell her that he loved her, though she knew very well that he did.

Still . . .

Would you repeat the Question?

Valerie lay awake for an hour, pondering an answer. She felt a bit frustrated that one wouldn't come. By the time she fell asleep, a little after 1:30 Saturday morning, the best that she had been able to do was to put it out of her mind—at least until the next night that she spent all by herself.

The taxicab that Valerie had phoned for arrived at her apartment at 10:15, at the same time that Alexander Doyle was introducing himself to the Baldwins in the coffee shop on Crescent Avenue in Avalon. It was a twenty-five-minute drive from Valerie's apartment to the John Wayne Orange County Airport. Valerie confirmed her reservation and picked up her boarding pass. She thought that the latter was a bit silly and unnecessary, since the eighteen-minute shuttle flight to Catalina carried a maximum of twenty passengers.

At 11:15, as Trevor, Markie, and Brad were heading for the Airport-in-the-Sky, Valerie Heath was crossing the tarmac from the rear of the Channel Islands Air Service terminal to board the small, twin-engine Beechcraft that would carry her and thirteen other passengers, along with a crew of four, to Santa Catalina Island.

The small plane left on schedule, taxiing easily, lifting off gently from the runway, then banking gracefully to the southwest. The morning sunlight glinted off its wings.

Valerie glanced down at her wristwatch at 11:55 and smiled to herself, thinking that she hoped Trevor was getting his money's worth. Her one-way ticket to Catalina had cost forty-five dollars . . .

Something tickled her cheek, and she brushed it away by reflex, not really noticing what it was. It landed on her forearm, and Valerie looked down to see a small honeybee. She shook her arm, but not quickly enough to prevent a burning sting just below her wrist. She cried out—at the same instant that the plane's nose suddenly dropped, hurling all of the passengers against the seats in front of them. Someone very close to Valerie was screaming.

The plane righted itself, and Valerie looked ahead to see the cockpit doors flop open. Out staggered one of the two flight attendants who had greeted the passengers. The woman was clawing at her face, at what appeared to Valerie to be a strange, moving, black cowl that covered the attendant's upper body. All the while the woman was screaming and screaming.

The plane tilted crazily again, and Valerie

William Relling Jr.

wrenched her shoulder trying to jerk herself free of her seat belt, but at last she managed to pop the belt loose. She pulled herself up by the back of the seat in front of her.

Valerie glanced forward. For a moment she could see past the flight attendant into the cockpit itself, where both the pilot and the copilot of the plane were flailing away madly at the cloud of insects that seemed to fill the space. The living cloud parted just long enough to allow Valerie a glimpse through the plane's windshield at the dark mass that loomed just ahead of the craft.

Valerie lost her grip as the plane whipped down again, tossing her into the seat across the aisle from her own. She cracked her head hard against the seat window, spidering the glass.

Valerie could feel herself slipping into a red and black unconsciousness; the screaming that filled the passenger cabin echoed farther and farther away from her.

Fight it, Valerie cried to herself. *Fight* . . .

But she was blessedly unaware of the last few seconds of her life, when Channel Islands Air Flight 73 slid, belly-down, screeching, along the asphalt at the end of the Airport-in-the-Sky's solitary runway; caught fire; then careened over the cliff that marked the runway's end—a blazing fireball tumbling down the side of a mountain toward the sea . . .

Fourteen

At the time of the crash of Flight 73, Chief of Police Ray Buckler was only four miles away from Catalina Airport at El Rancho Escondido. He had just finished instructing the pair of officers he was leaving behind to wait for the investigators from the Los Angeles County sheriff's office. Buckler had called the sheriff earlier that morning, after he had gotten the first reports of the grisly scene his men had discovered. It was obvious to Chief Buckler that neither of his officers relished the thought of having to stay at the ranch.

Not that he could blame them. The two men

William Relling Jr.

had been there since before 8:00 A.M., when they had been sent by Sergeant Ritter as backup to Jim Medina, whose body they discovered only minutes after they arrived. Katy Wylie huddled in the corner of the bunkhouse, not ten feet from Medina's body. Katy was alive and apparently uninjured, but she was in a state of frightened shock that rendered her all but incoherent.

Katy Wylie's condition unnerved the two policemen, perhaps more than finding the body, particularly since it wasn't at first clear what had happened in the bunkhouse. Then they rolled Medina's body over and discovered the puncture marks on the dead man's throat, just below his swollen, purple jaw. Very carefully the two officers searched the bunkhouse for snakes. But they found nothing.

It wasn't until after they had wrapped Katy Wylie in a blanket and put her in the back of their Jeep, then radioed in to Chief Buckler, that the officers searched the rest of the ranch and found the mangled remains of Cap Willison in the stable. The old man had obviously been trampled to death by the very horses he had loved for years. Apparently the animals had then smashed through the stable's rear wall and run off into the hills surrounding the ranch.

Chief Buckler was just climbing into his own Jeep to leave when he and his men heard a flat, distant boom that was too soft and far away to startle them. Buckler knew instantly that the explosion had come from the airport. He leaped into the Jeep, and as he spun it in a 180-degree turn in the gravel drive, he shouted to his men to stay put until he radioed them to do otherwise.

Ten minutes later Ray Buckler's Jeep crested the man-made plateau that was Catalina's airport. Siren blaring, all four wheels left the ground as the chief sped onto the airport property. Buckler whipped the vehicle around in a spray of dirt and rock, toward the asphalt runway and the edge of the cliff, beyond which bloomed a thick column of oily, black smoke. The chief slammed on his brakes, jammed the vehicle's transmission into park, and was just reaching for the handle of his door when he paused.

Where the hell is everybody?

Buckler could see a Jeep convertible and a red, white, and blue hotel van parked near the airport's terminal. He eased back against the seat, allowing his mind to slip quickly and smoothly into what he thought of as its "cop mode." Sort it out, Buckler told himself.

The chief looked down at his wristwatch.

Twelve-fifteen.

Scene of an accident.

Somebody should be here . . .

Buckler stepped out of the Jeep, leaving the door open behind him. He crossed the parking lot to the edge of the runway, head cocked slightly as he approached the plume of smoke that rose thirty yards away. An acrid burnt-rubber and gasoline smell made him crinkle his nose.

Buckler was forty paces from the edge of the

plateau when he heard a man's voice screaming behind him: "No! Don't! Nooooooooooo!!!"

The chief swung around, dropping into a crouch as he reached for the service revolver holstered at his right hip. Buckler looked in the direction of the voice, and his eyes opened wide.

For the first time in his life, Ray Buckler knew what it felt like to have the hairs on his head literally stand on end.

A man had appeared from around the side of the terminal, near the picnic benches. He was zigzagging his way toward the chief, staggering drunkenly. But what had raised Ray Buckler's hackles was the way the man was swatting furiously at the buzzing, moving cloud that swirled about him. All the while the man was shrieking in agony, "Get away! Get *away* from me!!!"

Buckler recognized immediately what was attacking the man. As a boy, the chief had visited his uncle's vineyards in Fresno. His uncle had raised honeybees in a half-dozen boxed hives in the backyard, not far from the house. One afternoon, for no apparent reason, an angry swarm had decided to attack his uncle's collie. The pain from hundreds of bee stings drove the dog mad, and though the insects' venom would have killed the poor animal anyway, Buckler's uncle had been forced to shoot the dog with his Winchester before the tormented creature turned on someone else.

The man took another few lurching steps forward before crumpling to his knees, trying futilely to cover his exposed skin. The cloud of insects enveloped him, wrapping itself around the fallen man.

Ray Buckler dashed back to his Jeep, his cop mode already working out a plan to try and save the man who was writhing on the ground two hundred yards away. At the same time, the chief was dimly aware of something nagging at the back of his mind, an odd sensation, a feeling that if he himself weren't careful . . .

They know I'm here.

Buckler dismissed the thought. He settled into the driver's seat and pulled the door shut, tugging it hard one time to make certain it was secure. Then he quickly rolled up his window, closed the vent, and glanced at the passenger side, making sure that those windows were also closed.

The chief twisted around to reach underneath his seat and pull out the metal toolbox that he kept there. He set the box on his lap, flipped open the latch, and uttered a soft "Damn." He thought he still had several white-phosphorus emergency flares. There were only two left, and Buckler remembered that his daughter had borrowed the Jeep to go camping when she had come home for the weekend a month before. The chief himself had taught Carole years ago that one of the easiest ways to start a campfire was to use a flare.

Dammit, I should've checked . . .

Too late to worry about it now, Buckler told himself. Just have to make do.

He stripped the caps from both flares and set them on the passenger seat, shoving the toolbox to the floor. Then he reached across the seat and unsnapped the small CO_2-type fire extinguisher that was buckled to the passenger-side door.

I hope to God this works.

The chief set the extinguisher on the seat beside the flares. Then he took a deep breath, switched on the ignition, dropped the vehicle into gear, and stamped down on the accelerator.

The Jeep shot forward, covering in seconds the short distance to the man on the ground. The Jeep squealed to a halt less than a dozen feet from the man. Buckler left the vehicle idling, snatched up the flares and the fire extinguisher, and threw open the door.

The chief tumbled out and struck the first flare. There was a brief explosion of brilliant, blue-white flame, accompanied by a burst of noxious smoke that stung his eyes and nostrils.

As the flare went off, Buckler sprinted toward the man on the ground, thrusting the burning flare forward. He hoped that the insects would hate the smoke and fire as much as he did.

It worked. The living cloud dissipated as the bees scattered. As the smoke lessened and the flame diminished from a blazing blue-white to a sun-bright pink, Buckler laid the burning flare on the ground and used it to ignite the second one. Foul-smelling smoke from the second flare billowed almost instantly, enshrouding the two men.

Buckler knelt beside the fallen man. He swung the fire extinguisher around, then depressed the release pin. The chief sprayed carbon dioxide foam over the man's body. The chilling foam froze the insects that were still clinging to him. Buckler could feel his own fingers that were holding the spray nozzle starting to burn from the intense cold.

The chief felt something crawling on the back of his neck. He reached back to swat it, just as he felt the tiny stinger prick him. He grunted in pain.

He looked around and noticed that his second flare had stopped smoking. It lay side by side with the first. The tips of each of them were glowing hot pink.

Buckler dropped the extinguisher, bent down, and scooped the man into his arms. It took him a moment to steady himself with his burden, before he could trot back to the Jeep. Buckler rolled the injured man inside onto the passenger seat as gently as he could, then climbed in, pulling the door firmly shut behind him.

Panting, Buckler scrambled into the driver's seat. He turned to look at the man sprawled on the seat beside him.

The man was breathing through his mouth, short and shallow gasps. For the first time, Ray Buckler got a good look at the man's features and had to repress a shudder. The man's face was a misshapen mass of welts, his skin so stretched that in places it was cracked and bleeding.

The man suddenly shook violently, as if he were forcing himself to come to. He swung his head around to face the chief, trying to peer through eyes that had swollen shut. The man croaked, "Who . . . ?"

"Chief Buckler."

The man's breath rattled in his throat. "Name's . . . Carr . . ."

Involuntarily Buckler reached for the man's arm. Carr recoiled in pain at the chief's touch. Buckler pulled back quickly. "Don't try to talk," he said. "I'll get you back to town."

The injured man shook his head. "Inside," he rasped. He lifted an arm weakly and pointed toward the wood and brick structure.

Buckler looked at the terminal and was surprised to see a figure at the window. The figure was waving at the Jeep. It took the chief a moment to realize that he could hear the person in the window shouting. The window was wide open.

The bees had disappeared.

"Inside," Carr repeated, choking on the word.

Buckler rolled the Jeep forward and pulled around to the terminal's main entrance, on the opposite side of the building. Two men came running from the building to the Jeep as the chief braked to a halt. One of the men was dressed in grimy coveralls; Buckler guessed that he worked for the airport. The other was Brad Cusimano.

Buckler climbed out of the Jeep and went around to the passenger side to help the two newcomers lift out the injured air traffic controller. The three of them carried the man into the building. The chief eyed Brad Cusimano unhappily, bothered by the coincidence of Brad's presence at the scene of yet another "incident."

Brad noticed. "Something the matter, Chief?" he asked.

Buckler frowned, then said quietly, "Mr. Cusimano, I'm not real happy to see you here."

"I'm not real happy to *be* here," Brad grunted.

There were six people waiting inside the building. Only Enrique Flores, the Mexican kid who drove the hotel shuttle, seemed to be hurt. Buckler checked on the others: Patti Romano, the teenager who operated the snack bar and whom Buckler had seen waving at him from the window; Charlie and Anna Baker, the elderly couple from Los Angeles who had ridden up to the airport in the van; and Trevor and Markie Baldwin, who had gone off to one side of the waiting area, away from everyone else. The man who had come out to the Jeep with Brad Cusimano was a part-time mechanic named Jimmy Sutherland.

They carried Mr. Carr back into his cubbyhole, where Patti Romano could keep an eye on him while she tried to contact Avalon for help on the shortwave radio. Buckler doubted that even if they could get Carr to a hospital immediately it would do any good. The man had passed out in their arms on the way into the building, and the chief thought that it might be best for the poor guy if he didn't wake up again. Which, judging from the extent of his injuries, was likely.

Buckler found out what had happened, mostly

William Relling Jr.

from Brad Cusimano, who had witnessed a great deal more than either of the two other airport employees. The cloud of bees had wrapped itself around an incoming passenger flight—for, God knew, whatever reason—and the plane had skidded off the end of the runway and over the edge of the cliff, where it had crashed and burned. But immediately before the crash, the swarm had detached itself from the stricken plane, as if it had somehow realized that the aircraft was doomed. The swarm had chased everyone who was out of doors, including Jimmy Sutherland, who had come over from the hangar where he was working to find out what in the hell was going on. They had run into the terminal, and, fortunately, none of them had been caught by the swarm, although Enrique Flores had fallen down and, from the looks of it, broken an ankle.

Once inside, they found that while the telephones seemed to be in working order, they weren't able to complete any calls for help because no one answered any of the emergency numbers that they tried. Mr. Carr was about to use his shortwave radio when they spotted the chief's Jeep speeding toward the plane crash. Brad Cusimano had been about to make a run for the Jeep himself when Mr. Carr suddenly pushed him out of the way and ran outside instead.

While Brad was telling him this, Chief Buckler discovered that it surprised him a little that Cusimano was the one who had considered chancing the swarm of killer bees. Cusimano's friend

BRUJO

Trevor Baldwin had struck the chief as more the heroic type. Then Brad also told the chief that Trevor's girlfriend was one of the passengers aboard the plane.

"So now what?" Brad asked.

"We're gonna have to get out of here," Buckler answered. He motioned toward Mr. Carr, who was lying unconscious on the floor of the cubbyhole and breathing shallowly through open, raw lips. "If we don't get him to a hospital—"

The chief was interrupted by a *skeek* of static from the shortwave radio's speaker. "Anything?" he asked Patti Romano.

She shook her head no.

"Well," Brad said, "we sure as hell aren't all gonna fit in your Jeep."

"What's wrong with the van?"

Brad was shaking his head. "That kid driver told me it's like trying to handle a goddamn semi. I don't even know how to drive a clutch. He's the only one who does, and his ankle's busted—"

Jimmy Sutherland cut in. "Hell, I can drive it."

"Huh-uh," Buckler said. "You need to stay here with Patti. We don't know if there's anybody else flying in—"

Brad interrupted: "What about my Jeep? I can't just leave it up here."

"I want everybody together," Buckler told him firmly. "And I don't want anybody to be out in the open."

"I'll drive the van."

William Relling Jr.

The voice had come from the office's doorway. There stood Trevor Baldwin, his son beside him.

Trevor looked at the chief impassively. "I'll drive it," he repeated.

The chief began to say, "Look, Mr. Baldwin—"

Trevor cut him off. "It's like driving a truck, right? I've been driving trucks since I was fifteen."

"That's not what I was gonna say, Mr. Baldwin—"

There came another garbled blast from the radio. This time Chief Buckler could just barely make out the words. Someone was calling his name.

Buckler took the microphone from Patti Romano and pressed the transmit switch. "This is Chief Buckler," he snapped. "Go ahead."

The radio crackled; the voice faded in and out. ". . . hear me, Chief . . . ranch said you were at . . . back to town . . ."

Buckler reached for the radio's gain knob. "I'm losing it," he muttered.

The radio abruptly spat at him loudly: ". . . Chief, you got to come back to town! The shit's hit the fan!"

Fifteen

"They're still out there," Grace Mitchum whispered.

Alexander Doyle sat beside Grace on the floor of his darkened office in the Avalon library. Their backs were against the heavy oak desk which the two of them had dragged across the room to barricade Alex's office door.

Alex was listening to Grace breathe. Too much exertion for a fat man and an old lady, Alex was thinking. Mrs. Doyle didn't raise no son of hers to be no manual laborer . . .

That's it, Doyle, he said to himself. Make with

the jokes while something's right outside the door waiting to eat you alive.

Alex Doyle had gone to his library office immediately after breakfast that morning. He was tremendously excited about all that he had heard in the previous few hours—the stories of vicious sea gull attacks and rampaging red bats and nutty piano players who flipped out onstage and ran screaming into the night.

Alex was especially excited about the word he himself had heard from the mouth of a six-year-old boy who was supposedly quoting the mad musician from the El Capitan Hotel. *Chinigchinich*.

Not a word you hear every day, Alex thought.

Avalon's library was three blocks from the coffee shop where he had overheard Markie Baldwin. Alex had been in such a hurry to get there that by the time he unlocked the library's front door he was panting and out of breath. As he opened the door, he admonished himself for being so goddamn overweight and out of shape.

The library was supposed to be open on Saturdays from eleven to four, but Alex relocked the door behind him, leaving the "Closed" sign that hung on the door facing outward. He beelined for his office in the rear of the library building, switched on the overhead lights in the small, windowless room, and closed the office door, shutting himself off from the rest of the world.

Alex had personally designed the room for precisely that purpose. The walls and ceiling were covered with acoustic tile, the floor with thick pile carpeting, and the door was specially reinforced and cut to fit into its frame perfectly. All of which served to render Alex Doyle's office virtually soundproof and, if he switched off the lights, pitch-dark. The soft full-spectrum fluorescent lighting could be brightened and dimmed from controls on the antique oak desk that rested in the corner of the room, opposite the door.

All of the money for the remodeling had come from Alex himself, though it amused him to toy with the idea of sending an occasional purchase order to the Los Angeles County library system's accounting office: "One Barcalounger Wall-Hugging Recliner. Custom Design. Deliver. $1,050." It would no doubt throw some accountant into a shit-fit—they were used to librarians who were intimidated by the people who approved their budgets.

They would never get used to Alex Doyle, however, because Alex was LA County's only *millionaire* librarian.

He worked for the Avalon library because he enjoyed it. Alex could probably have assumed just about any vocation he desired. Seven years earlier, he had been in his last year of law school at Berkeley when both of his parents were killed in an automobile accident. Alex's father had been a successful investment counselor in Santa Barbara, and as his parents' only child, Alex Doyle had fallen into an inheritance of nearly eleven million dollars. Alex completed his Juris Doctor—third in

William Relling Jr.

his class—but didn't bother taking the bar exam. Instead, he moved to Catalina, to his favorite of the three houses that he now owned. He had been there ever since.

Alex saw himself as one of only a handful of people whom he had ever known who was genuinely satisfied with his life, though he recognized that it had a great deal more to do with luck than with any real effort on his part. He loved the library, the books, the whole feeling of being at the center of so much information—merely for its own sake. Alex thought of himself as a dilettante, a literatus, a seeker after arcane knowledge.

And, by coincidence, Alex Doyle was the world's youngest authority on the history of the state of California, and particularly of the various Indian tribes that had existed before the land was discovered by white Europeans in the mid-sixteenth century.

The centerpiece of Alex's office was a DEC Rainbow 100 personal computer, which he had bought as a present for himself two Christmases before. Alex sat down at his desk, in front of the computer, and opened the top right-hand drawer where he kept his floppy disk files.

The disk that he wanted was one on which Alex had stored a series of articles that had been published in *American History Illustrated* the previous summer and fall. Alex had recounted a detailed history of the Indian tribes that inhabited the Channel Islands at the time of the islands' discovery by Spanish explorer Juan Cabrillo in 1542. Alex's fourth and final article, published only a few months before in November, discussed the now-extinct tribe that had occupied Santa Catalina Island until the beginning of the nineteenth century, when the tribe was wiped out.

It took him only moments to call up on the computer what he wanted:

> ... Cabrillo left San Miguel (San Diego), and four days later he and his men reached the island that Cabrillo named "Vitoria." As Cabrillo's boat neared land, his men could see a great number of Indians signaling to them to come ashore. It took very little time for Cabrillo's men and the Indians to lose what fear of each other they possessed; the Spaniards warmly greeted a boatload of visitors from the island, presenting the Indians with gifts of beads and other trinkets.

Alex scrolled the computer forward, looking for something else. He paused when he found it, letting out a satisfied "Ahhh."

> The Spanish showed little interest in the island until 1602, when Sebastián Vizcaíno rediscovered "Vitoria" while looking for a port where the Spanish galleons could hide from pirates. Vizcaíno's diarist, a priest named Antonio de la Ascensión, wrote of the expedition:
>
> > A few leagues farther, they [the men of Vizcaíno] saw a large island, almost twelve

leagues away from the mainland, and went to inspect it. This was the day of the martyr Saint Catherine, and for this reason it was named "Santa Catalina." As the ships were approaching the Isla de Santa Catalina to cast anchor, the Indian inhabitants began to raise smokes on the beach, and when they saw they had anchored, the women, children and old men began to shout and make demonstrations of joy in proof of their happiness. They came running to the beach to receive the guests who were arriving.

As soon as the ships anchored and the sails were furled, the General ordered the *Almirante* to go ashore and take with him Father Antonio, Captain Peguero with some soldiers from the *Capitana*, and Captain Alarcón with twenty-four soldiers, all armed with harquebuses and with their matches lit, to see what the Indians wanted, what there was on the island, and to bring back the information at once. When those who were with the *Almirante* landed, many old men, women and children came up with much familiarity, friendship and affability, just as if they had seen Spaniards before.

The soldiers ran all over the island, and in one part of it fell in with a place of worship or temple where the natives perform their sacrifices and adoration. This was a large flat patio and in one part of it, where they had what we would call an

BRUJO

altar, there was a great circle all surrounded with feathers of various colors and shapes, which must come from the birds they sacrifice.

Inside the circle there was a figure like a devil painted in various colors, in the way the Indians of New Spain are accustomed to paint them. At the sides of this were the sun and the moon. When the soldiers reached this place, inside the circle there were two large crows, larger than ordinary ones, which flew away when they saw strangers, and alighted on some nearby rocks. One of the soldiers, seeing their size, aimed at them with his harquebus, and discharging it, killed them both. When the Indians saw this they began to weep and display great emotion. In my opinion, the Devil talked to them through these crows, because all the men and women hold them in great respect and fear. I saw with my own eyes some Indian women cleaning some fish on the beach for food for themselves and their husbands and children. Some crows came up to them and took this out of their hands with their bills, while they remained quiet without speaking a word or frightening them away, and were astonished to see the Spaniards throw stones at them.

"Asshole Spaniards," Alex muttered.

He read on:

Father Antonio had recorded the first evidence of the *Chinigchinich* cult, which was centered on Santa Catalina Island. (The island was called "Pimu" by its inhabitants, who referred to themselves as "Pimugnan.") *Chinigchinich* was the main god of the Pimu Indians, their sun god. The Pimugnan's worship of the god was highly structured and moralistic, and the precepts of *Chinigchinich* were strongly impressed on the minds of Pimugnan children at a young age, that they might become good people and reject evil.

At the age of six or seven, each boy was assigned a personal protector, an animal in whom he was to place his confidence and who would defend him from dangers, particularly in battle against his enemies. The protector also served as the link between a boy and the god *Chinigchinich*.

The boy encountered his "spirit-brother" through a ceremony in which he was made to ingest an infusion of jimsonweed (*Dataura Stramonium*), a dangerous hallucinogenic drug. Boys being initiated into cult membership took the drug and would lapse into unconsciousness for several hours. Then, under careful supervision of the tribe's elders, the boy would be deprived of food and water for three days. During that time the tribe's shaman would exhort the boy to stay awake, to remain alert, to be ready for when the coyote or raven or rattlesnake might come to express *Chinigchinich*'s desire for the initiate. Through the visionary experience, the boy gained power of one sort or another—to be a great hunter, to be courageous and skillful in battle, and so on. Once in every generation, one special boy who had demonstrated unusually strong qualities of courage, intelligence, and spiritual awareness would be chosen by the shaman as an apprentice. The boy would then be adopted by the shaman and instructed in the ways of *Chinigchinich*, and upon reaching manhood, he himself would assume the mantle of shaman of the tribe.

Alex scrolled ahead again.

For the next two centuries, the Pimugnan were mostly left alone by the Spanish, who preferred to concentrate their efforts on the California mainland. The *Chinigchinich* cult continued to thrive on Santa Catalina Island—in contrast to the mainland, where cult worshipers were almost unanimously converted to Catholicism by mission priests. The followers of *Chinigchinich* on Santa Catalina Island flourished peacefully, largely ignored, except for the occasional smuggler's ship or storm-tossed vessel that made landfall on the island, seeking shelter.

What brought about the extinction of the Pimu Indians, at the turn of the nineteenth century, was the discovery on the island of an animal whose fur commanded fabulous prices from merchants in Europe and Asia. Sea otters abounded in the Channel Island waters. The Indians were doomed.

In 1806 Captain Joseph O'Cain, an officer of the Russian-American Fur Company, landed a shipload of hunters—many of them Aleut and Kodiak Indians from the Alaskan peninsula—on Santa Catalina Island.

At first the Pimugnan welcomed O'Cain's men with open arms; the Indians were used to strangers after almost two hundred years of continuous contact with the Spanish. The Spanish, however, were much different from these newcomers; for the most part, their priests and seamen had always treated the Pimu Indians well.

O'Cain's men were little more than pirates. They terrorized the Pimugnan for sport, killing hundreds of the tribesmen whose clubs and arrows were no match for the hunters' musketry. By the time O'Cain's ship came to retrieve them, the hunters had virtually decimated Santa Catalina Island's Indian population.

The remaining Pimu Indians fled the island in 1811 and were rescued by Spanish priests who took them to the San Gabriel Mission on the mainland. But, sadly, within two decades the last of the Pimu Indians died—from starvation, from overwork, from diseases which they caught from the white man. By the year 1830 the Pimugnan of Santa Catalina Island no longer existed.

* * *

BRUJO

Alex Doyle leaned back, thinking. His desk chair groaned softly from the stress of his shifting bulk.

The words angered him as much as they had when he first wrote them, more than eight months before. *By the year 1830 the Pimugnan of Santa Catalina Island no longer existed.*

Alex had been a student of American history for many years, and his cynicism had long since superseded any horror he might have felt when he read of the atrocities committed by white Europeans upon those who were living in the land before they came. The Indians themselves treated their enemies barbarously. In the case of the Pimugnan, the Aleuts and Kodiaks were equally responsible for the slaughter of Catalina's native inhabitants as the whites were, if not more so.

It was not the horror of the act that enraged Alex so much as the *waste*. Judging from what few records existed, the Pimu had one of the more advanced cultures of all the California tribes. They were certainly among the most artistic, as indicated by what few carvings and pottery they had left behind. The Pimugnan were also greatly fascinated with the mystical, the supernatural. There was evidence in the art that the Pimu Indians held very specific beliefs regarding the spiritual nature of the universe.

But most of that was conjecture, because any firsthand information—that which might come from descendants of the tribe itself—simply was not there. There were no descendants of the Pimu Indians. Not one.

So what has this got to do with Mark Baldwin?

The thought intruded on Alex's dark abstraction. That was what he was trying to figure out, how the boy had known the name of the Pimu Indians' sun god. Alex doubted that Markie had picked it up from Saturday morning cartoons.

A sudden, insistent rapping at his office door startled him. Alex put a hand over his heart and could feel it beating hard against his chest. But his momentary fear passed when he realized who it had to be at the door.

Alex glanced at his wristwatch, nodded, then wheeled his chair to the office door. He pulled the door open and smiled.

"Good morning, Grace," he said brightly.

Alex Doyle and Grace Mitchum had been friends for more than six years, ever since the day that Grace had come to the library to meet the new librarian and ask him if he could arrange a transfer of a certain volume of Italian Renaissance history that was available only at the library's main branch in downtown Los Angeles. (At the time, Grace was planning to write a biography of the artist Raphael.) The two of them hit it off immediately; Alex was an admirer of Grace's books, and Grace recognized Alex as a man of rare perception.

Not long after their initial meeting, Alex and Grace had their first Friday night coffee-and-dessert gin rummy match at Grace's house, something that over the years became a ritual for them. Every other week—barring unforeseen interruptions—

Alex would be on Grace's doorstep no later than nine o'clock, and the two of them would play cards and talk for hours. Grace never seemed to mind that Alex was an abysmal card player. She often told him that she was happy to take his money.

Last night, though, Alex had won for a change. He knew that Grace was still distressed about what had happened to her dog, Bridey, that morning. She told Alex very little about it—in fact, Grace had been understandably reluctant to discuss anything all night—but Alex could sense how upset Grace was over Bridey's death.

Earlier in the week Grace had asked Alex if she could come into the library on Saturday to use his computer, something that she often did when she needed to do research. As Alex was leaving Friday night, he asked Grace if she still wanted to come over the next day. Grace recognized the concern in Alex's voice, and she smiled at him gratefully. She would be there, in his office, at noon. The best thing to do, she said, would be to work. It would take her mind off everything else.

Grace arrived at the library promptly at twelve on Saturday. She was surprised to find the front door locked and the "Closed" sign hanging up, even though the library was supposed to be open.

It wasn't like Alex Doyle to forget an appointment, Grace thought, and if something had come up he would have called her. Not that it mattered, because Grace had her own key—Alex had given it to her for her fiftieth birthday. ("What do you give the literate woman who has everything? Her own key to the library.") The key had turned out to be a terrific present; often Grace had come in at odd hours to look up bits of information that she lacked at home, but without which she could not proceed with whatever she was working on.

Grace felt a little funny about using Alex's computer when he wasn't around. Not that Alex minded, but Grace believed that she had a lifetime's worth of technophobia to overcome before she would be comfortable with microprocessors and data bases and such all by herself.

Grace pulled out her key to the library and inserted it into the lock—then she paused, struck by a momentary feeling of apprehension. It was the same feeling she had had when she went out to look for Bridey yesterday morning . . .

What if something's happened to Alex?

Grace frowned. Stop it, she told herself. Just stop it.

She pushed the door open and went inside. Grace left the door unlocked and reached for the switch beside it that turned on the library's overhead lights—after all, it was supposed to be open. Alex would be grateful, and it wasn't as if Grace hadn't helped him out before, when he went out of town . . .

She couldn't shake the thought that nagged her in the back of her mind: Something's happened to Alex.

Grace was surprised to find that Alex was just fine. He was in the office working at the computer. Grace was so relieved to find him that she didn't even bother to ask him why he had closed himself in.

Alex telephoned a number that had been given to him by a friend of his, a professor of library science at UCLA. Then he plugged his phone into the modem attached to his computer. The phone number allowed Alex access to UCLA's BITNET system, a nationwide computer linkup that was, in effect, a massive card catalog file that listed sources of information on virtually any subject. Alex made frequent use of his friend's access number and password code—which, while it wasn't exactly illegal, would likely get Alex's friend into hot water with his superiors if they were to discover that he had passed on such privileged information to a university outsider.

Within twenty minutes Alex had called up a substantial list of possible sources for what Grace wanted to know. After instructing his own computer to record the list, Alex logged off the BITNET system and disconnected his phone from the modem.

Alex was just about to print out a hard copy of the list for Grace when a jagged green line flashed across the computer's display terminal. Then the screen went blank, just as all of the lights in the library building—including those in Alex's office—blinked out.

"God*dammi*t!" Alex barked.

"What's the matter?" Grace asked him.

Alex was pushing buttons furiously on the computer keyboard, barely visible in the fading light from the terminal screen which remained blank. "Goddamn power failure," he muttered half to himself. "I just hope we haven't lost—"

Alex stopped in midsentence. A strange, puzzled look crossed his face.

Grace said, "Alex . . . ?"

"Shh. Listen."

Grace did as Alex commanded, and all of a sudden she could hear a low sound, a strained, faraway growling. She clutched Alex's shoulder. He pushed himself out of his chair and stepped into the library proper. Grace was right behind him.

The growling was louder among the gloomy library stacks at the front of the building, near the main entrance. Alex and Grace rounded the corner of a tall shelf of books and came within sight of the library's front door.

And froze.

On the other side of the front door were three huge German shepherds. The dogs were trying to force their way inside; the biggest of the trio had managed to wedge his snout into a crack in the doorway. The other two were pushing him from behind, and all of them were snarling viciously.

The dogs stopped trying to force the door when they saw the two humans. For a moment people and dogs stared at each other. Then, as if the sight of prey drove the animals into a blood frenzy, all three of the dogs charged the door, yapping madly.

Then they were inside.

By then Alex and Grace were running back toward Alex's office. They shut themselves in, an instant before the pack reached the office door.

The two of them could hear the dogs scratching at the door, occasionally barking in frustration. It sounded as if one of the animals was actually gnawing at the door's wooden frame.

Alex moved forward carefully in the darkness, groping blindly for his desk. He cracked a shin against his desk chair and grunted, "Son of a bitch!" He reached for the edge of his desk and found the upper right-hand drawer. Alex slid the drawer open, grabbed the flashlight that he kept there for emergencies, and flipped the light on. He shined the beam on Grace. She was leaning spread-eagle against the office door, as if trying to barricade it with her body. Her face was white.

Alex set down the flashlight on his desk chair, then motioned for Grace to grab the other end of the desk. The adrenaline brought on by sheer terror gave both of them the strength to slide the huge desk in front of the door to block it. Then they collapsed to the floor, side by side, exhausted.

"They're still out there," Grace repeated. "I can hear them."

"I heard you the first time," Alex whispered back.

"How long are we going to be in here?"

Alex snapped, "How the hell should I know?"

"I'm just asking."

"Dammit, Grace, I don't know what's going on any more than you do!"

Grace looked at him crossly. Alex shook his head, then looked down at his watch to check the time.

He turned back to Grace, hoping that he could make himself sound calm. "Look," he said, "we haven't even been in here ten minutes. There's no way those dogs can get through that door."

"Can you tell me how we're going to get out?" Grace interrupted.

Alex sagged. I give up, he thought.

Grace said, "Alex, I don't want to be a pain—"

"You *love* being a pain, Grace."

Alex brought up his face slowly, and Grace Mitchum could see that he was smiling strangely. "C'mon now," Alex said. "Admit it. Didn't you always . . . didn't you always dream of a situation like this . . . with a man like me . . . *alone* . . ."

Grace stared at him incredulously. Then, before she could catch herself, she started to laugh. "You bastard . . ." she sputtered.

"Who, me?" Alex asked innocently.

They were both laughing. "You planned this," Grace said, trying to catch her breath. "Just to get me in here with you . . ."

"How can you say such a thing."

Alex paused, his smile faded, and he tilted an ear toward the door. Grace was still laughing, and Alex shushed her.

"What is it?" she whispered.

"Shhh!"

Alex was listening very hard. Then he whispered back to Grace: "I can't hear the dogs. They—"

From the other side of the door came the muffled report of a gunshot. The first blast was followed almost immediately by another three shots in succession.

Alex climbed to his feet as quickly as he could manage. "Help me," he ordered, and Grace rose to take the other end of the heavy desk and move it away from the door.

Grace held the flashlight as Alex squeezed between the desk and the door. From the other side, a faint voice called out, "Anybody in there? Hey, anybody in there?"

"We're here!" Alex shouted. He threw the door open and found himself facing a uniformed patrolman whose service revolver was in his hand. Alex spoke as he moved to the officer: "Man, you got no idea how glad we are to see you—"

The policeman cut him off. "You're Mr. Doyle, right? The librarian?"

Alex nodded.

"Listen, Mr. Doyle," the man went on, "I don't know why the hell you let them dogs in here—"

"We didn't let them in, Officer," Grace said.

The policeman looked past Alex's shoulder to Grace and frowned. "Yeah, well, it was a damn lucky thing that somebody saw 'em come in. You both gotta come with me—"

"You mind telling us just what in the hell is happening around here?" Alex cut in.

The policeman frowned again. "All I know is

that in the last hour I've heard about a dozen reports of people being attacked by everything from birds to dogs to snakes, and a lot of 'em are dead. The whole goddamn city's in a panic . . ."

He paused and gestured behind him to where the three German shepherds lay dead. The dogs' blood was seeping into the carpeting that covered the library floor. In the dim light the blood was black and glistening.

"You tell me what's going on, Mr. Doyle," the policeman said. "You tell me and we'll both know."

Sixteen

Trevor Baldwin sat behind the wheel of the Dodge van, driving almost mechanically. He kept his eyes on the Jeep in front of him, trying to stay no more than a hundred yards behind it.

There were five others in the van with Trevor: Markie, Brad Cusimano, Enrique Flores, and the Bakers. Chief Buckler had the injured air traffic controller with him. Patti Romano and Jimmy Sutherland had remained behind at the Airport-in-the-Sky, as Buckler had ordered. The chief told the two airport employees to wait until his men came up from the Wrigley Ranch to pick them up, and

William Relling Jr.

they were also to stay on the radio to warn any pilots who might be wanting to land at Catalina's airport to reroute their planes to the mainland.

Trevor knew that Ray Buckler hadn't been anxious to let him drive the van back to Avalon. The chief had agreed to it only when he realized that he was faced with no other choice.

What the hell did Buckler think I was going to do? Trevor wondered. Go crazy? Drive a vanload of people over a goddamn cliff myself?

Probably.

Trevor grimaced. Maybe I am going nuts, he thought. Why else would I be carrying on a conversation in my head with the guy in the Jeep ahead of me?

Maybe you are going nuts.

So tell me how I'm supposed to deal with this, Trevor thought. Tell me how I'm supposed to deal with Markie. Tell me how I'm supposed to deal with what happened to Valerie . . .

It's all your fault—

"It's not your fault, Dad."

Markie's small voice had come from the passenger seat beside Trevor. He turned to look at his son, feeling as if he were coming out of a trance. Markie was wearing the same worried expression that he had worn the day before on the bridge of the *Long Beach King* when Trevor had come to.

But there was something else about Markie's expression that disturbed Trevor, a peculiar look in the boy's eyes.

BRUJO

The back of Trevor's neck was tickling.
How does he know what I'm thinking?
"It's not your fault, Dad," Markie said again quietly.
"What's not my fault?"
The boy seemed to be having trouble finding words. "This," Markie said at last. "All of this."
Trevor steeled himself, then asked softly, "You mean Valerie?"
Markie was still regarding his father with strange eyes. He nodded.
Trevor felt an odd chill. "Mark—"
Markie cut him off. "Dad, you have to save us."
The boy's vehemence took Trevor back. But before he could answer, a low voice spoke from over his shoulder: "He's right."
Trevor glanced back. Brad Cusimano had slid into the seat directly behind him. "Markie's right," Brad continued. "Your main concern right now is taking care of the two of you."
"Brad, I don't need you to tell me what to do—"
Markie cut in. "That's not what I meant."
The two men turned to look at the boy, both of them stunned into silence by the insistence in his voice. Markie winced, as if struck by a sharp pain. His eyes were unfocused and far away.
Markie opened his mouth to speak, but the voice that came out was remote and unfamiliar, not at all the voice of a little boy. "You have to save us, Dad," the voice said. "You have to save all of us. The beasts—"

William Relling Jr.

Brad suddenly clapped a hand on Trevor's shoulder and shouted, "Look out!"

Chief Buckler's Jeep had rounded a curve and disappeared behind the side of a bluff seconds before. But as Trevor made the turn himself, the Jeep was sitting at a dead stop in front of the van. Trevor jammed on the brakes, bringing the van to a halt mere inches from the Jeep's rear end.

Ray Buckler was out of the Jeep and climbing up the side of the small bluff. He glanced down at the van and motioned for Trevor to follow him.

Trevor shifted the van into neutral, set the emergency brake, and was just reaching for the handle to his door when he heard Markie whisper to him, "Dad, don't."

Trevor turned to his son. Markie's voice was his own again. But the boy sounded frightened.

What is it you're not telling me?

Trevor looked at his son sternly. "What's the matter, Mark?" he asked.

Enrique Flores called from the back of the van, "Hey, man, the chief wants you!"

"Please don't go out there, Dad," Markie begged quietly. "Please don't go with him."

"Why, Mark?"

The boy shivered.

Trevor repeated, "*Why*, Mark?"

Markie swallowed. "Because."

"Dammit, because why?"

Markie hissed, "*Because he's gonna die!*"

An icy hand seemed to clutch Baldwin's stomach. He gaped at his son incredulously, suddenly realizing that he was no longer so much afraid *for* Markie as he was becoming afraid *of* him. Trevor had to fight back an urge to grab the boy and shake him.

But he saw that Markie's own expression was terrified, his eyes wide with fear. It was as if Markie had no control over whatever it was that had entered his mind and was manipulating his words.

Just then Enrique Flores called out again, "Hey, man, ain't you gonna find out why he stopped?"

"You better go, Trev," Brad said. His voice was a soft, dry croak. "I'll watch Markie."

Trevor looked at his son. "I'll be right back," he said quietly.

"Please, Dad—"

"Mark, I said I'll be right back."

For a moment, Trevor wanted badly to add: *No one is going to die.* Instead he pushed the door open and stepped from the van.

The bluff rose at a sharp angle, almost perpendicular to the road. Its crest was about twenty feet above him, and Trevor had to climb carefully, feeling his way. He forced himself to concentrate solely on the steep climb.

As he was about to reach for the top of the rise, his foot slipped from its precarious hold. Trevor cried out in alarm. A strong, khaki-uniformed arm snaked over the edge, and the hand grabbed Trevor's forearm. He looked up to see Ray Buckler's face, which was showing the strain of the chief's effort to pull Trevor up. With a final, hard kick Trevor tumbled over the rim.

The top of the bluff was a small plateau that afforded a view of most of the southern half of Catalina. Trevor came to his feet, looked around and noticed that to the southwest lay a line of dark thunderclouds, heading in their direction. He guessed that the storm had to be no more than six hours away.

"Come over here," Buckler said.

Trevor followed the chief to the opposite edge of the plateau. The view overlooked Avalon Bay.

"I finally got through to town," Ray Buckler was saying as they walked to the rim. "Somebody with a CB radio. I talked to one of my men. They're trying to evacuate everybody to the Casino."

Trevor felt the odd chill return. "Evacuate?"

Buckler nodded grimly. They had come to the edge of the plateau, and below them, perhaps three miles away, lay the city of Avalon, spread out like a picture-postcard village. The chief pointed toward Avalon.

Trevor looked.

The city was *burning*.

But now ask the beasts, and they shall teach thee; and the fowls of the air, and they shall tell thee:

Or speak to the earth, and it shall teach thee; and the fishes of the sea shall declare unto thee.

The words had come to the Brujo as he oversaw the destruction of the Evil Ones, the invaders, the despoilers of the sacred place. The slaughterers of his people, who were now themselves led to the slaughter.

Ask the beasts.

They were the words of the white priests, spoken to the Brujo when he was a young man. The words now returned to the Brujo, across the dim mists of his memory.

Speak to the earth.

In his mind the Brujo saw himself long ago, fighting the Evil Ones who had destroyed his people. His struggle then had been futile, his power not sufficient to deter them. They struck him down and took hold of him. They tortured him and buried him alive.

The Brujo saw himself falling into the pit. He struck bottom, and as his mind slipped into blackness the words had come to him:
Ask the beasts.
The Brujo *reached*.

Seventeen

Arthur Harris hated Saturdays. Not that he liked any other day much better, but Saturday was the day that he could see the damage that had been wrought during the rest of the week by the little bastards he was always cleaning up after.

Arthur had been the janitor/handyman at the Avalon public schools for seven years. The job never changed: at the beginning of every school day make sure the furnace was working; check the vents in each of the three separate buildings that housed the grade school, junior high school, and high school; check that he had not missed wiping clean any chalkboards or mopping any halls or overlooked any full wastebaskets or failed to perform any of his other piddley-ass chores from the afternoon before. Then wait during the day for something to come up—like some wimpy second grader puking his beans 'n' franks all over the cafeteria floor, or a bunch of ninth-grade boys stuffing paper towels into a toilet and flushing it till it backed up and walking into the boys' john was like walking into a sewer, or having to take more shit from that walking turd of a high school principal about the inside of the gym looking more like the aftermath of an atomic bomb explosion than a sock hop. But mostly during the day Arthur Harris tried to stay out of sight in his "office" in the boiler room, where he could quietly sip on the pint of Wild Turkey that he kept in the back pocket of his bib overalls and think about how much he despised this fucking job and all these fucking kids.

At least on Saturdays it was quiet, and he didn't have to listen to eight zillion ghetto blasters blowing out Van Halen and Madonna and Judas Priest and all that other horseshit that gave him a headache. Not that he was old—for Christ's sake, he was only fifty—or didn't like rock and roll, but the stuff these kids listened to these days was pure shit. Whatever happened to fucking Chuck Berry? he wondered. There was never anybody around on Saturdays, and Arthur never had to worry about somebody catching him outside nipping at the ol'

BRUJO

Wild Turkey or taking a whiz in the bushes outside the high school principal's office.

But Saturday was still a workday. Sweep the sidewalks, rake the leaves, check the walls on the outsides of the buildings for graffiti; Arthur told himself that if he had to whitewash one more "Locals Only" or "Stoners Rule," he was going to fucking scream. Then go through the week's worth of trash in the dumpsters behind the three school buildings, separate the bottles and cans and shit that the school recycled, then haul the rest out to the incinerator at the rear of the school grounds and burn it.

Shortly after noon, Arthur Harris was sitting at a table in the grade school's faculty lounge. He had finished eating the braunschweiger sandwich and potato chips that he had brought along for lunch. The bottle of whiskey lay open on the table beside the crumpled Saran Wrap, potato chip bag, and brown paper sack. Arthur reached for the bottle and took a long swallow, letting the stuff burn down his throat. He burped one time, and rubbed his belly.

Time to get back to work, he told himself, and made a disgusted face. He stood up and capped the bottle and slipped it into his pocket, then picked up his trash, rolling everything into a ball that he stuffed into the paper bag.

He went outside and grabbed the rake that he had left leaning beside the door to the lounge, next to a roll of plastic trash bags that he also retrieved, and started for the corner of the building. Around the corner, he faced the dumpster, a massive metal box painted Rustoleum brown. The thing was as tall as Arthur himself, and he had to strain to push it far enough from the building so that its lid could be flipped open. He lifted the corner of the lid and tossed it over, sending it crashing against the back of the dumpster with a loud clang.

The stink of the garbage inside the thing overwhelmed him. Arthur held his nose and whistled: "Whee-ooh"; then he pulled a pair of work gloves from an overall pocket, put them on, and grabbed the rim and hoisted himself up to peer inside. The dumpster was about three-quarters full with trash. Just the usual shit, Arthur said to himself. He dropped to the ground, picked up the rake and the roll of trash bags, then pulled himself up again, over the edge, climbing in.

He marched around, settling himself, feet sinking in the trash, then tore a trash bag from the roll, shook it open, and began rooting through the dumpster, pulling out empty soda bottles and other pieces of glass and dropping them into the bag. He was reaching for the top of a Coke bottle when he saw briefly, near the bottle, a flash of bare flesh, the photograph of a naked woman. Arthur Harris thought to himself: Now what the fuck is that?

He bent down and tugged at the picture. Arthur pulled it free and was holding the center spread of a *Penthouse* magazine. He held the magazine open in front of him and turned the pages, smiling evilly as he muttered, "Well, I'll be damned . . ."

One of the little peckers must've brought the nudie magazine to school with him, Arthur thought. He could hardly believe it—but then he told himself, Hey, kids these days, man, they're jumping on each other's bones before they're even growing any hair you-know-where. God knows he had seen enough of them, goddamn junior high school kids, groping each other in the halls . . .

Maybe there's more.

Arthur crouched and rummaged around in the trash, pushing stuff aside, reaching down deep—

He shouted "Ow!!!" and jerked his hand out quickly. He tore off his glove and saw the speck of blood staining his index finger. He sucked at the blood, thinking to himself, Goddammit, something bit me right through my goddamn glove—

He froze.

Arthur knew instantly what it had to be, and he swung around behind him to reach for the rake, saying out loud, "Fucking rat, I'll show you. Bite me, willya, motherfucker . . ."

He turned around and saw the thing poking its head from under the trash, just looking at him. Arthur raised the rake just as he heard a sound.

From outside, on the sidewalks, along the ground, from in between the buildings. A kind of skittering, the sound of many tiny claws *skritching* over asphalt and bare earth. Arthur could feel his skin crawling. He looked down at the filthy gray rat beneath him, and the thing just stared at him.

A dark motion caught the corner of his eye as the sound of the skittering claws grew louder, and Arthur turned around.

The grounds were swarming with rats.

There were hundreds of them everywhere, covering the grounds like a furry, living carpet. All of them silent. All of them running in the same direction, toward the dumpster where Arthur Harris was trapped, unable to move even if there had been a way for him to escape. Some of them already scrambling up the sides of the metal box. All of them coming.

For him.

Marcie Wetzel was wondering whether or not her husband, Rob, had said if he would be home in time for lunch. She couldn't remember exactly what he had told her when he left at 5:30 that morning—while it was still dark outside, for heaven's sake—whether this was just supposed to be a morning fishing trip with their neighbor Judd Mayfield or if it was another of Rob and Judd's all-day affairs.

If it was the latter, Marcie knew she could expect the two of them to come staggering in, half in the bag, sometime after sundown, each of them lugging a line of sea bass or whatever it was that they pulled out of the water, which they would then plop into her kitchen sink. Then they would roll into the living room and switch on the TV and watch *Love Boat* or *Movie Macabre* or something and swill more beer. She would have to throw the cat outside before the fish smell drove it nuts, and spend the rest of the night cleaning the damn things, all the while listening to hear if the baby woke up from the noise those two drunk chowderheads made, because it was for damn sure Big Rob wasn't going to get up and take care of Little Robbie.

She frowned. It wasn't Rob so much as it was Judd, who was retired and a widower and just happened to have a lot of time on his hands. It was kind of neat, though, the way the two men got along with each other—Judd was sixty-six years old and Rob was only thirty-one, and you would think that their relationship would be some sort of father-son thing, but that wasn't the case at all. Rob and Judd were out-and-out pals, had been ever since Marcie and Rob had moved in next door three years ago. Judd had also become Rob's first legal client on the island, when he allowed Rob to rewrite his will, and had sent at least a dozen more customers in Rob's direction since then.

Marcie sighed. Men, she thought. Can't live with 'em, can't live without 'em.

At least Robbie had been good today. This past week had been the first nights that Robbie had slept straight through without waking up. She could put him to bed after feeding him at ten o'clock, and every night since Tuesday, Robbie had slept until six the following morning, which was when she and Rob got up anyway. Not bad for a two-month-old baby, Marcie thought. This morning he had slept until almost 7:30.

William Relling Jr.

Marcie was sitting at the kitchen table, eating a bowl of Campbell's cream of asparagus soup she had heated for her own lunch. Robbie would be waking from his morning nap anytime now, and he would be hungry. She turned to check the cat dish that lay on the floor near the back door. Their cat's name, Brutus, was painted on the side of the dish, and Marcie was surprised to see that the half can of Nine Lives Gourmet Liver that she had scooped into Brutus's dish a couple of hours before was untouched. It was funny, because that godawful liver was the old fat tom's favorite stuff, and it was usually gone not fifteen minutes after Marcie put it out. But Brutus had been acting strangely all morning. Maybe he was getting sick or something . . .

She could hear the baby whimpering, the sound coming from the back of the house. At least *some*body's hungry around here, she thought to herself, smiling. She swallowed another spoonful of soup, just as Robbie started to wail. "All right, all right," she said. "I'm coming."

Marcie got up from the table, carried her bowl to the kitchen sink, and rinsed it. Then she reached for the towel hanging over the sink and began to dry her hands.

The house was suddenly *silent*.

The humming of the refrigerator and the ticking of the electric clock above the stove had stopped. But neither of those was what made Marcie's stomach tighten with apprehension.

She called out tentatively: "Robbie . . . ?"

The towel fell from her hands as she dashed out of the kitchen. He's all right, she told herself. He's just quiet . . .

Marcie had drawn the curtains in the baby's room that morning. She reached for the light switch near the door. The switch clicked but the room stayed dark. The power had indeed gone out.

She took a step into the room, toward the baby's crib, and said, "Robbie . . . ?"

Marcie's eyes adjusted to the gloom and she could see into the crib. Robbie was there, lying on his back, not moving. There was something furry wrapped around his head, almost as if he were wearing some kind of hat that had slipped down over his face.

The furry thing moved, then growled at her: "Meeoowwwwwww . . ."

Marcie said puzzledly, "Brutus?"

The cat lifted himself from the baby's face and turned to look at her. His muzzle was smeared with red. Brutus pawed his whiskers, then casually licked the blood off his paws.

Marcie Wetzel screamed.

The cat smiled.

An army of animals in the city of Avalon had gone on a rampage against their masters. They had learned from the voice that directed them how to bite and tear at the gas lines that fed into the houses from the tanks on their owners' property, how to create sparks by chewing electrical wires, how to make things burn. Then they had been set loose upon the streets, pursuing any human beings they might encounter. To hunt. To kill.

The raven saw.
And the Brujo was pleased.

The Brujo *reached* for The-One-Who-Would-Serve. From The-One the Brujo had gotten the knowledge that he had passed on to the beasts, how to destroy the places of the Evil Ones. But there was still much to be done . . .

There was darkness. The-One did not answer.

The Brujo was suddenly struck by a feeling of uneasiness. He knew that his thoughts were touching The-One-Who-Would-Serve. But somehow he was not being heard.

The Brujo became angered.

Speak to me, the Brujo commanded.

At last The-One responded to him. *I hear*.

The Brujo instructed him, all the while becoming aware of the darkness in the mind of The-One. For the first time, the Brujo sensed that a part of The-One might be uncontrollable. There was a black area in the soul of The-One-Who-Would-Serve. A madness.

The Brujo completed his instructions and sent The-One to carry out his bidding. Then the Brujo *reached* the raven, instructing the bird to watch The-One closely.

Afterward the Brujo withdrew into himself. That The-One-Who-Would-Serve did not answer when he first called had disturbed him. Something may have to be done, the Brujo thought.

The-Other . . .

The Brujo had once more felt the presence of The-Other, had touched him briefly. The Brujo knew that The-Other was a special one, as the Brujo himself had been special when he was chosen by the sun to lead his people so long ago. The-Other was one whose own spirit could learn to *reach*.

But only if the Brujo could *reach* him. Then he would no longer have to rely on The-One-Who-Would-Serve . . .

He had to give a warning along with his instructions. *Do not fight me*, the Brujo had whispered to The-One-Who-Would-Serve. *Do not fight me, or you shall be destroyed.*

Eighteen

You shall be destroyed.

Casey Harrison listened to the voice that spoke inside his head. The voice was warning him. Somehow it had become aware that Casey's resolve was waning.

Casey answered, "I won't fight you."

The raven returned to Casey and led him to the place where the voice had wanted him to go. The bird guided him to a narrow stretch of rocky beach that lay at the southernmost tip of Santa Catalina Island. The voice ordered Casey to remain there and wait. Then the bird left him, and Casey was alone on the beach.

William Relling Jr.

Casey waited, as he was told to do, and while he waited, he convinced himself that he had lost his mind.

Casey sat cross-legged in the sand, watching the jagged, gray-green ocean waves. The waves were coming very hard and fast.

He looked to the sky and saw the line of dark squalls approaching. Casey watched the coming storm, and he listened to the crash of the water on the shore.

The waves were speaking to him. They said, *Remember . . .*

Casey remembered sitting in his hotel room all day Friday, remembered watching the nightmare over and over in his mind's eye, even though he was wide awake. He remembered going to work Friday night, and he remembered that instant in the middle of his set when he first heard the voice speaking to him, moments before the flock of bats burst into the bar. The voice had sent the bats to lead Casey away.

Waiting for Casey outside the bar was the raven who had visited him that morning. The voice told Casey not to be afraid of the raven and to follow the bird into the hills. Casey told the voice that he wasn't afraid.

The bird took Casey to the top of Mount Orizaba, from which he could see all of Santa Catalina Island. Casey sat on top of the mountain for hours, enthralled, watching the mist roll in from the ocean to enshroud the island and blot out the twinkling lights of the mainland.

There Casey had allowed the voice to empty his mind and read his thoughts. While at the same time, Casey was able to absorb from the voice a sense of its purpose.

The voice was seeking revenge. Casey Harrison was to be its instrument.

Rather, *one* of its instruments. Casey came to understand the power that the voice controlled, the power to bend creatures to its will, to manipulate animals like the birds and the bats and the wild pigs. Casey understood that the raven was different from the other beasts, that the black bird was associated with the voice in a more mystical, spiritual way. The raven served as the eyes and ears of the voice, as an extension of the voice itself. Casey, however, was simply another creature that it could control.

But Casey didn't mind. The voice gave him comfort, in exchange for that which it took from him. By the time the sun had risen on Saturday morning, Casey Harrison found himself filled with an incredible sense of well-being.

It was the gift of the voice. Casey had slept very little the entire night, yet he was refreshed and alert, ready to do whatever the voice wished him to do.

So the voice allowed Casey to see visions. It allowed Casey to become one with the beasts, to share the sensations of the creatures that it controlled.

The visions were overwhelming. Casey saw, through the eyes of the rattlesnake, the frightened horses whom the voice had tried to manipulate but somehow could not. Fear of the snake drove the horses mad. They broke free on their own, trampling to death the old man who tried to calm them. Casey-the-Snake had heard the call of his brother, and he slithered across the cool ground to the place where his brother had trapped the young woman. Casey moved up oh-so-stealthily behind the man that held a gun pointed at his brother's head. Then he shot forward and he felt his fangs sink deep into the man's leg, and Casey tightened the muscles of his jaw, forcing the poison from its sacs. Casey watched his brother strike the death blow to the man's throat as he felt the vibrations of the young woman's screams cut the air.

After that, the voice had had Casey draw back into himself for a time. The voice wanted to watch the rising of the sun through Casey's eyes. The voice used Casey's lips to form a name that it called to the sun, a name that Casey did not know.

The name *Chinigchinich*.

But with the coming of the sun had come Casey's understanding. *Chinigchinich*. The sun.

Chinigchinich was God. And God spoke to Casey Harrison.

It is time, the voice told him.

For the next several hours Casey Harrison's corporeal self—his physical body—sat entranced and unmoving atop Mount Orizaba while his spiritual self accompanied the minions of the voice on their holy charge. Casey was transfixed by the visions that flooded over him. He became one with the beasts, sharing the animals' selves as they carried out the commands of the voice of God.

Casey was everywhere.

Casey was a gray whale, swimming the channel with a trio of his brothers, making their way north. The voice touched them. *Beware*, it whispered. *The Evil Ones approach.* Then a boat appeared, and Casey's human memory recognized it as a passenger boat similar to the one he had sailed on from the mainland. The boat's decks were filled with people.

Casey-the-Whale and his brothers glided to the surface and Casey exhaled a fierce spray of triumph from his spout. Then he and the other whales charged the boat at full speed, and as they approached, Casey watched with satisfaction the expressions of terror on the faces of the people watching from the decks. The whales rammed the boat, smashing into it with all of their might. With their massive tails they thrashed at those who fell from the boat into the water. Casey and the other whales smashed the boat again and again until they demolished the craft, sending all those aboard into the arms of the chilly sea.

The voice called to the whales: *I am pleased. But you must remain on guard. There will be others.* The whales did as the voice instructed.

At the same time, Casey was one with the mass mind of the hive. He was the swarm of bees that attacked the crew of the plane that carried Valerie Heath and the others aboard to their deaths. He was that same swarm when it attacked the air traffic controller on the ground minutes after the crash.

At the same time, Casey was also part of another huge swarm that enveloped the Coast Guard installation at Two Harbors. The swarm drove most of the seamen to their boats, where Casey and his brother whales could smash and sink them. Casey was also the smaller swarms that attacked campgrounds at Parson's Landing on the northern edge of the island, at Little Harbor just west of El Rancho Escondido, and at Black Jack Mountain a mile east of where Casey himself sat, watching, from Mount Orizaba.

At the same time, Casey was one of a herd of wild pigs that invaded and destroyed the Marine Science Center at Fisherman's Cove on Two Harbors' eastern side, opposite the Coast Guard installation. Casey was one of a flock of gulls that savaged a group of hikers who were resting at Eagle's Nest Lodge a dozen miles to the south. He was one of a pair of buffalo that attacked an Inland Motor Tour tram that had paused at West Point, the small mountain above Land's End at the northwestern tip of Santa Catalina Island. The ten people from the tram had been watching the two great, shaggy beasts grazing peacefully until the voice touched the minds of the buffalo and sent them charging. The passengers all managed to scramble back aboard the tram, but before the driver could start its engine, the buffalo had slammed into the side of the vehicle. It took only that single solid smash to send the tram tumbling down the side of the mountain, flipping over and over till it smashed on the rocks below and exploded into a fireball that blossomed high into the early afternoon sky.

Then the raven had reappeared to Casey and he drew back into himself. *Go with the raven*, the voice commanded him.

The black bird led Casey back to Avalon.

The city was aflame.

Casey knew what had happened; the images had flashed through his brain as he made his way over the hills toward Avalon. In his mind Casey saw the people of the city in an utter panic, able neither to comprehend what was happening nor to defend themselves. Great numbers of people—those who did not or could not find a place to hide on their own—were retreating to the Casino. The city's policemen were shooting at what few mad animals made targets of themselves, and they killed many, but nowhere near all. The animals, guided by the voice, were too numerous, too clever, too powerful.

Casey came to the rise that stood above the botanical gardens at the city's southern edge, nestled at the end of Avalon Canyon Road. Somehow he knew that already more than a hundred people were dead. The beasts, the instruments of the voice of God, had effectively isolated the survivors of their first savage attack. The animals were patrolling the sea and air as well as the land, guarding against any escape or invasion from the outside.

Somehow Casey knew that the hundreds of human beings left on Santa Catalina Island would all soon be dead. The voice would have its revenge.

But as Casey climbed over the rim of Avalon Canyon and could see the smoke from dozens of fires in the city below, he paused.

For a fleeting instant it was as if Casey's brain were bathed in a brilliant light. For that instant his mind was his own once more. It was Casey Harrison's last moment of sanity.

He was suddenly, lucidly *aware*.

He was horrified.

Casey choked, "My God—"

The voice whispered to him immediately. *Speak to me*, it said.

But Casey stood still, ignoring the voice.

The voice commanded him: *Go with the raven*. Its anger registered on Casey, but the young man remained still.

Then, without warning, the voice snapped at Casey, roaring its rage, driving shards of ice into his brain. Casey's hands shot up from his sides, clutching the sides of his head in agony. He fell to his knees.

For what seemed an eternity, the pain in his head was so intense that Casey could not make a sound, not even a whimper.

Then the pain was gone.

There was only the voice. *Go with the raven*.

Casey answered, "I hear."

* * *

BRUJO

The bird led Casey to the beach, where he now sat by himself, awaiting its return. After a time alone, Casey had come to understand. His disobedience had incurred the voice's wrath. He had displeased God, and God had lashed out at him, causing his pain. But Casey realized that he was not being punished, exactly. The voice had brought him to this deserted place for a purpose. The voice wanted Casey to *remember*.

Thou shalt have no other gods before me.

Casey recalled the words from when he was a boy. He remembered other words as well: *I the Lord, thy God, am a jealous god.*

Casey told himself not to doubt the voice that spoke to him. The voice of *Chinigchinich*. The voice of God.

He heard a rustle of wings overhead, and he looked up to watch the raven as it landed in front of him. The bird regarded Casey dispassionately with red eyes.

Then the voice returned. It gave Casey his instructions, along with a warning. *Do not fight me*, the voice told him, *or you shall be destroyed*.

Casey acknowledged, and came to his feet to follow the raven, to carry out his task.

Nineteen

Pacific Bell, the telephone company for southern California, maintained a microwave transmission tower at the top of East Mountain, two miles southeast of the city of Avalon. The microwave tower was Catalina Island's primary communications link to the mainland; the original trunk cable that had been laid along the bed of the San Pedro Channel in the 1920s had been officially "retired" in 1981.

None of that mattered to Officer Dave Romero as he steered his Jeep along the south road out of the city. All he knew was that he was under orders

William Relling Jr.

from Sergeant Herb Black, the Avalon Police Department's second-in-command, to drive up to the microwave tower and make sure that it was secure. They had to be able to maintain contact with the mainland during the emergency, and if anything went wrong with the tower . . .

Dave Romero recalled what Sergeant Black had said to Chief Buckler. Romero was standing beside the sergeant when Black finally got through to the chief at the airport. (They'd had to use an ancient shortwave radio that the sergeant found in a storage closet in the chief's office, because all of the local phone lines seemed to be fucked up.)

Sergeant Black barely had time to say anything to the chief before the radio gave up the ghost. But Black managed to get out, "The shit's hit the fan!"

That was the understatement of the year, Romero thought ruefully.

Romero had no clue as to what had driven the animals on Catalina Island out of their minds. There was no rational explanation for it, but goddammit, there it was. And the really scary thing about it was that it seemed so . . . organized. Dave Romero knew that he wasn't the only one who couldn't shake the feeling that there was something in charge of what was happening, that there was some kind of grand design to it all.

Romero thought, It's like being in a goddamn horror movie.

All of the power in the city was out. There was no way that the Avalon Fire Department could handle the number of fires in the city—half the town seemed to be in flames. The internal phone system for the island was dead, but surprisingly the lines to and from the mainland were still working. That was when Sergeant Black had remembered that the local lines and the off-island lines were two separate systems with two separate switching centers, and ordered Dave Romero to haul ass up to the East Mountain tower.

The road before him ended at a gate that was the entrance to Pacific Bell's tower compound. The tower itself was one of three structures within the enclosure that was surrounded by a ten-foot-high Cyclone fence. There were two buildings, the larger of which was nearer to the gate and housed the switching center and control room. The smaller building, some sort of equipment shed, Romero figured, rested alongside the tower itself.

The approaching storm had darkened the afternoon sky, and Officer Romero saw that there were lights on inside the main building. He sounded the Jeep's horn. A door opened in the side of the building, and a young black man dressed in dungarees and a telephone company shirt stepped out for a look. Romero waved to the young man, who then came trotting out to the gate to let the policeman in.

Romero parked the Jeep, then he followed the young man into the main building. Inside was a single large room filled with electronic equipment—monitors, banks of knobs and switches, several computer keyboards—all of which was completely alien to Dave Romero. A small black and white TV, showing a rerun of *F Troop*, sat on the edge of a counter, in front of a computer console.

The young man introduced himself as Bill King, and he told Officer Romero that he was the tower's weekend supervisor, though the only one he supervised, King said, was himself. Running the tower was strictly a one-man operation.

"How come you still got power?" Romero asked.

The young man looked puzzled. "Why wouldn't I have power?"

"You didn't hear? You didn't see the smoke from the fires?"

Bill King was astounded. "*What* fires?"

Dave Romero told the young man what was happening on the island. Bill King stared at the policeman incredulously. "You got to be foolin' me, man," he said.

"I wish I was," Romero told him. "The goddamn electricity's out all over. But you haven't been cut off or anything?"

Bill King shook his head no. "Even if there's an interruption we got our own auxiliary generator. It'd kick on automatically."

"Did it?" Romero asked.

"I'll check. I didn't notice if it did before." King leaned over the console and reached for a toggle switch. He flipped the switch.

Nothing happened. King frowned.

"What's wrong?" the policeman asked.

"Circuit must've blown," Bill King answered.

He looked up from the console to the other man. "I'll go and take a look at the generator."

Before Romero could say anything else, Bill King was gone. The policeman let out a deep sigh and he fell into Bill King's swivel chair in front of the small television. On the screen a pair of U.S. Cavalry soldiers stood on the set of the Indian camp. One of the Indians was telling a joke, and the faint sound of canned laughter floated up from the television's tiny speaker.

Dave Romero grunted in disgust, thinking that he couldn't believe this guy King was sitting here watching this crap while everything around him was going to hell in a handbasket.

Just then the television screen and all of the lights in the room started to flicker. All at once the power went out, and Dave Romero sat in the dark.

He felt a momentary flush of panic. Far away he heard a low rumble of thunder. Swell, Romero thought. What a time for the goddamn storm to break.

Romero decided to see if Bill King needed a hand. He pushed himself up from the chair and walked out of the building. Once outside he noticed that the sky had darkened considerably in the few minutes he had been at the tower. A light, chilly wind whipped about him, and Romero could smell the storm in the air. He shivered.

Romero called out, "Hey! Hey, King!"

He waited, but there was no answer. Grumbling to himself, Romero headed for the rear of the main building, toward the tower and the storage shed. He supposed that the auxiliary generator had to be someplace back there.

Romero found the generator where he had guessed it would be, resting on a concrete slab set into the ground, near the base of one of the microwave tower's metal legs, a few yards from the back wall of the storage shed. But as soon as he came within sight of the generator, a twinge of fear caused Dave Romero's spine to tingle.

Someone had smashed the auxiliary generator to pieces.

The policeman moved up to examine it. The generator's metal housing had been caved in and ripped open, exposing the guts of the equipment. Whoever had done it had used something with which he could hack away at the generator's insides, and even Dave Romero's limited knowledge of machinery told him that the thing was beyond repair.

Suddenly Romero's ears perked up. He heard *something* . . .

There it was again. A soft, scraping noise—a footstep that sounded as if it had come from around the front of the storage shed. Romero called out tentatively, "King? That you?"

Dave Romero listened hard for several seconds. All he could hear was the sound of the wind blowing around him, whistling through the spidery legs of the microwave tower.

Romero unholstered his service revolver and stepped cautiously to the side of the shed. He moved toward the front of the small building, one hand holding his pistol, the other pressing along the side of the shed.

Twenty paces brought him to the forward edge of the building. Romero took a deep breath, then sprang around the corner of the shed and dropped into a firing position, both hands braced on his weapon.

There was nothing there. The door to the shed was open, wavering slightly in the wind.

Romero straightened. Whatever it is, he thought, it's in there.

Romero tried to steady the tremor in his voice. "King?" he called into the open shed.

There was no answer.

Romero moved forward, gun in hand, stopping when he reached the door to the shed. It was very dark inside the small, windowless structure.

Dave Romero stood in the doorway, peering inside, letting his eyes adjust to the dim light. It took only a few moments for his vision to sharpen enough to allow him to distinguish shapes in the gloom.

On the floor of the shed lay Bill King.

Romero whispered, "Jesus . . ."

The policeman immediately knelt beside the young man, vaguely aware that he was fighting an impulse to turn away and run. Romero had to choke back a swallow of bile that clogged his throat.

Bill King was alive, but barely so. The front of his shirt was torn and soaked with a dark, spreading stain. His mouth jerked spasmodically, and a thin, dark line of blood trickled down his chin.

King's eyes were open, and he was staring at the policeman who was kneeling beside him. He seemed to want to say something, but the only sound that he could make was a faint gurgling.

"Don't talk," Romero urged quietly.

The policeman holstered his revolver and slid an arm under Bill King's neck, lifting the young man's head from the floor. King's entire body shuddered violently, startling Romero so that he almost let go. Then Bill King seemed to gather his strength momentarily, and he gurgled at Romero again.

Bill King shot out a bloody hand to grab the front of Romero's shirt. The policeman jerked away instinctively, but the injured man held on to him. King was staring up past Romero's shoulder, his eyes bulging.

Dave Romero turned around.

Romero's brain recorded flash impulses from all of his senses at once. He heard the whisper of the wind and the gurgle of Bill King's almost-words; he felt the chill air from outside on his skin, felt the hard concrete beneath his knee, felt the back of the young man's neck resting on his forearm; he smelled the metallic aroma of Bill King's blood, like freshly sheared copper; he tasted the acid bile in the back of his throat.

And he saw:

The figure stood above him, outlined in the doorway, arms raised overhead. The figure was a grotesque scarecrow of a man, dressed in a tattered, grimy T-shirt and filthy jeans. Long, scraggly, dirty hair framed the figure's head. Its eyes

Brujo

glittered yellow, the color of madness. In its hands the figure held an axe, poised for a killing blow. The last thing that Dave Romero saw was the axe.

Coming down.

The Brujo once more allowed himself a feeling of pleasure. His power over the beasts, granted him by his god, *Chinigchinich*, was complete and absolute. The beasts had carried out the Brujo's will and had isolated the island, trapping the Evil Ones who yet remained alive. Soon, however, they would all be destroyed. The spirits of the Pimugnan would be avenged.

But the Brujo's pleasure was fleeting. There came to his mind the image of The-One-Who-Would-Serve. The Brujo could feel that he was losing control of The-One, and his pleasure dissipated.

He was disturbed because at first the link between the Brujo and The-One had been very strong. The-One-Who-Would-Serve was capable of understanding visions, which was a gift that few men possessed. And from the beginning the Brujo had sensed that the spirit of The-One seethed with an anger that the Brujo himself could well understand.

Now, however, the Brujo was concerned that the madness within The-One could no longer be channeled. The Brujo tried to read the dark area of The-One's soul, but he could not see into the blackness.

The Brujo prayed to *Chinigchinich*, asking for guidance. Should he abandon The-One? Should he try again to *reach* The-Other?

The Brujo sensed that *Chinigchinich* needed time to reflect. With the eyes of the raven the Brujo watched as the sun disappeared behind gray clouds.

The approaching storm frightened the beasts, and the Brujo had to calm them. *Be still*, he whispered. *It is* Chinigchinich, *gone to rest. He will return.*

The rain began to fall.

Twenty

The thunderstorm hit Santa Catalina Island on Saturday afternoon at 3:30.

In one way the storm was a blessing. The rain came down hard and steady, and by sunset nearly all of the fires in Avalon were extinguished. Which was fortunate, because Avalon's half-dozen full-time fire fighters had by then retreated to the Casino, along with the rest of the city's surviving population, those who hadn't already found hiding places on their own.

After they had barricaded everybody inside the Casino, Buckler's men had taken a head count.

Thirteen hundred and sixty-six men, women, and children were taking refuge in the Avalon Casino's downstairs movie theater and upstairs ballroom.

Most of the people had been taken up to the ballroom, since it had been designed to handle three thousand dancers on more than twenty thousand square feet of floor space. Members of the Avalon Community Hospital's staff, led by Dr. Judy Wong, set up a small triage area in one corner of the ballroom, curtained off by hanging blankets. Fortunately, most of those whom they treated suffered from relatively minor injuries—animal bites, a few broken bones, first- and second-degree burns. Everything had happened so fast that the hospital's personnel had been able to bring along very little equipment and very few supplies; they, too, had been evacuated at a literal moment's notice.

More than a hundred people had to be treated for varying degrees of shock. Chief Buckler's men and several of the Avalon fire fighters assisted the hospital staff in administering first aid to many of the shock victims, but there was little that any of them could really do, beyond keeping the victims as warm and as comfortable as possible.

Still, the majority of those who camped upstairs in the ballroom were unhurt, and by nightfall the initial panic that had swept with them into the Casino had subsided. Most of them sat huddled together in clusters on the huge dance floor, their only light coming from various candles and lanterns that had been placed around the room. The panic had given way to a dull atmosphere of confusion and disbelief.

Outside, the thunderstorm raged.

In the late 1950s the Avalon Casino had been designated as Catalina Island's Civil Defense Emergency Shelter. But unlike many of those that had been established on the mainland, the Casino shelter had been consistently and properly maintained. The shelter's stocks—hundreds of cases of emergency rations and bottles of water, first-aid supplies, lanterns and candles, blankets and cots—were rotated regularly over the years, as the twenty-six-mile separation from the southern California mainland did not allow Avalon's residents the luxury of letting things slide. On more than one occasion their prudence had borne them out—for example, in 1971 when an earthquake centered in Sylmar rattled all of Los Angeles County, and as recently as 1980 when the coast was battered by eight straight days of rainstorms, the fact that the Casino shelter had been kept up had saved more than a few lives.

As Trevor Baldwin and Brad Cusimano moved down the wide concrete ramp that led from the upstairs ballroom to the Casino's ground floor, they overheard one of the three men who were walking ahead of them congratulate his companions on their foresight and planning. Brad had introduced the men to Trevor as three of Avalon's five City Council members. The entire group, including Brad and Trevor, was on its way to a meeting with Chief Buckler, who was waiting for everyone in the theater auditorium.

Trevor had reluctantly left Markie upstairs, in the care of Dr. Wong. The boy had gone into a mild state of shock when the storm hit—Markie had long been afraid of thunder, and the storm, on top of everything else that had happened, had pushed the boy over the edge. In an odd way Trevor felt grateful. He knew deep down that Markie would be all right, but his concern for his son shouldered out much of the grief and guilt over Valerie that Trevor had been trying hard to repress.

Dr. Wong gave the boy a sedative, and Markie fell asleep quickly on a cot in one corner of the triage area. Trevor wanted to stay with his son, but the doctor assured him that Markie would be carefully watched, that she would call Trevor immediately if anything happened. It would be a good thing for Trevor to go and get something to eat, Dr. Wong had told him. Besides, she added, the hospital personnel could use the space.

Trevor and Brad had gone to the other side of the ballroom, where volunteers had set up a kind of soup kitchen. Trevor had no appetite, but accepted a cup of black coffee. He moved away, looking around the ballroom at the groups of people who were huddled on the floor, wrapped in blankets. The people were shadows among the dim, flickering lights. They reminded Trevor of prehistoric men and women, gathered in their caves, praying that their fires would keep them safe, praying that whatever lurked outside would stay away . . .

An Avalon policeman appeared from downstairs to announce that the chief was calling an open meeting to let everyone know what was going on. Anyone who wanted to attend was invited.

The Avalon Casino's massive theater auditorium held twelve hundred seats, and those closest to the front were filling with people. Chief Buckler's men had placed Coleman lanterns along the aisles leading to the stage in the front of the theater, providing the people with just barely enough illumination to let them see where they were going.

Trevor and Brad came into the auditorium and saw Ray Buckler standing on the stage. Buckler was talking to a man whom Trevor recognized as the fat librarian who had spoken to him that morning at breakfast. The three City Council men moved away from Brad and Trevor and pushed their way to the front. Trevor saw the chief acknowledge the three men, then wave them to seats in the first row.

Trevor and Brad were among the last people to enter, and a policeman steered them to aisle seats fifteen rows back from the stage. Other officers moved along both aisles, directing people to sit down, and Trevor noticed that the theater looked to be a bit less than a quarter full. Within moments the low murmurs of conversation that he had been hearing since he first came in had all but died away.

Trevor watched Alex Doyle awkwardly climb down from the stage and take a seat in the front row. Ray Buckler turned to face the audience gathered in front of him and raised both hands, gesturing for quiet.

"You're all gonna have to just sit there and not say anything for a while," Buckler called out. His voice was strong and commanding, carrying well to the rear of the theater. "Just bear with me until I finish letting you know what we know about our situation, then you'll get your chance—"

A woman's voice shouted to him: "Ray, where's the mayor?"

Buckler frowned toward a spot a few rows in front of Brad and Trevor. "Virginia, didn't I just ask you to bear with me?" he said. The chief paused, not really waiting for an answer, then continued. "Frank is in San Bernardino visiting his wife's folks. The rest of the City Council is right here except for Mary McCarty, who . . . who didn't get out of her house . . ."

Buckler paused again, looking pained, then he went on. "Now, basically what's happened, what most of you already know, is that we're under siege. None of us have got a clue as to why all the animals on the island all of a sudden decided to turn on us, not even our resident expert on everything, Alex Doyle. I know that it probably seems like something out of a damn sci-fi novel, but . . ." The chief took a deep breath. "Anyway, regardless of why it's happened, it's still *happened*. Everybody who's in here is safe for the time being. We've got plenty of food and water and plenty of room, and we've got enough doctors and nurses to take care of people. My men have secured every entrance and exit to the Casino on both floors, so nothing's gonna get in here."

That's fine, Trevor Baldwin was thinking. Now tell us how we're going to get out.

"Now for the bad news," Buckler was saying. "As far as we know, all our communications are cut off. Our local switchboard was destroyed in the fire, and the Bell tower's been cut off. How, we don't know, 'cause the man who went up there to check it out didn't come back, and I'm not about to risk sending somebody else up there right now. The only communication we got is a couple of battery-powered shortwaves, but the storm is screwing them up. We're trying, though. The weather's also made flying in or off the island impossible."

"Where's the Coast Guard, Chief?" someone yelled.

"They got their own problems," Buckler said. "The last word we got from Two Harbors came about four this afternoon, and it sounded like they were in a helluva fix." Buckler shook his head, pressing his lips together. "This is the craziest goddamn thing of all," he added, "but apparently any boat that has attempted to leave the island or cross the channel has been sunk. By whales."

William Relling Jr.

There was an immediate buzz of surprise and consternation, spreading through the people in the auditorium. Ray Buckler called for the audience to settle down. "Look," he said, "we're just gonna have to keep doing what we're doing and treat this as a disaster situation until we can get some relief. We've decided to send out search-and-rescue teams at daybreak—we'll divide the whole island into sections. What I want are volunteers—and I only want those of you who know how to handle a gun, you hunters, anybody who's been in the army, whatever. Men or women, it doesn't matter. Just so you're familiar with firearms."

Buckler paused for a moment, and he looked to Trevor as if the weight of everything that had happened was suddenly pressing down upon his shoulders, crushing him. Buckler was visibly exhausted, and Brad Cusimano leaned over to Trevor and whispered, "You couldn't pay me enough to want to have his job."

Then the chief took a deep breath, drawing himself up, reaching up for the last reserves of his strength. He called out firmly, "Any questions?"

There were none. Buckler nodded. "Okay. Volunteers, give your names to my men so we can work out your assignments, then go upstairs and get some sleep." He paused for a moment, then went on. "I want you all to get some rest, because you're gonna need it," he said. "First thing tomorrow morning, we're going out."

Sunday

The storm broke during the night, and the Brujo sensed that his communion with *Chinigchinich* was once again restored.

The voice of his god spoke to him. *There is an enemy.*

An image formed in the mind of the Brujo. It was the face of one whom he knew, the face of one whom he had seen through the eyes of the raven. The face of one who was dangerous.

The enemy can destroy us, said the voice. *The enemy is most powerful.*

Of that the Brujo was already aware. He had had the raven watch the enemy carefully, though he had told the bird to keep its presence invisible to the enemy's eyes.

The voice told the Brujo that the enemy was the key. To destroy him would mean the certain eradication of the rest of the Evil Ones.

The Brujo asked, *How can he be destroyed?*

In his mind the image of the enemy blurred, becoming indistinct. Then the image re-formed, taking on a new shape.

It was the image of The-Other.

The Brujo whispered to himself, *At last* . . .

It was the will of *Chinigchinich*.

The-Other could at last be *reached.*

Twenty-one

The dreams came to him during the night. They were dark and foreboding dreams, strange wisps of shadow and light.

Usually, when he woke up, he was able to recall only the last visions of his sleep, any dreams which had preceded the last one all but forgotten. On this night, though, *all* of his dreams remained with him when he awoke.

He lay in the darkness, remembering.

The first dream had frightened him more than the two that had followed it. He had seen himself a prisoner of horrible creatures, beings who inhabited his worst nightmares. They were beasts—half human and half animal—and their faces were featureless, save for their glittering red eyes. The leader of the beasts was a man-thing with huge black wings that enabled him to fly above the others and direct them. The dreamer saw the nightmare beasts carrying his dream self to a place over which the bird-man hovered. The bird-man gestured, and a black pit opened wide in the ground beneath him. The nightmare beasts tossed the dreamer high into the air, and his body floated above the pit. The bird-man dipped toward him, black wings brushing against the dreamer's face. Then he was falling, falling into the open maw of the pit, ever so slowly. And all the while, he screamed . . .

Then he heard the voice. It whispered to him, *Stop*.

He hung suspended in blackness. He had stopped falling. His fear dissipated.

Listen, the voice whispered. *See*.

He heard a sudden rush of wind, and he opened his eyes to find himself standing atop a black mountain in the middle of an island that lay surrounded by a charcoal-gray sea. The sky above him was pure white. Another sound, a faint humming, the sound of a mighty engine approaching him. He turned to look in the direction of the sound and saw an airplane made of solid, sparkling silver winging its way toward him. As it neared, the roar of the plane's engines grew louder, almost deafening him, and its silver sparkle hurt his eyes. Then the plane was whooshing past him, its underbelly a scant few feet over the top of his head. He spun around as the plane flew past and saw the great silver machine slide on its belly along the top of the mountain, its metal skin screeching in agony. The plane slid off the edge of the mountain and disappeared from his sight. Then there came a tremendous explosion, and a blazing, red-orange spout of fire rose from the far side of the mountain. He followed the fire with his eyes as it rose higher and higher, growing brighter and brighter. He stared into the fire and watched as it settled above the horizon and turned into the sun. He stared into the brightness until he became aware that his sight was dimming. Then the blackness returned to surround him, and he thought, I'm blind . . .

The voice whispered, *No*.

He lay suspended in the blackness once more. He waited for the voice.

At last it returned to him. It whispered, *Feel*.

The last dream came to him. He was standing against a wall in an immense room. The room's walls glowed with a soft pastel hue, the color of a pearl, and the edges of the walls—where they met the ceiling, the floor, and each other—curved slightly at their point of juncture, so that he could not tell how large the room was. Opposite him, at the other end of the room, was a group of people. He knew them. They beckoned for him, but as he stepped toward them they seemed to back away and grow smaller, as if he were looking at them through the wrong end of a telescope. He broke into a run, but they moved away from him all that much faster, shrinking in size as they got farther and farther away. He reached out desperately to touch them and was suddenly pressed against the chest of a man who had appeared as if by magic in front of him. The man blocked his way. He looked up into the man's face.

The voice whispered, *He is the enemy.*

The dreamer could feel powerful, conflicting emotions welling inside him: frustration, fear, loneliness, grief, anger.

The voice repeated, *He is the enemy.*

The dreamer woke.

He lay there in the dark, remembering the dreams. All of the emotions that had raged within his dream self in the moments before he had awakened were gone. They were replaced by a solitary, cold, black feeling. Hatred.

The face of the man in the dream floated before him, and he heard the voice once more, whispering, *He is the enemy. You have the power. Destroy him.*

But the hatred was suddenly tempered by something else, by other feelings: guilt, compassion. Another part of him spoke, telling him, *It is wrong.*

The first voice repeated to him, *He is the enemy.*

He groaned out loud softly, "Nooo . . ."

Do not fight me, whispered the voice. *He is the enemy.*

The face floated before him seductively.

The voice said once more, *The enemy* . . .

"Destroy him," he mumbled aloud softly, echoing the words in his mind, giving in to the voice. He lay there for a moment more, letting the image of the enemy solidify in his mind's eye. Then he came to his feet and moved off into the darkness.

Twenty-two

Ray Buckler concluded his open meeting shortly after nine o'clock and spent the next three hours with his two sergeants, Herb Black and Carl Ritter, organizing and coordinating search-and-rescue teams for Sunday morning. They had nearly a hundred volunteers, and after weeding out a third of them, settled on twelve groups of five people each. The groups would be headed by Ray Buckler or one of his officers. Buckler and his sergeants had taken a map of Santa Catalina Island and divided it into sections, concentrating on the areas where they would be likely to find people hiding from the marauding animals.

William Relling Jr.

The chief's day caught up with him around midnight. By then he had been awake for twenty-one straight hours, and his energy stores were depleted. All he had eaten in the past ten hours was a sandwich that one of the volunteers had brought him before the start of the meeting, then a cup of tea and a doughnut while he and his sergeants made their plans. By twelve o'clock none of what he had eaten was sitting very well with him, and his indigestion merely served to make him irritable on top of everything else.

One of the chief's men came downstairs to let Buckler know that they had their first casualty: Mr. Carr, the air traffic controller, had died. Buckler followed the officer back up to the ballroom, arriving in time to see Dr. Wong and a pair of nurses wrapping Carr's body in a sheet. The doctor had been able to do little for the man aside from treating him with pain relievers and making him as comfortable as she could. She told the chief that even if she had had access to full hospital facilities, she doubted that she would have been able to save him. It was remarkable to her that Carr had lasted as long as he did.

Buckler helped three of his men carry Carr's body to the makeshift morgue that had been set up in a storage room behind the ballroom stage. As the four men laid the body on the floor, Ray Buckler twisted awkwardly and felt a sudden, sharp twinge in his left shoulder. He grunted in pain, and the officer nearest to him asked, "You okay, Chief?"

Buckler sat on the floor and rubbed his shoulder, then crooked his elbow and moved his left arm around, trying to work out the soreness. "Think I strained something," he said, fatigue evident in his voice.

The policeman looked at Buckler with concern. "Chief, I don't want you to get mad or anything," he said, "but you look like hell. You oughta get some rest."

All at once, Ray Buckler felt completely done in. He managed a rueful smile, then came to his feet and stretched. "I think I'm gonna do that right now," he said. "Do me a favor and tell Sergeant Ritter to make sure that somebody gets me up at sunrise."

"Okay, Chief," the man answered.

Buckler walked into the ballroom. He paused for a moment to look at the hundreds of sleeping bodies that lay sprawled on the dance floor in front of him.

The chief shook his head tiredly, trying once again to make some sense of what was happening. No one had been able to come up with any rational answers, which disturbed Ray Buckler. Not because he possessed a strong imagination which would create a frighteningly bizarre explanation, but because he was faced with a problem whose cause he could not fathom.

Buckler walked over to the triage area, where he found Carl Ritter talking to Dr. Wong. Ritter had been looking for the chief, to tell him that they had finally gotten through on the shortwave and described their situation to authorities on the mainland. All rescue attempts were being held off until morning. The mainland was very concerned about a new cold front that was moving in rapidly from the Pacific Ocean. More thunderstorms would be hitting the coast by no later than 9:00 A.M. Sunday, which would seriously hamper the rescue efforts.

Chief Buckler nodded, barely taking in the information. Dr. Wong noted the chief's weariness and directed him to an empty cot in a darkened corner, away from the rest of the triage area. She had set up the cot specifically for him.

Buckler tried to protest, but Dr. Wong was adamant. The chief wouldn't be good for anything if he didn't get some sleep, she told him, and he was going to lie down on that cot if she had to strap him down personally. Until he did, she wouldn't be able to sleep herself. So that was that.

Buckler asked Ritter to awaken him at dawn. He sat down on the cot heavily, pulled off his shoes, and swung his legs up, settling himself comfortably. Folding his arms behind his head, he lay there, thinking, running through his weary mind the preparations for the next morning, wondering if anything they had planned could really do any good. Buckler was certain that the people inside the Casino would end up safely transported to the mainland—but how many people could they hope to find outside, still alive . . .

Ray Buckler's heavy eyelids closed. Within minutes he was deep asleep, snoring softly.

What woke him four hours later was an aching pain that seemed to radiate from his left shoulder and down his arm. Buckler's consciousness returned slowly, his brain thick with sleep. For a moment he felt a panicky disorientation as his eyes opened and focused on his unfamiliar surroundings. The only sound he could perceive was the rushing of his own blood in his ears.

Then he remembered where he was, and he became aware of the pain. Buckler thought to himself: I must've fucked up my shoulder worse than I thought.

Ray Buckler became aware of a constricting tightness in his chest. That frightening, familiar sensation snapped him fully awake. He knew instantly what was wrong.

I'm having a heart attack!

Buckler pleaded silently: Dear God, not now! He tried to push himself up from the cot, but was dismayed to find that he couldn't move. It was as if he were being held down by a giant invisible hand. Buckler opened his mouth to cry for help, but could only produce a choked whimper.

The clutching pain in his chest grew tighter. His skin felt damp and clammy, and his breaths were coming short and fast.

Buckler tried to lift himself once more, but the effort was futile. A feeling of helpless terror began to rise within him, and he wondered dimly why no one came to help.

From the corner of his eye, he saw a shadow separate from the gloom. The shadow moved toward him, then stopped beside the cot. A rush of fear almost caused the chief to black out, but he steeled himself, grasping at the edges of his consciousness. With tremendous exertion he managed to turn his head to face the shadowy figure.

Buckler recognized who it was, but before he could speak, the pain exploded in his chest. His face twisted into a mask of agony.

The figure stood beside him silently.

At last Ray Buckler managed to gasp: "Mark . . . get help . . . Mark . . ."

Markie Baldwin looked down on the chief, his face blank and expressionless.

"Please . . ." Buckler whispered. "Mark . . ."

The voice that came from Markie was cold and hollow. "You're gonna die," the boy said.

Ray Buckler was suddenly aware that he could no longer feel his arms and legs. The pain in his chest was also diminishing, as the numbness enveloped his whole body. This is what it's like, he thought. This is the big one.

"You're gonna die," Markie repeated in his strange, sepulchral voice. "You're the enemy and you're gonna die."

The chief looked at the boy through a misty, gray fog that had settled over his vision. Markie's features had grown faint and indistinct.

But for a moment, Ray Buckler thought he saw something else. Superimposed over the boy's face was the face of another, almost the face of a skull.

Then Ray Buckler allowed the numbing fog to settle over him and take away his pain.

Forever.

It was as the Brujo had wished. He had finally *reached* The-Other, and the enemy, the leader of those against whom the Brujo sought revenge, lay dead.

The enemy's followers were in disarray. They were not aware that The-Other was among them, awaiting the Brujo's instructions. When the time came—very soon—The-Other would open the way for the Brujo's minions to strike. The Evil Ones would be obliterated.

The time would come with the rising of *Chinigchinich*, the sun . . .

Suddenly there came a voice, calling to the Brujo: *My God, my God, why have you forsaken me?*

The voice intruded upon the Brujo's thoughts. He was angered. He knew to whom the voice belonged, but he disregarded the plea.

The-One-Who-Would-Serve was of no further use to him.

The voice begged: *My God, my God—*

The Brujo turned away.

Twenty-three

Casey Harrison had taken shelter from the storm in the abandoned café where Trevor and Markie Baldwin and Brad Cusimano had eaten breakfast Saturday morning. Casey smashed his way into the restaurant with the same bloody axe that he had used on the two men at the microwave tower, the same tool he had used to wreck the tower's generator and the control equipment inside the main shed. He had done as the voice of God commanded him to do, destroying the Evil Ones' ability to communicate with the outside.

His task completed, Casey had suddenly felt a

peculiar sense of *release*. The raven left him, and as the storm clouds rolled in, darkening the sky and covering the sun, Casey's will had once more become his own. But all that he had seen had destroyed his sanity; his thoughts were no longer rational.

Some primitive sense of survival warned Casey to seek shelter. That same sense reminded him that it had been two days since he had last eaten, and Casey was suddenly ravenous. The shattered pieces of his mind formed the image of the small restaurant, and with a howl of hunger Casey had leaped the fence surrounding the tower property and was running back to Avalon.

Casey loped through the streets of Avalon, oblivious to the eeriness of his surroundings. The structures in the southeast part of the city had not caught fire, but they lay dark and deserted and silent.

The rain was falling heavily, and Casey was soaking wet by the time he reached the café. He hurled the axe through the glass of the front door, shattering it, then kicked out the shards still jutting from the door frame before squeezing through.

Inside was evidence that those who had been in the restaurant had evacuated in a tremendous hurry. A good third of the booths and tables and counter space were covered with the remains of partially eaten meals—plates of half-eaten sandwiches, desiccated salads, piles of stone-cold French fried potatoes, cups of coffee gone to mud. Casey scrambled from table to table, cramming food into his mouth with both hands, grunting and slobbering like a wild animal tearing into prey.

Suddenly the room was momentarily flushed with brightness, and seconds later there came an explosive crash of thunder. The light and the noise startled Casey, causing him to drop the hamburger that he had snatched from a plate on the front counter.

He spun around quickly, peering toward a plate-glass window at the front of the café, twenty feet in front of him. Casey caught a glimpse of his own reflection in the glass and stared, puzzled by what he saw. He took a step toward the glass cautiously, hand extended to touch the image that was at the same time reaching for him.

Another flash of lightning illuminated the street outside, burning the image in the glass into Casey's brain. What he had seen was barely human: a thin, unshaven, pathetic creature, its hair hanging in snarled strings, its clothes soaked and grimy and stained with blood. Its eyes shined madly, pupils wide and black, eyeballs yellow and bulging.

Casey wondered, Is that me?

Another crack of thunder made him jump, and he tore himself away from the glass.

All of a sudden Casey felt very tired. He moved toward the rear of the restaurant, to the darkest part, and found an empty booth. He climbed onto the Leatherette seat and curled himself into a fetal ball. For a time he listened to the falling rain, then fell asleep.

He awoke, hours later, in pitch-blackness. A

faint odor of spoiling food tickled his nostrils. The sound of the rain was gone. Casey lay still on the seat of the booth. All he could hear was the soft sound of his own breathing.

He shifted on the seat, tearing his bare skin away from the plastic. Casey frowned. Something disturbed him, an odd, unfamiliar feeling that he had never known before. It wasn't a physical sensation, like the hunger and fatigue that had driven him to this place many hours earlier. Rather, it was a kind of spiritual hollowness, an emptiness. Casey felt suddenly, sharply *alone*.

And he was afraid.

Casey sat up and looked around the dark café. His eyes quickly accustomed to the gloom, and the shapes of the objects in the restaurant—the tables and chairs, the counter, the cash register in front—all stood clearly outlined. Casey turned to look through the front window to the street. The air seemed to be diffused with a faint silver and violet glow. There was no movement anywhere, no sound save that of his own breathing.

Casey sucked in a gulp of air and held his breath. He sat there, listening intently, waiting for a sound—*any* sound—to come to him, something that would convince him that he needn't be afraid, that he was not completely alone.

He sat for two full minutes, hearing nothing but the pounding of his blood in his ears. The pounding grew louder and louder. Casey's lungs began to ache and he closed his eyes, forcing himself to hold on. Tiny fireworks exploded on the under-

BRUJO

sides of his eyelids, the blood roared in his ears, his lungs burned—until at last the air exploded from his mouth. He clutched the table in front of him for support, panting for breath, swallowing gulps of air. Gradually Casey's breathing slowed, but his heart was still beating very fast.

He was *alone*.

He had to fight back a rush of panic. His scrambled thoughts tried to arrange themselves into some semblance of order.

My God, what's happened to me?

The voice. The voice that had summoned him, that had sent the raven to him, had led him into the hills, shown him visions, commanded him to kill. The voice of God . . .

The voice was no longer there.

Casey reached into his memory for words of supplication that he had learned as a child, words that he had been taught long ago.

He prayed: "My God, my God, why have you forsaken me?"

Casey waited patiently for an answer. His fear was diminishing, because he sensed that his prayer had been heard, that the voice was still *there*. He was not alone.

But the voice refused to acknowledge him.

Casey repeated his prayer: "My God, my God—"

Before he could finish, Casey felt a coldness wash over his mind. An icy chill froze him, cutting off his prayer.

The voice had *scorned* him.

Casey was alone.

William Relling Jr.

But he was not afraid. Other emotions roiled inside him—rejection, shame, anger.

"What did I do?" Casey pleaded. "Tell me what I did?"

There was no answer. The voice had abandoned him.

Casey sat in the dark for some time, thinking mad thoughts. His shame and anger passed, were replaced by a new sense of determination. Somehow he had displeased God, and for that God had rejected him. Casey had no idea what he had done to cause disfavor, but he decided that he would have to make up for whatever it was. He would redeem himself in God's sight. He would hear the voice of God again. He would once more feel God's *power*.

Casey rose from the booth and found the axe, lying beneath a counter stool. He climbed back through the jagged hole in the shattered front door that he had made the afternoon before. He stood outside, drawing chilly, damp air into his lungs.

Ahead of him, to the east and across the channel, Casey could see the faintest glimmer of the sun as it tinged the edge of the horizon. Daybreak was not long in coming, though above him still hung a clear, dark sky and a handful of stars that twinkled in the fabric of night.

Casey could smell the approach of yet another storm.

He turned, slowly, to look up Crescent Avenue. A half mile away from him stood the Avalon Casino, atop a slight rise. Huge and foreboding, the structure glowed white against the dark sea and sky.

Casey had decided what he had to do to win back God's favor.

He gazed at the Casino and thought: *There*. They were waiting for him . . .

Casey hefted the axe and started up the street.

Twenty-four

Trevor Baldwin had finally fallen asleep from sheer exhaustion around 1:30 A.M. Judy Wong had allowed him to arrange a pair of folding chairs near the cot where Markie lay sleeping, so long as he didn't disturb his son or any of the other patients in Dr. Wong's makeshift ward. Brad Cusimano had sacked out a dozen feet away in a sleeping bag. Trevor wrapped himself in a blanket and suspended his tall frame uncomfortably, sitting up in one chair while using the other for a footstool.

After checking on her patients one final time, Dr. Wong had gone to the far side of the ballroom

William Relling Jr.

for a much-needed few hours' rest of her own. She left the supervision of the patients in the hands of another doctor, an older man named Ziegler, who was a general practitioner in Avalon and who had volunteered to cover the night shift. Dr. Ziegler sat at the far end of the ward, away from Trevor and Markie, beside one of a handful of Coleman lanterns that glowed in various spots around the huge ballroom.

Once Trevor had settled himself, he looked around the room. It appeared as if the entire upstairs space had been converted into a kind of refugee camp. Several families had strung blankets on lines to separate themselves from their neighbors, to give themselves at least the illusion of privacy, like squatters laying claim to their own piece of territory, however small it might be. Trevor thought it was fortunate that the Casino's ballroom and theater had been designed to accommodate more than three thousand people; there was plenty of space and enough food and water, and the lines to use the Casino's toilet facilities had never grown too long—no worse, it seemed, than being at a football game and having to wait for a few minutes to use the john. His overall impression was that he and his son were on some sort of macabre camping trip with a thousand other campers—a strange thought, and it might have been funny had the circumstances not been what they were.

Trevor sat for some minutes, listening to the rustlings and snorings of the hundreds of sleepers around him. It was the first chance he had to think about what had happened in the past two days to him, to his son, to Brad Cusimano . . .

To Valerie.

No one could confirm that Valerie had been aboard the plane, but the sense of loss that had overwhelmed Trevor convinced him that Valerie was gone.

Except for a few moments in the airport terminal before Chief Buckler's arrival, Trevor had not had time for grief or sorrow to affect him. And at that time, moments after the crash, with the horrible scene so fresh in his mind, the shock had simply been numbing. Trevor's mind had reacted by treating the crash as if it hadn't really happened at all, as if it were just a bad dream. The pandemonium and horror of the day's subsequent events—including Markie's illness—had prevented Trevor from even thinking of Valerie.

Now, however, in the comparative peace and quiet of the ballroom, the terrible pain and guilt and sorrow seemed to swell inside of him. Valerie was . . .

Say it, Trevor told himself harshly. Say it.

Valerie's dead.

Realization was a dull, heavy ache in Trevor's chest. He had known her for such a short time, but had envisioned spending the rest of their lives together. Now all of that was gone, destroyed in a flash of fire and smoke, and Trevor felt as if a part of himself had been mercilessly cut away. All that was left was this gaping emptiness.

He wondered how many times he had told Valerie that he loved her; sadly, he felt that he could probably count the number on his fingers. Did she know that I loved her? he wondered. It was a question to which Trevor would never have an answer.

Trevor told himself, I have to think about something else . . .

He glanced over at his son's still form, curled beneath a blanket. Markie's small chest heaved slowly and rhythmically, his breathing quiet and regular. The boy looked so much at peace that no one watching him, not even his father, could have guessed at the nightmares that even then were unreeling in Markie's unconscious mind.

Trevor watched the boy for some minutes, and his feelings of guilt and grief over Valerie were augmented by similar feelings for his son. It's all my fault, Trevor thought bitterly. It had been his idea to bring Markie and Valerie to Catalina. Never mind that he had no way of knowing what would happen—he was still responsible for both of them.

Trevor wondered about his son's mental state after this ordeal—assuming that Markie even survived. Face it, Baldwin, Trevor told himself. You're a failure. You failed as a husband, you failed as a father, you failed as a lover. You even failed as a goddamn hero on the boat, because somebody had had to come out and rescue *you*. Just what the fuck good are you . . .

Trevor caught himself and drove the black thoughts from his fatigued brain, along with the helpless despair that seemed to be settling over him.

Brad was right, he thought. Trevor's main concern had to be taking care of his son, and an "Oh, me—poor me" act wasn't going to do anybody any good.

He felt his resolve strengthen, however slightly, and he pledged silently to his son: I'll get us out of this okay, Mark. The thought was still with him when Trevor at last slipped into an exhausted slumber.

But like that of his son, Trevor Baldwin's sleep was plagued by nightmares. In Trevor's case the dreams were little more than shadow plays; what happened was vague, the shapes and settings and dream players themselves ghostly and insubstantial, almost as if Trevor's nightmares were being filtered to him through the mind of another.

The only clear image in Trevor's nightmares was that of Markie—and in the dream that had awakened him, Trevor saw his son spinning away from him into a void, as if Markie were falling into a bottomless tunnel. All the while the boy strained to reach his father, but the effort was in vain. Neither could Trevor's dream-self will his own arms to reach out for Markie. All that he could do was stand by helplessly, staring into the blackness into which his son disappeared . . .

Trevor's eyes snapped open. The dream had filled him with such dread that his heart was hammering. He whispered his son's name out loud as he swung around to look at the cot where the boy lay sleeping.

Markie was gone.

Trevor kicked his feet free of the chair on which they rested, shrugged the blanket off his shoulders, and scrambled to the side of Markie's cot. His brain was still fogged with sleep, his thoughts still colored with a residue of dread left over from the nightmare that had awakened him. Trevor felt an absurd hope that Markie was perhaps hiding beneath the cot or curled in the tangled bedclothes. He searched, but the boy wasn't there.

Trevor sat down on the edge of the cot. He tried to force his weary mind to function, tried to shake it free of cobwebs. He wondered where Markie could possibly be, and it took some time for the logical answers to his question to creep into his thoughts.

Perhaps Markie's sedative had worn off and the boy had woken up hungry or thirsty, or had had to go to the bathroom.

Then he noticed something. At the opposite end of the ward, a group of people were gathered together, working over someone on a cot. Whatever it was they were doing, they appeared to want to work as quickly and as quietly as possible, so as not to disturb the other patients or the hundreds of sleepers in the dark ballroom. But there was something about their activity that suggested urgency to Trevor. The people were trying to fix something—or someone—that had gone terribly wrong.

Trevor's mind flashed: *Markie!*

He leaped from the cot and dashed across the ward. Trevor recognized the people who were bent over the still form. Two of the figures—a nurse and the police sergeant, Ritter—held lanterns, while Drs. Wong and Ziegler performed cardiopulmonary resuscitation. A second policeman looked on, his face a tangle of worry, anger, and fear.

Sergeant Ritter saw Trevor coming and nodded to the other policeman. The officer moved away from the cot to intercept Trevor before he got close enough to the group to see whom they were working on.

The policeman grabbed Trevor's arm to restrain him, but he jerked away angrily, and barked at the officer, "That's my kid!"

"No, it's not!" the policeman shot back. But Trevor had slipped from the man's grasp and shoved him aside.

He came up behind Dr. Wong just as she turned to look from the cot to Sergeant Ritter. Her face was a mask of professional calm, but her words held defeat and pain. "I'm sorry, Carl," she said softly.

Trevor's heart dropped. He choked: "Oh, my God, no . . ."

Dr. Wong heard Trevor's voice over her shoulder and turned to look at him. Her expression shifted; she was puzzled to see him there. She came to her feet.

"I've got to see him," Trevor said, pushing past

her. Before Dr. Wong could stop him, Trevor was standing next to the cot.

Staring down at Ray Buckler.

Trevor heard Dr. Wong call his name, but her voice sounded very far away. He looked at her dumbly. She repeated Trevor's name and started to say something else to him, but he blurted aloud, in surprise and relief, "It's the chief!"

The loudness of Trevor's voice seemed to startle Dr. Wong and the others. She shushed him harshly, then laid a hand on his arm and led him away. "Please, Mr. Baldwin," she said in a hushed tone that made Trevor think that she was speaking to him as if he were a child. Or crazy.

"Chief Buckler had a heart attack," Dr. Wong said. "But you can't let anybody else know. Not yet."

Trevor felt as if he were waking from a deep trance. He shook himself, then turned to Dr. Wong and saw that she was looking at him peculiarly, but with concern.

"I . . . I'm sorry," he stammered at last, keeping his voice low. "Doctor, I just . . . I thought he was—"

"It's all right, Mr. Baldwin," she told him.

Trevor said, "I thought he was my son."

The look of puzzlement again crossed Dr. Wong's face.

"Markie's disappeared," Trevor told her. "I woke up and he wasn't in bed."

Dr. Wong thought for a moment, then said, "He's probably gone to the toilet."

Trevor pressed his lips together and nodded.

"Please go away, Mr. Baldwin," she said. "And please, don't say anything to anyone about Chief Buckler. We need your . . . cooperation."

She waited for his assent, but Trevor stood unmoving. Dr. Wong frowned. "Please," she said, "you have to understand—"

"I understand," Trevor snapped, cutting her off. He was suddenly very angry with Dr. Wong, with the police, with everything. Without another word, he turned away from Dr. Wong and walked back to his son's empty cot.

Trevor considered waking Brad Cusimano to ask him to help search for Markie, but decided against it. In the mood that he was in, he didn't feel like having to talk to anyone.

He didn't understand why he had gotten so angry at Dr. Wong. Trevor knew why it was important not to broadcast Chief Buckler's death. The news would have to be broken to the Casino survivors in such a way as to minimize its emotional impact, because everyone there looked to Buckler as the group's leader, trusting him to get them out safely. The other civic types would have to convince the people that Buckler's death changed nothing. Rescue plans would proceed as the chief himself had outlined. Everything would be fine.

Trevor understood all of that. What angered him was that they were all acting as bureaucrats usually did—covering their own asses before worrying about the safety of an individual, who in this case happened to be Trevor Baldwin's little boy.

Dammit, maybe I am being irrational, Trevor thought to himself. But it's *my* kid who's lost.

But there was more to it than that. As Trevor looked for his son—systematically checking the places where Markie was likely to have gone—his quiet, gnawing fear returned. It was the same feeling that Trevor had first felt aboard the passenger boat on Friday afternoon, then again yesterday as he was driving the van back to Avalon from the airport—the feeling that he had when Markie announced in that remote, hollow voice that Ray Buckler was going to die.

Trevor paused midway through a silent, cursory search of the sleeping bodies that covered the expanse of ballroom floor. He stood there, thinking.

Markie knew.

It hadn't registered on Trevor until that moment. He remembered that Markie's dire prediction had frightened him at the time, but almost as soon as Trevor had returned to the van, Markie had been terrified into a state of shock by the thunder from the coming storm. There had been no time for Trevor to consider the boy's strange behavior, and he had forgotten all about it. Until now.

Trevor repeated to himself: *Markie knew.*

The realization chilled him.

What in the hell is going on here?

It dawned on him slowly. Trevor Baldwin was not a man who possessed an especially vivid imagination, but for the first time, he began to consider the possibility that what was attacking them was *supernatural*, something so far out of the realm of ordinary experience that there was no rational way to deal with it.

But whatever it was, it had his son.

Trevor thought, I really *am* going nuts.

The sleeping figure on the floor near Trevor's feet rolled over and snorted loudly. Trevor looked down, and despite his preoccupation with Markie, seeing the man on the floor made Trevor think of an old joke. The guy should be careful about falling asleep in public, because somebody was liable to paint "Goodyear" on his side.

Then Trevor recognized the man, and after only a few moments' consideration, he bent down to wake him up.

Trevor shook him gently. "Mr. Doyle?" he whispered. "Mr. Doyle, I need your help."

"I don't want you to take this the wrong way, Mr. Baldwin," Alex Doyle said quietly, "but I think you're out of your fucking mind."

The two of them were standing at the end of a long table on which volunteers had set out gallons of coffee and boxes of doughnuts. At the opposite end of the table, out of earshot, were two of the policemen who were working night duty—one of whom, Trevor noticed, was the man who had helped Sergeant Ritter carry away Ray Buckler's body to the makeshift morgue.

Trevor looked at Alex Doyle, who was chewing

on a doughnut. "A few minutes ago I was thinking the same thing myself," Trevor said.

Alex discerned the note of desperation in Trevor's voice. "Look," he said apologetically, "I didn't mean . . . you're worried about your boy, I know—"

"It's okay."

"I just don't know what you think I can do," Alex said.

Trevor thought hard for a moment, then asked, "How well did you know Chief Buckler?"

Alex shrugged. "Not very."

Trevor said, "Markie told me Buckler was going to die."

"So?"

"So don't you think that's awfully goddamn strange—"

"Mr. Baldwin, what do you want from me?"

Their voices had risen enough to attract the attention of the policemen at the table's other end. Trevor frowned.

Alex Doyle reached for another doughnut. "What are you trying to tell me?" he said softly.

Trevor could feel his frustration rising. "I don't know," he answered, keeping his voice low. "It's just . . ."

Alex was looking at him impassively.

Trevor said, "I know that whatever's happened to Markie, you can fix it."

"How?"

"I don't *know*. But I know that something's got hold of him and it's taken him to wherever he is now. I don't know how I know, but I know."

Alex picked up a cup from the table and filled it with steaming coffee. He sipped at the coffee, waiting for Trevor to go on.

Trevor was trying hard to think of how to put what he wanted to say into words. "Mr. Doyle," he said at last, "I don't understand this, but it's got something to do with that stuff you told us yesterday. That Indian stuff."

Alex Doyle looked at Trevor over the rim of his cup.

"Markie knew that word," Trevor said.

"*Chinigchinich*."

"Yeah. What is that?"

Alex set down his coffee and regarded the other man seriously for a moment, wondering what he was getting himself into. Then he gave Trevor Baldwin a brief version of the history of the Pimu Indians.

When Alex had finished, Trevor asked him, "The Indians worshiped animals? You're sure about that?"

Alex nodded.

"And they took kids when they were six years old?"

"Six or seven, yeah," Alex answered. "They figured that a boy that young was the most receptive. The hallucinations wouldn't scare them as much, because their sense of wonder and belief would be a lot stronger at that age . . ."

Alex paused, noticing the dark expression that had crossed Trevor's face. "What's the matter?" Alex asked.

"Markie," Trevor said. "He's six and a half years old."

Neither of them spoke for several seconds. Alex Doyle was looking at Trevor as if he were trying to make up his mind whether or not Trevor really *was* crazy.

"What about that other guy?" Trevor said. "That singer. Casey Harrison."

"The one who went nuts in the bar?"

"Yeah. How come everybody's forgotten about him? How come nobody knows what the hell's happened to him?"

Alex shrugged. "How should I know? Something's probably eaten him by now—"

"He knew that word, too," Trevor cut in. "Remember? *Ching*-whatever. Markie told us that that's what Casey Harrison was saying when the bats came in. Maybe if we found him . . . maybe whatever's got Markie . . ."

Trevor paused, letting the words hang in the air.

Alex sipped his coffee. "Mr. Baldwin, what you're thinking . . ." The librarian shook his head, pushing away the notion that had struck him. "It's just not possible," he said.

Trevor's voice was stony, without inflection. "What's not?" he asked.

Alex found the words difficult to say. "It's not possible that what's killing the people on this island . . ." Alex's face registered his displeasure. "What you're thinking is . . . dammit, it's just not possible that your son's been . . . *possessed* by the god of a tribe of Indians who were wiped out two hundred years ago!"

Trevor's mouth twisted into a bitter grimace. "You said it yourself, Doyle," he grunted. "I'm out of my fucking mind." Trevor's expression tightened and his tone became deadly serious. "But I want my son back."

Before Alex Doyle could reply, a commotion at the other end of the table drew both his and Trevor's attention. A third policeman had come up to the other two, and though he spoke in a quiet voice, the newcomer was obviously excited about something. All three moved off quickly, heading for the concrete ramp that led downstairs.

Trevor broke away from Alex Doyle and trotted after the policemen who had disappeared down the ramp. "Hey!" Alex called to Trevor's back, trying to get his attention. But an instant later Trevor, too, was out of sight.

Trevor jogged down the ramp and caught a glimpse of the three policemen as they pushed open the lobby door that led to the outside. He was out the door after them seconds later.

The chilly, predawn air stung Trevor's face. The sun would be up shortly, though, and it had already begun to lighten the night sky to gray. As soon as he was outside, Trevor heard a voice coming up from the bottom of the Casino drive.

The screaming voice of Casey Harrison.

The young musician stood at the end of the driveway, glaring at the trio of policemen who

William Relling Jr.

were very slowly moving forward, revolvers in their hands.

Casey held the bloodstained axe threateningly, as if to challenge an attack. The young man was shrieking like a demented banshee, in the same strange language that he had used that night in the El Capitan Hotel's bar. Only this time, Trevor recognized one of the words—the one that he now knew was the name of a supposedly long-dead Indian god.

The policeman nearest to Trevor looked back for an instant and yelled at him, "Get back inside!"

Casey Harrison suddenly slumped, his face contorting in agony. Then he straightened, his insane gaze riveted on Trevor. "The-Other!" Casey screeched. "The-Other came from you!"

Trevor suddenly heard Alex Doyle's out-of-breath whisper coming from behind him: "Who the fuck is that?"

"You!" Casey screamed at Trevor. "You want the power! But I've got it! I've—"

He stopped abruptly, then turned to face the east, the rising sun. "*Chinigchinich*," Casey breathed. He held the axe outward, as if in offering. "Show them the power."

And Casey Harrison *reached*.

Nightmare.
The five men—Trevor, Alex, and the three policemen—became one with Casey Harrison. Their minds were filled with dazzling brightness, the light of the sun. Then the light faded, and the six-who-

BRUJO

were-now-one found themselves in a place that had existed many years earlier.

They saw the villages, the people. They saw through the eyes of the one who was the emissary of their god, the sun. The white priests of the land across the channel called him Brujo.

They saw the Evil Ones.

The Evil Ones were invaders. They were all those who differed from the Brujo and his people, those who were not Pimugnan. The Evil Ones were outsiders who wished to steal the island from the Brujo's people. They were despoilers of the sacred land.

The Evil Ones destroyed the Pimugnan. The hunters who sought the fur of the otter also hunted the Indians.

Their ships had left them behind to hunt. The Evil Ones remained to kill, to maim, to ravage the people of the sun.

His people begged the Brujo, "Help us."

The Brujo fought the Evil Ones, fought them with the power of Chinigchinich, *the god of the Pimugnan. But the Evil Ones defeated him.*

They took him prisoner, and they tortured him.

Then they buried him alive.

The Brujo prayed to the sun, Help me. Help me.

But there was only darkness.

And at last the Brujo slept.

The nightmare lasted only a few seconds, though to Trevor it felt as if it had gone on forever. He

William Relling Jr.

realized that he had returned to his own reality only when he heard Alex Doyle's hushed voice behind him, muttering, "Holy *Christ* . . ."

Then Trevor heard Casey Harrison crying aloud, in agony, "My God, my God, why have you forsaken me!"

As if in answer, there came a savage *skreek* from overhead. As Trevor watched, there appeared as if by magic a black, winged shape that dived at the young musician. The black bird struck Casey Harrison full in the face, its claws extended to gouge at the man's eyes.

Casey screamed. He flailed at the bird with his axe, but the creature dodged his blind swipe. It rose away from him gracefully.

Casey swung around to face the three policemen, his weapon at the ready. Clear fluid tinged pink with blood dribbled down his cheeks from the torn sockets where his eyes had been.

The policeman nearest to Casey shouted at him, "Put the axe down, man! You need help!"

Casey whirled around at the sound of the policeman's voice, raising the axe to strike.

"Drop it, goddammit!" the policeman commanded.

Casey shrieked, "Noooooooo!!!"

He leaped at the policeman.

The others opened fire.

Twenty-five

The gunshots shattered the unnatural stillness of the morning air, the explosions so loud that both Trevor and Alex covered their ears reflexively. In as many seconds a dozen bullets smashed into Casey Harrison, the shots literally blowing him off his feet.

Casey crashed to the ground, and for a brief moment the figures outside the Avalon Casino stood frozen in a grim tableau: Trevor Baldwin and Alex Doyle near the building's front door; the three policemen crouched, their hands bracing weapons that were trained upon the crumpled body that lay in a bloody heap at the end of the drive.

Casey's body gave a sudden, spasmodic jerk—his muscles twitching from one final, involuntary spark of electricity shot from his brain—and it was as if someone had flipped a switch to turn everything on again.

The policemen edged forward cautiously toward the dead man on the ground, until one of them was close enough to kneel beside the body. The officer held his gun up with one hand and rolled the musician over with the other. Then he looked up at his partners and nodded curtly, and the other two officers came forward to examine the man whom they had killed.

Trevor was curious to find out what was happening, but he was too far away to hear what the policemen were saying to each other. Their figures blocked his view of Casey Harrison's body. Trevor had taken a step forward when he felt a beefy hand grab his arm to restrain him.

Alex Doyle ordered him softly, "Listen."

Trevor stood still, and slowly he became aware of an eerie sound that broke the quiet surrounding them. The sound, faint at first, came from his left, in the direction of the city of Avalon itself. A kind of breathless panting—not at all the kind of sound that human beings would make—was accompanied by the padding of dozens of small feet, scratching on the pavement. The sound grew louder.

"Look," Alex said.

Trevor peered toward the storefronts clustered

on Crescent Avenue, at the bottom of the slight rise on which the Casino was situated. The buildings were only a half mile away, but their outlines were fuzzy and difficult to make out in the peculiar light of not quite sunrise.

At first Trevor thought that the light might be playing tricks on his eyes. Then he was sure that he could see the dark, rapidly moving shapes that separated themselves from the surrounding buildings. The dark shapes joined into a single, snarling pack that raced up the street toward the Casino.

Trevor shouted to the policemen at the end of the driveway: "Get back! *Dogs!*"

The three men had seen the animals coming even as Trevor had called out his warning and were already running up the driveway to safety. Alex jerked open the lobby door and held it while Trevor and the policemen dashed inside.

Just in time. They watched as a pack of at least thirty dogs of all breeds and sizes scrambled up the driveway, yapping and growling madly. The men pulled back as the pack pressed against the outside of the door, and the pack's leader—a vicious-looking Doberman pinscher—snapped at the men, whom he could see through the glass but could not reach.

There was a furious howling at the end of the driveway, and the dogs at the door turned away to join the animals that had discovered the body of Casey Harrison. The men inside the door watched in absolute horror as the beasts ripped the dead musician's body to bloody shreds.

William Relling Jr.

* * *

The sounds of the gunshots that had killed Casey Harrison and the insane yelping and growling of the pack of maddened canines that devoured him had awakened almost everyone inside the Casino. Fortunately the majority of the people resisted any urge to panic—in fact, they managed to help comfort and calm those few who had succumbed. Most of the refugees seemed resigned to their situation, if a bit numbed by it. Nearly all hoped for an imminent rescue.

Chief Buckler's death was announced to the Casino survivors in another community meeting at 7:00 A.M. The meeting was led by Dr. Judy Wong, Sergeant Herb Black, and the ranking member of Avalon's City Council, a man named Richard Sundermann.

The news badly upset a few people, in particular those who had considered themselves among the chief's close friends. But all of the people in the theater auditorium were assured by Mr. Sundermann that what had been planned the night before would occur. Sergeant Black, as second-in-command of the Police Department, was assuming the role of acting chief of police for the duration of the crisis.

Mr. Sundermann and Dr. Wong turned the meeting over to Herb Black, who then passed on to the people gathered in the theater what little new information he had. Herb Black was older than Ray Buckler, his personality more easygoing, but he radiated a similar kind of take-charge authority. It was a good thing that he did, because it made the group's acceptance of him easier.

Sergeant Black told everyone that shortwave radio contact with the mainland had been reestablished, at least for the time being. A Coast Guard official in San Pedro had reported that the channel was closed to all traffic and that the Guard had made an attempt at crossing at first light, shortly after 6:00. Unfortunately the attempt had failed, and the rescue cruiser and its crew had been lost.

The Coast Guard was planning another, more heavily defended crossing for 7:45 A.M., but the storm due that morning was moving faster than had been anticipated, and it would probably hit before their rescuers got to the island.

"How come you don't give us the *bad* news, Herb?" a man's voice called from the audience. There followed a titter of uncomfortable laughter.

Sergeant Black rolled his eyes unhappily. "I'm glad you're all takin' our situation seriously," he said. "Myself, I'm pretty damn tired of this little Boy Scout Jamboree we got goin' on in here."

Black waited to hear if there were other remarks from the group before he continued. "We're gonna go ahead here as planned," he said. "The problem is that without Chief Buckler, we're down to eleven police officers, counting me, and three men have been up all night. The Coast Guard wants us to send somebody out to their facility on the other side of the island and find out what the hell's gone

William Relling Jr.

on out there, and that'll take two more of my men right there. That leaves us with six teams to go out, so we're gonna have to restrict our search parties to the city for now."

Sergeant Black outlined how he wanted the teams to go through Avalon, assigning sections to the various officers, whom he introduced to the audience. Then he read from the list that Ray Buckler had prepared the night before, assigning volunteers to the various search parties.

Trevor Baldwin was sitting in an aisle seat beside Brad Cusimano, eight rows from the front. Directly in front of them sat Alex Doyle and Grace Mitchum, whom Alex had introduced to Brad and Trevor as they were coming into the meeting.

Trevor was only half listening to Herb Black. He was thinking about the vision.

Neither Trevor nor Alex had said a word to each other—or to anyone else—about what had happened to them outside, what they had seen in their minds. But on their way into the theater Alex had caught Trevor's attention briefly. In the librarian's eyes Trevor had noted a strangely troubled, yet knowing expression, and Trevor was suddenly aware that he and Alex Doyle shared a dark secret.

And it made both of them afraid.

Brad Cusimano nudged Trevor with an elbow. "That's us, Trev," he said.

Trevor looked at Brad, uncomprehending.

"They just called our names," Brad said. "We're on that guy's team." He pointed to a policeman who was standing up a few rows ahead of them and to the right, the same policeman who had driven Trevor and Markie from the boat dock to the hospital on Friday afternoon.

"Your chauffeur," Brad said. "We're supposed to get together with him as soon as they adjourn . . ." Brad paused, noticing the vacant expression in Trevor's eyes. "Trev?" he asked.

Alex Doyle twisted around in his seat and fixed Trevor with a hard look. "We have to talk," he said, his voice low but determined. "Now."

Trevor looked at Alex for a moment, then nodded. The two of them rose and started up the aisle together, heading for the lobby.

The big man lumbered alongside Trevor as they moved from the dimly lit auditorium into the comparative brightness of the deserted first-floor lobby. Alex spoke in a low voice, making sure that only Trevor could hear him even if someone else were around. They had to keep the search parties from going outside. He and Trevor were the only ones who really knew what it was that they were fighting.

Trevor followed the librarian down a curving corridor that led them to a pair of oak doors on which was lettered in gold leaf: "Catalina Museum." Alex pushed the doors open, and the two men walked inside.

The room was large, with tall windows that allowed the gray, early morning light to filter through. On the walls of the room hung historic photographs of Santa Catalina Island and Avalon, many of which were faded and discolored with age. Glass display cases around the room were filled with specimens of flora and fauna indigenous to the island, semiprecious stones, topographical and geological maps, and various antiques.

Alex paused beside one of the display cases. Inside lay Indian relics—bits of bone and pottery, soapstone sculptures, a whistle that had been carved from the femur of a dog, several tools, and a long ceremonial smoking pipe.

Alex leaned on the case. It seemed to Trevor that he was almost caressing the glass. "It'll kill them," Alex said. "They don't have any idea what it is they're up against."

"Do we?" Trevor asked.

Alex looked at Trevor as if trying to make up his mind whether or not the question was serious. He decided that it was.

"I think so," Alex answered. He spoke almost as if he were trying to convince himself as much as he was trying to convince Trevor. "You can't think about finding a logical explanation anymore, because there isn't one," he said.

Alex paused and rubbed his forehead, pressing away a pain behind his eyes. Then he looked at Trevor again. "Whatever you want to call it—a ghost, a spirit, a demon . . . hell, I don't know what it is any more than you do. But it's there. It's real.

"We both saw it," he said with finality. "Those cops saw it, too, but they're too fucking stupid to know what it is. But we know. And we're the ones—the *only* ones—who can do anything about it."

Trevor remembered the words that his son had spoken in the van yesterday.

You have to save us, Dad. You have to save all of us.

It was as if Alex Doyle were reading his mind. "It's got Markie," Alex said. "This Brujo thing, whatever it is. If we find it, we'll find your son."

Alex reached into a pocket of his trousers for a handkerchief, which he wrapped around his right fist. He raised his arm to smash the glass in the display case when a voice suddenly called from behind him, "What in hell is wrong with you two?"

Alex and Trevor turned around. Brad Cusimano and Grace Mitchum were coming into the museum. Brad had called to them. Both he and Grace were looking more than a bit confused and angry as they joined Trevor and Alex by the display case.

Alex said to Brad sharply, "We don't need you. You've done enough already—"

"What's the matter with you?" Grace snapped, cutting him off. She eyed her friend coldly. "You know, you've been acting awfully strange, ever since . . ."

Grace's voice trailed off and her anger dissipated as she noticed the pain and fear in Alex Doyle's eyes.

Then she asked him in a quiet voice, "Alex, what happened to you out there?"

William Relling Jr.

Alex turned from Grace Mitchum to Trevor. "I'm no hero," he said. "But I think I know where it is. I know the place." Alex took a deep breath. "You were right before, Mr. Baldwin. I know how to fix it."

Trevor nodded. "Both of us have to go."

Brad cut in, bewildered. "Go where?"

Trevor ignored him. "You're sure about Markie?" he said to Alex Doyle. "He's there?"

Alex nodded. "I think so."

"Go *where*?" Brad demanded.

Alex and Trevor looked at Brad with surprised expressions, as if they were first noticing him standing there.

"Goddammit, Trevor," Brad Cusimano said angrily. "Wherever you're going, I'm going, too."

Alex Doyle shot back, "You can't—"

Trevor's hand on his arm stopped the librarian from saying any more. Trevor had seen something in Brad's eyes, behind his fury. It was a look that said, I'm the one who brought you into this. You've got to let me help you get out.

Trevor nodded once to Alex Doyle, then turned back to Brad. "All right," he said softly.

In his wrath the Brujo had lashed out at The-One-Who-Would-Serve, sending the raven to destroy him.

BRUJO

He was furious because The-One had tapped into the Brujo's own power while he had been distracted, reading the thoughts of The-Other. Somehow The-One had learned to manipulate the power himself, had somehow absorbed the power from the Brujo.

The Brujo was also furious for underestimating The-One-Who-Would-Serve. He should have realized that what had brought him into contact with The-One in the beginning was his sensing the dormant ability to use the power of *Chinigchinich* that lay within The-One. Just as the Brujo had learned the strengths and weaknesses of the Evil Ones by *reaching* into the mind of The-One-Who-Would-Serve, so had The-One been able to learn of the power.

The Brujo had felt The-One-Who-Would-Serve *reach* him while he was occupied with The-Other, had felt the dream ripped from his own memory. He had felt the dream-sharing that The-One forced upon his enemies.

The-One's *reaching* wrenched the Brujo away from The-Other. The sudden, unexpected linking of his mind with the minds of Evil Ones filled the Brujo with disgust that quickly gave way to rage. The Brujo *reached* the raven. Then he watched through the bird's eyes as The-One-Who-Would-Serve was murdered by those with whom The-One had blasphemously shared the Brujo's power.

After the death of The-One-Who-Would-Serve, the Brujo withdrew from his spirit-brother and from the pack of dogs whom he had sent to devour the body of The-One. He returned to The-Other, who was waiting where the Brujo had left him, in a secret place.

The Brujo read The-Other's thoughts.

As he *reached* into the mind of The-Other, the Brujo felt gratified that this time he had chosen the proper instrument for his revenge. The-One-Who-Would-Serve had been a poor choice. Though he had served the Brujo well for a time, The-One had been from the beginning bent on his own destruction. The Brujo had warned The-One not to fight him, but The-One disobeyed.

Still, it had disturbed the Brujo that The-One-Who-Would-Serve had been able to tap into his power. If The-One had been able to learn to manipulate the power to his own ends, could not The-Other learn as well? When at last he had *reached* The-Other in the last hours before dawn, had not The-Other tried to resist him, if only for a few moments?

The Brujo *reached* into The-Other's deepest thoughts.

No. No, The-Other was not like The-One-Who-Would-Serve. The-One had been tainted by madness. The-Other was not.

The Brujo withdrew from The-Other to *reach* the beasts who were massing near the place where the Evil Ones were hidden. The beasts were waiting for his instructions, and after he finished with his brother-creatures the Brujo would return once more to The-Other. The final destruction of the Evil Ones would at last be at hand.

Twenty-six

Alex Doyle was mistaken when he guessed that Markie Baldwin had gone to the place that Alex and Trevor had seen in their vision, the place where the Brujo was buried alive nearly two hundred years before. Alex would be surprised to discover that the boy was very close by.

Markie had never left the Avalon Casino. The voice that spoke to him in his nightmares led Markie to a small dark room where the boy had since remained hidden. *The Evil Ones will not search for you here*, the voice told Markie. The room was a place for their dead, and they would be certain that the boy would be afraid of the place, as they themselves were afraid.

On the floor of the small room lay the bodies of those Evil Ones who had been killed. It was to this room that they had brought their leader, the one whom the voice had called its enemy. From the shadows behind high wooden shelves Markie had watched them lay the body of the enemy alongside the body of the other man who had died.

As Markie watched from his hiding place, he heard the voice whispering to him. The voice was pleased. It had been able to turn the boy's dislike for its enemy into hatred, then it had used that hatred to ensure the enemy's death.

The voice indicated its pleasure with Markie by rewarding him with a new name. It whispered to him, *You are The-Other*.

The voice called to Markie, urging him to come forward from his hiding place.

The boy stepped away from the shelves. He could see as clearly as if it were day in the pitch-blackness of the small room, though he gave no thought as to how he could do that—it simply *was*.

The voice led him to the body of its enemy. It commanded Markie to look.

The boy bent down and unwrapped the blanket that covered the dead man. Markie pulled the blanket away. Then he stood erect, staring down at the still, waxen, expressionless face of Ray Buckler.

The boy stood there, staring, for some time. He listened to the voice.

The voice inside his mind abruptly and unexpectedly rose in pitch from a whisper to a skull-splitting screech of rage. The pain caused by the sound was so sudden and so severe that Markie was unable to cry out. He crumpled, falling to his knees.

Before Markie Baldwin's eyes passed the *vision*.

Markie saw what was unreeling in the minds of the five men who were outside of the Casino with Casey Harrison. And all the while the vision played before him, the boy could hear the voice screaming in fury.

Then it was gone.

Markie lifted himself from the floor slowly. He turned his head slightly, as if to listen for some faraway sound.

He listened for a long time, but there was nothing there. The voice had gone.

In the dark Markie gradually became aware that he was kneeling beside the still body of Ray Buckler. He felt puzzled, but unafraid. Where am I? he wondered. Where's my dad?

He looked down at the dead man's face, and he remembered.

Markie scrambled to his feet and backed away from Ray Buckler's body, unable to take his eyes from the dead man's face.

What did I do? What did I do?

He wanted badly to scream . . .

But Markie caught himself. He remembered that it was the voice that brought him here. It was the voice that had told him of the man who lay at his feet. The voice had whispered, *He is your enemy.*

"His name is Ray," Markie croaked aloud.

But he's *not* that Ray, Markie told himself. Not the one you don't like, the one who keeps talking about wanting to be your new dad, the one your mom won't tell that you already *have* a dad. This man isn't the same as the other Ray—just his name . . .

That's no reason for him to die.

Markie could feel himself grow cold with anger. All of a sudden, everything had become very clear to him.

The voice had *lied.*

The dead man who lay at Markie's feet was not an enemy. He was a good man, and Markie hadn't been fair to him, and now it was his fault that the man was dead . . .

Markie told himself harshly: No.

It was the voice's fault. Everything was the voice's fault. The voice had tricked him, had forced him to go to the policeman named Ray while he was sick and scare him and watch him die.

The voice was *bad*. It had hurt the policeman, it had hurt Valerie and his father.

Markie swore to himself: No more.

After a time the voice returned. It whispered to Markie as it had done before. Markie listened to the voice, allowing it to come inside him. But at the same time, he hid part of his thoughts.

The voice spoke to him for a long time.

Just before it finished telling Markie what it wished him to do, the voice fell silent, as if it sensed that there was something wrong with the boy. Suddenly it *reached* deep inside of Markie, pulling at him, urging him painfully to answer its question.

Will you disobey me, too?

Markie prayed that the voice could not know the truth. "No," the boy lied. "I won't fight you. I'll do as you say."

The voice left him again.

Markie did as he was instructed, waiting in the dark room for the voice to return with its final instructions. While he waited, Markie made plans. He knew that the voice was very powerful, and he knew that he would have to fight it alone. But he would be ready.

Markie Baldwin sat in the dark, waiting for the voice to come back, waiting for the battle to begin.

The beasts were gathered to hear the Brujo. *There*, he said to his brother-creatures. *Your enemies are in that place.*

William Relling Jr.

In the minds of the beasts the Brujo conjured the image of the great structure where the Evil Ones lay hidden. The Brujo could feel the frenzy of the beasts. The dogs yipped excitedly. An eagle *skreeked* in triumphant anticipation.

It is time . . .

But before the Brujo could release the beasts, he was interrupted by the raven. His spirit-brother demanded the Brujo's attention.

The Brujo *reached* the raven, and the bird carried him away to show him what it had seen. The bird flew high over the hills, away from the city, toward the center of the island.

It whispered to the Brujo, *There*.

Below him the Brujo could see a machine of the Evil Ones, one of their vehicles. *They have escaped*, whispered the raven.

The Brujo was not concerned. The beasts had already destroyed many of the machines.

This one is not like the others, the bird whispered. It asked the Brujo to *reach*.

The Brujo did as his spirit-brother requested. He touched the minds of the men who were inside the machine. The Brujo recognized the men. And he learned of their purpose.

For the first time in almost two hundred years, the Brujo knew fear.

The raven whispered, *They would destroy us*.

The Brujo remonstrated his brother gently. *No*, he said. *They will be too late*. All he needed was to find creatures who could destroy these dangerous men before they could reach him.

Brujo

He commanded the raven to search, and almost immediately the bird answered him.

The beasts that the Brujo sought were so near the men in the machine that he was convinced it was the handiwork of his god *Chinigchinich*. The Brujo ordered the raven to cry its thanks to the newly risen sun.

Then the Brujo *reached* in several directions at once. He touched the beasts in the hills, near his enemies in their machine. He touched the beasts in the city, waiting outside of the hiding place of the Evil Ones. He touched The-Other . . .

And only the raven heard him scream.

Twenty-seven

Herb Black shouted, "Goddammit, Grace, I know you know what they're up to—"

Grace Mitchum snapped back angrily, cutting him off. "Herb, I'm getting pretty sick and tired of people addressing me as if my first name was 'Goddammit Grace'!"

Richard Sundermann spoke up tiredly, "This is getting us nowhere . . ."

The three of them were in the Casino's theater auditorium along with the other City Council members, Sergeant Carl Ritter, and a pair of uniformed patrolmen. Everyone else had gone upstairs to the

William Relling Jr.

ballroom to have breakfast or to coordinate with the half-dozen Avalon policemen who would be leading them on search parties into the city.

The two officers were the men whom Herb Black had assigned to drive out to the Coast Guard facility at Two Harbors. When the policemen had gotten to their Jeep, they discovered that it wouldn't start. A subsequent check of the vehicle showed them that its distributor cap was missing, as were the distributor caps of the other two Avalon Police Department Jeeps parked near it. The Jeep belonging to the chief of police was gone as well.

When they reported what they had found to Herb Black, Black's first reaction was one of dumbfounded surprise. Given their situation, whoever had stolen the Jeep must have had a very good reason . . .

Sergeant Black then remembered that toward the end of the early morning meeting, he had seen four people get up and leave the auditorium and go out into the lobby. One of them was that Baldwin guy who had been raising a stink about his missing kid. With him was Alex Doyle . . .

Herb Black thought of something else. Trevor Baldwin and Alex Doyle were outside when Black's men blew away that nutty musician. Something weird happened out there, something that shook the cops pretty badly. None of them seemed to be able to remember quite what it was, other than that it had scared the living shit out of them—even *before* those motherfucking dogs showed up.

Black ordered his men to find Alex Doyle, Grace

Mitchum, Trevor Baldwin, and Baldwin's curly-haired friend whose name he couldn't remember—the guy with the condo project that had been stirring up all sorts of shit, especially now that the actual building of the goddamn things was about to get under way. Sergeant Black had seen Grace and the condo guy walk out together right after the first two had left his meeting.

The officers returned minutes later with only Grace Mitchum in tow. By then Carl Ritter and the three City Council men had joined Herb Black in front of the auditorium stage, and he had told them as much as he knew about the business of the Jeeps. All five of them were anxious for Grace Mitchum to provide some answers.

She told them only what Herb Black had already surmised—that Alex Doyle, Trevor Baldwin, and Brad Cusimano had taken Ray Buckler's Jeep after making sure that nobody could use another vehicle to follow them. Alex had told her quite vehemently that absolutely no one was to leave the Casino, that it was too dangerous for anybody to be outside, even the police. That meant no search-and-rescue missions.

Herb Black then asked Grace the obvious question: Why? But they had gotten from her all the information they were going to get.

That was when the acting chief of police finally lost his temper.

Herb Black and Grace Mitchum glared at each other as Richard Sundermann moved between them. "There's no reason why we can't keep this discussion rational," the councilman said.

"Sure there is," Herb Black grunted. "Grace."

"I've told you everything I know, Herb," said Grace. "Alex didn't say where they were going, and I don't think those other two knew at all. Maybe Trevor did, I don't know. But Alex thinks he's figured out what's wrong, and he thinks he knows what to do to take care of it."

Carl Ritter asked, "Why didn't they come to us?"

"I don't know," Grace said, exasperated. "Maybe they were worried . . . maybe they were afraid that the more people who were out there, the more likely that what Alex wanted to do wouldn't work. And the more likely too many people would get hurt." She looked pointedly at Herb Black. "I really don't know what they're doing."

Black snorted his displeasure and disbelief.

"C'mon, Herb," Richard Sundermann said, trying to be conciliatory. Then he turned to Grace. "That's all Alex told you? Just that everybody is supposed to stay inside?"

Grace nodded. "That's what he said."

"Till when?" Carl Ritter asked.

Grace shrugged. "I guess till they come back."

Herb Black grumbled, "*If* they come back."

Grace frowned at him, then said, "Alex thinks the Casino is safe. That's why he wants everybody to stay put."

One of the other councilmen spoke up. "And you believe him?"

BRUJO

Grace looked into each of the faces of the men who were surrounding her. "I trust him," she said simply. Then she walked away.

Grace was fuming as she climbed the ramp that led upstairs to the ballroom. Why do men always have to be so damn stubborn? she asked herself. And they wonder why I give them a hard time.

Even Alex. She couldn't understand why Herb Black didn't believe her when she told him—honestly—that Alex hadn't told her where he and Trevor and Brad were going.

Better if you don't know, Alex had told her.

She had seen the utter seriousness on Alex's face—an emotion he rarely expressed—and had not pressed him further. When she told Herb Black and the other men in the auditorium that she trusted Alex, she was speaking the simple truth.

Still, she worried about him. A lot.

On her way upstairs, Grace passed a dozen men who were heading down the ramp. Several of them were armed with guns.

The search parties, Grace thought unhappily.

One of two policemen with the group of men knew Grace and he gave her a thin, tight smile in greeting. She didn't smile back. Grace knew that Herb Black would be sending out the search parties anyway, in spite of what she had told him. As the last man passed her, Grace muttered angrily, under her breath, "Bloody fools."

Grace walked into the second-floor ballroom where some thirteen hundred people were camped or milling about or eating breakfast—all very quietly. To Grace, the scene seemed oddly analogous to when she had last registered for college classes. At that time the university enrolled students en masse by setting up booths and tables in its field house—an attempt at registering twelve thousand students in as orderly and expeditious a fashion as possible. Except that it hadn't worked out as intended, and at any given time during registration you could find a thousand or more confused, angry, tired, or simply lost students wandering about the massive room, trying to find someone who could answer a simple question: What am I supposed to do now?

The only difference was that there was considerably less activity in the Casino ballroom, and an oppressive, unnatural quiet pervaded the space. A thousand people should make some noise, Grace thought.

She skirted the main floor of the ballroom, heading for the tables where several volunteers were serving breakfast. Grace wasn't hungry, but she wanted a cup of tea. The tea proved to have been steeping for some time and was only lukewarm, but bitterly strong. Grace sipped it and made a face. She was about to say something snappish when she looked up at the teenage boy who had proffered the tea to her. He was smiling at her wearily, and she could almost hear Alex Doyle's voice in her mind, chiding her: "C'mon, Grace, lighten up. Be nice for a change."

She returned the boy's smile, then said to him,

"Listen, if you're tired, I can cover for you for a while."

The boy shook his head. "I just came on an hour ago," he said. "I look a lot worse than I feel. But thanks for offering."

Grace smiled again, then turned away from the table. She walked over to the tall windows that encircled the ballroom. Looking to the northwest, away from the hills that surrounded Avalon, she could see only a sliver of gray-green ocean to the right of the land. The first few sprinkles of rain dotted the glass, and Grace could tell that the morning light illuminating the ballroom was growing darker.

She sipped at her bitter tea and thought about Alex Doyle and the two men who had gone out *there* with him. Grace knew that it was ridiculous for her to try to guess what they were doing.

But they weren't the only ones Grace was concerned about. Trevor Baldwin's little boy—whose name, she remembered, was Markie—had disappeared during the night. Somehow, what the men were doing out there involved looking for the boy. Alex seemed certain that Markie was wherever they were going, though Grace hadn't a clue how he could know something like that. Grace had sensed that finding his son wasn't Trevor Baldwin's sole motive for accompanying Alex. There was more to it than that.

And what if Alex was wrong?

The thought stayed with her. Grace began to wonder how Markie Baldwin could have gotten out of the Casino on his own. He certainly couldn't have moved the metal barricades from the lobby doors all by himself, and it was more than likely that he would have been seen by someone—one of the policemen who was on guard during the night—if he tried to use one of the other exits. The more Grace turned it over in her mind, the more she became convinced that the boy wasn't outside at all. Markie was here, someplace. Alex was wrong.

But where was he?

Trevor Baldwin said that he had searched the entire building for his son but hadn't found him. Of course, Grace thought, Trevor would have assumed that Markie wanted to be found . . .

She turned away from the window and looked around the massive ballroom. If I wanted to hide from all these people, she thought, where would I go? Where is a place where nobody would look for me?

The answer came to her.

Grace's first impulse was to disregard it completely. Of course no one would look for Markie there, she told herself. He would never go in there . . .

A place where nobody would look.

Grace drained the last of her tea and crumpled the Styrofoam cup. She stepped away from the window and moved back toward the breakfast tables, where she tossed her cup into a trashcan. She was still considering what she should do when she saw resting on the table, near an empty coffee urn, a five-cell flashlight that one of the policemen had left for the food service volunteers to use. Grace looked around to see if anyone was watching her, then picked up the flashlight and walked back in the direction of the stage.

Grace crossed the ballroom floor to the stage as surreptitiously as she could, hoping that she appeared nonchalant. She climbed onto the stage and stepped out of sight of the ballroom, through a door in the wings. It was very dark backstage, and Grace flipped on the flashlight.

She and Alex had watched Ray Buckler and his men carry the body of Catalina airport's air traffic controller back here. Grace had to stop walking when she realized that had happened only eight hours earlier. It seemed like ages ago.

Grace paused outside the door of the storage room that was serving as the morgue. She could feel the hairs tickling on the back of her neck, as they had done two mornings before when she had found her dog's mutilated body in the backyard. Grace shook herself, trying to thrust aside the memory and drive away the unpleasant feeling.

Hesitantly she reached for the handle of the door.

Grace stopped. She could hear from someplace not far away the *pok-pok-pok* of gunfire. It took her a moment to recognize what the sound was, and then Grace thought to herself, Who could be shooting?

Then she pushed open the door.

Grace shined the light ahead of her, examining

the cramped, dark room. Its walls were lined with wooden shelves that were filled mostly with cartons and housekeeping supplies, much of which looked as if it hadn't been disturbed in some time.

Grace stepped all the way into the room and brought the light to play on the figures that lay, wrapped in blankets, at her feet. She shined the light on the body that was nearer to her and was filled with relief that it was completely covered and she didn't have to look at it. Then Grace shined the flashlight on the second figure, and she had to choke back an urge to cry out in fright.

Ray Buckler's head and upper body lay unwrapped and exposed, the light falling on his still, dead face.

From somewhere in the tiny room, Grace heard a whimper.

Her free hand jerked upward involuntarily to cover her mouth. Grace listened very hard. Then, slowly, she pulled her hand away and whispered, "M-Markie?"

Just then the door to the storage room flew shut behind Grace, and small fingers shot out from the darkness to clutch the wrist of her hand that held the flashlight. Grace cried out, startled. She dropped the light, and it fell onto the chest of the corpse at her feet with a soft thud, then rolled off the body and clunked to the floor. A small hand gripped Grace's wrist tightly, and suddenly she could hear a child's voice that seemed to come from everywhere and nowhere. It spoke directly to Grace's mind.

The voice was in pain.

I have him, the voice whispered to Grace. *I have him . . . with me . . .*

Grace tried to will herself to pull away from the hand that clutched her wrist, but her muscles were frozen with terror. She could see the flashlight on the floor; the light was shining on a pair of small feet in tennis shoes. The feet stood right beside hers.

Help me, the voice pleaded. *I've got him trapped . . . but he's too strong . . . he'll get away . . .*

Startlingly the voice came to life. It said aloud, agonized, "Dad . . . I'm trying . . . Dad . . ."

The boy's hand gripped Grace's wrist more tightly.

Her mind seemed to explode with brightness, and Grace was no longer in the dark room. She was in another place, a battleground. Two figures were locked in a struggle before her. The smaller of the figures was pleading with her: *Help me*.

The realization of what was happening came to Grace Mitchum in a flash of *satori*, of enlightenment. There was no question in her mind.

She was witnessing the fight for the soul of Markie Baldwin.

The raven asked, *My brother, what is wrong?*

The Brujo could not hear the bird. He was engaged in battle with the spirit of The-Other. The Brujo's awareness of everything else had been driven away.

It had happened at the moment that he *reached* The-Other, after he had released his brother-creatures on their final assault upon the Evil Ones. The Brujo had touched the mind of The-Other to order him to open the way for the beasts . . .

And The-Other had seized him.

You *are the evil one*, The-Other cried to the Brujo. *I will destroy you.*

The Brujo tried to strike him, but The-Other was able to repel the blow. The strength of The-Other's spirit was great.

The Brujo struck again, much harder.

He felt The-Other's pain.

The Brujo heard him call out for help—and almost immediately the Brujo sensed the presence of another, someone who had heard The-Other's cry.

Brujo

Another shape, a female shape, came out of the darkness. The shape reached for The-Other, trying to pull him away from the Brujo, who lashed out at her in fury. The Brujo knocked her away viciously.

The Brujo could hear The-Other calling, *Dad . . . I'm trying, Dad . . .*

By distracting the Brujo, the woman had given The-Other a brief respite, allowing him to recover his strength. He struck the Brujo again with an unexpected blow. The fierce attack knocked the Brujo away for an instant, but he recovered quickly. The blow enraged him.

The Brujo struck back at The-Other with all of his power.

At the moment that the raven called urgently to the Brujo, *Brother, you must see. They come. They come . . .*

Twenty-eight

It hadn't taken Alex Doyle very long to convince Trevor Baldwin and Brad Cusimano to take the Jeep belonging to Avalon's chief of police, and it turned out that Brad and Trevor knew a simple way to render the other police vehicles inoperable. Alex's reasons for wanting the other Jeeps disabled were fairly obvious: First of all, if none of the other Jeeps could run, then the three men would not have to worry about being pursued; and second, if the search-and-rescue teams lacked transportation, then the teams would be forced to remain inside the Casino, where it was safe. Or so Alex hoped.

All three of them had been surprised at how smoothly their escape had gone. Alex had led the others to a barricaded rear exit door not far from the Casino's museum. They tore away the obstruction, which was replaced by Grace Mitchum after she sealed the exit behind them. Then they crept around to the front of the building to where the four police Jeeps were parked.

Two of the vehicles were unlocked: Ray Buckler's CJ and one other patrol Jeep. In the latter vehicle Brad Cusimano found a 30.06 shotgun bolted to the underside of the dashboard and a box of shells in the glove compartment. He also removed a handful of signal flares from a metal case underneath the driver's seat. By the time Brad finished popping off the Jeep's distributor cap, Trevor Baldwin had done the same to the other two Jeeps that they were leaving behind.

Brad found Trevor and Alex waiting for him in the chief's idling CJ. Trevor was behind the wheel, Alex in the back, cradling the relics that he had brought with him from the museum. As Brad settled himself into the passenger seat and Trevor eased the Jeep forward as quietly as possible, it was Alex Doyle who remarked on what they had all been thinking. Never once, Alex said, had they encountered the least interference from anybody. Trevor wondered if that was a good omen or a bad one.

Alex directed Trevor to drive into Avalon. The Jeep moved slowly, south along Crescent Avenue.

The three men kept an eye out for marauding beasts, but the city seemed deserted.

At the point where Crescent Avenue curved to the left toward the cruise-boat docks, Alex ordered Trevor to turn right, up a narrow residential street lined with wood-frame cottages. Alex Doyle's house—a small, sky-blue, two-story structure that was virtually indistinguishable from its neighbors—was at the top of the street.

Brad Cusimano accompanied Alex into the house, carrying the shotgun with him for protection. Trevor waited in the Jeep and kept its engine running, ready to blast its horn at the first sign of danger.

When Alex and Brad came out of the house, minutes later, each was loaded down with a shovel, a gasoline can, a large canvas laundry bag, and a length of rope. They tossed the stuff into the back of the Jeep. Trevor noticed that the librarian was also carrying a manila file folder stuffed with papers. Alex had wrapped the folder in plastic.

The librarian then led them on a circuitous route out of town, one that got them onto the main road, heading northeast, toward the island's interior, without bringing them within sight of the Casino. Fifteen minutes later they were moving up the spine of the island, past East Summit, fifteen hundred feet above sea level. Droplets of rain speckled the Jeep's windshield.

Except for when Alex gave directions, none of them said a word. Trevor drove steadily, lost in his own thoughts. Alex sat cross-legged in the back, looking like an uncomfortable Buddha, examining the pages from the file folder in his lap. Brad Cusimano looked from one man to the other, unhappily puzzled.

Alex glanced up from the folder to peer through the front windshield. "Check the odometer," he said to Trevor. "We've got about two miles to the cutoff. When you see the radio station tower on the left, you've got about a third of a mile to go."

Brad grumbled, "You ever gonna tell us *where* we're going, Doyle?"

Before Alex could reply, Brad continued. "I think I've been awfully goddamn patient with you two and your secrets. How the hell am I supposed to help if I don't know what it is I'm helping with?"

Alex said, "That wasn't part of the deal—"

"Who the fuck said anything about a deal, fat man!" Brad exploded. "I just want to know what you know!"

Trevor said quietly to Alex, over his shoulder, "Why don't you tell him?"

Alex's eyes narrowed slightly as he looked from Trevor to Brad, as if considering what to say. He shook his head. "You're not going to believe it," he said to Brad.

Brad snorted derisively. "Pal, I just spent the night with a thousand people who were hiding out in a goddamn ballroom to keep from being clawed to death or pecked to death or trampled to death. And now I'm out here with you two. I already don't believe it. I just want to know where we're going and what we're gonna find there."

Alex closed the file folder. "It's funny," he said.

Brad frowned. "What's funny?"

Alex seemed to smile slightly. "You going with us. You know, Cusimano, you're a lot more responsible for what's going on than you know."

Brad's face darkened.

"To answer your first question," Alex said, "we're going to a campground called Ben Weston Beach on the west side of the island. I recognized the spot in . . ."

Alex caught himself before he could let out the words: *the vision.*

Brad was looking at him impatiently. Alex continued. "It's just a beach," he said. "Some picnic tables and campsites, stuff like that."

"What else?"

Alex Doyle's face twisted into a small frown. He didn't know how he could convince somebody else of something that was so incredible that it took everything he had to convince himself.

"What else?" Brad repeated.

"Tell him about it," Trevor said to Alex. "Tell him the name. Brujo."

Brad asked, "What's 'brew-hoe'?"

"Not what," Alex said. "Who. It's a person, an Indian shaman. A medicine man. 'Brujo' is the Spanish word for 'sorcerer.'"

Brad looked at the librarian in disbelief. "We're going after a *sorcerer*?"

Alex nodded. "I think so."

Brad shook his head. "This is a hundred times nuttier than I thought," he said under his breath.

Then he looked up at Trevor. "You believe it, Trev?" he asked.

"I know it's something," Trevor said. "It's got Markie."

"Trevor and I both saw it," said Alex. "We had . . . a kind of dream. Outside, when we saw the cops shoot that guy, that musician. Trevor and I, the cops, that guy Casey Harrison—we all shared some kind of . . ." Alex had to force the word out. "We had a vision. How it happened, I can't explain. I don't know. But the vision . . . it was a vision of the Brujo."

Trevor made a left turn onto another road, past a sign that read: "Middle Ranch—5 Miles." Beneath it was a second sign: "Ben Weston Beach—9 Miles."

"A vision," Brad grunted.

"I don't know what else to call it," Alex said. "But I saw it—"

"*We* saw it," Trevor cut in.

Brad looked to Trevor and could see that he wasn't joking. "The Brujo's what made all the animals go crazy," Trevor said. "He wants revenge."

"Revenge for what?"

"That's where you come in, Mr. Cusimano," Alex Doyle said. "*You* brought the Brujo back."

Brad frowned at Alex. "What are you talking about?"

Alex took a deep breath, not sure how to tell the story that he knew was true.

"First off," Alex said to Brad, "you know about the Indian tribe that was living on Catalina at the time that the Spanish discovered the island in the sixteenth century. The Indians had a pretty weird religion—they were a drug cult and animal worshipers and nature worshipers, that kind of thing. They believed that they got power from their gods, the power to communicate with animals and manipulate their environment. The tribe's medicine man was the go-between for the people and their gods, like a priest.

"Anyway, the Indians had been on the island for hundreds of years before any white men came, and they stayed pretty healthy and happy for a couple hundred years afterward, mostly because the Spanish left them more or less alone."

Alex paused, as something else came to mind. "Something else that's funny," he said. "I never thought of it before. For almost the last two hundred years, Catalina's had a history of violence. It all started in the early 1800s, when the Indians were wiped out."

"What do you mean?" Brad asked.

"Well, that was when the pirates and the fur trappers started coming to Catalina to hunt or to hide out," Alex said. "A whole shipload of cutthroats and pirates who were supposed to be hunting otters landed in 1806. But they got tired of animals after about a month and decided to start hunting the Indians instead."

Alex's tone turned bitter. "At the beginning of 1806, there were still a couple thousand Indians on Catalina. But by the end of the year, when the fucking hunters were through with them, there were maybe three hundred left. The ones that survived were rescued by Spanish priests and got taken back to the mainland, where they all starved or got smallpox or some damn thing. Anyhow, within twenty years there weren't any more Catalina Indians. The whole tribe is extinct, and has been since about 1830."

Alex fell silent.

None of them spoke for a few moments, until Brad asked, "So what does that have to do with *this*?"

Alex drew another deep breath. "The part I just told you is history," he said. "You could look it up if you wanted to. But this other part . . ."

Alex paused and seemed to be trying to convince himself of the veracity of what he wanted to relate. "I'm speculating," he said to Brad. "What I saw . . . what *we* saw . . ." The librarian paused again, thinking for a moment, then added, "It isn't just what we saw, but what we *felt*. That's how I know."

Brad shook his head, confused. "I still don't know what you're talking about, Doyle," he said.

"We saw the Brujo," Trevor told him. "In the vision we saw the hunters who murdered the Indians, and we saw the Brujo try to fight them."

"The Brujo was the last medicine man of the tribe of Catalina Indians," Alex said. "He had this . . . power. But he wasn't strong enough then to fight the invaders—the Evil Ones, he called them—and they caught him and tortured him. Then they

BRUJO

dragged him to the beach and buried him alive. And now . . . he's come back."

For a while there was no sound save that of the slap of the Jeep's windshield wipers. Brad turned away from Alex Doyle to look out at the rain that washed the blacktop road lying before them. He looked at Trevor as if to try and read something in his friend's face, then swung around to speak to Alex again. "You know where he's buried?" Brad asked.

Alex nodded. "I think so."

Brad pointed to the shovel that rested beside the librarian. "We're gonna dig him up?"

Alex nodded again.

"This is insane," Brad muttered, shaking his head. Then he looked at Alex Doyle and said, "What did you mean, I brought the Brujo back?"

Alex regarded Brad seriously, then tapped the folder in his lap. "There's an Indian ceremony called *keruk*," he said. "It's a ceremony to honor the dead. The Indians had a place on the island that was sacred to them—a kind of outdoor temple where they performed a lot of their important religious ceremonies, including *keruk*. If I'd remembered it before, when we were trying to stop your fucking condos, it would've been one more piece of evidence I could've used against 'em."

"Get to the point," Brad said, his anger rising.

"The site was a small natural amphitheater near Two Harbors. For the Indians it was a place for them to worship their main god, *Chinigchinich*. For some reason that land was never touched in the two hundred years since the Indians were wiped out. Nobody ever used it or grazed on it or built on it." Alex eyed Brad Cusimano, then added, "Until three days ago.

"We're gonna take what's left of the Brujo to your property, and I'm going to perform the *keruk* ceremony to consecrate his spirit, so it no longer remains earthbound. And angry." Alex Doyle's mouth was set grimly. "God knows this particular spirit's got enough to be angry about."

"This is nuts!" Brad exclaimed. He turned to Trevor and said harshly, "Is that what you think, Trev? You think that some fucking ghost has got Markie and it's all my fault?"

Before Trevor could answer, Alex cut in vehemently: "Goddammit, Cusimano, it makes sense! Casey Harrison's being possessed by the spirit makes sense, because he was probably some kind of druggie and maybe borderline psychotic, so he was receptive! And a kid like Markie . . . with his imagination . . . the Indians indoctrinated kids into the religion when they were just his age! It sounds crazy, but it makes sense!"

"I believe what he says," Trevor said quietly to Brad, trying to keep the pain and frustration out of his voice. "I—"

Trevor abruptly stopped speaking. He had felt something touch his mind, a fleeting *presence*. Mere tendrils of smoke had danced through his brain, then vanished as quickly as they had appeared.

But he knew what it was.

It had touched the other two men as well. Trevor heard Brad Cusimano say in a hushed voice, "What in God's name was *that*?"

Alex Doyle answered Brad in a voice that was just as frightened and far away: "The Brujo . . ."

Then they saw the beasts.

A hundred and fifty yards ahead of them, the road was blocked by at least a dozen shaggy shapes. Long, curving horns extended in a flattened "Y" from their heads. They stood still, facing the oncoming vehicle.

Alex leaned forward, between the two front seats. "Goats," he said quietly.

The Jeep had reached a point where the road ran along a narrow hilltop. The shoulder of the road tumbled away steeply, and the only guardrails were thin wire fences that ran alongside the edges of the road. The men knew that should the animals choose to charge, the goats would have little difficulty pushing the Jeep over either side.

Brad cradled the shotgun nervously. Trevor had been driving carefully along the slick, rain-swept road, but now he slowed the Jeep to a crawl, shifting into neutral.

The vehicle eased forward from its own momentum, until the goats were touched by its headlights. Trevor braked to a stop. He stared at the beasts' black eyes—eyes that seemed to have an unnatural glitter.

Trevor reached for the gearshift, just as the goat nearest to the Jeep shook its shaggy head vigorously, sending a fine spray of water into the air. The spray formed a halo around the animal's head.

Alex Doyle rested a thick hand on Trevor's shoulder and said, "Wait."

Until that moment the animals had been silent. But now many of the goats began snorting and bleating, and as the three men watched, the herd began to disperse, to open a way for the Jeep.

"Now," Alex said.

Trevor shifted the Jeep into gear and it jumped forward. The goats moved aside, seemingly to allow the vehicle to pass through.

Then a sudden, violent thump shook the Jeep. The blow had come from the driver's side, and Trevor jerked away reflexively.

He glanced out and saw that a half dozen of the animals were butting against the side of the Jeep, shoving it off the road. Trevor stomped on the brakes, but he could feel the wheels sliding sideways on the slick blacktop.

Alex Doyle yelled, "Go!"

"I can't!" Trevor shouted back. The goats ahead of them had closed together, hedging them in. With a crunching sound, the Jeep's tires slid off the road and onto the shoulder. Trevor looked over, and he saw Brad Cusimano working frantically at the handle of his door. As Brad popped the door open, the Jeep went tumbling over the edge.

Trevor saw Brad disappear through the passenger door, just before the world outside the Jeep's windows began to whirl about crazily. Trevor and

BRUJO

Alex were tossed around the vehicle's interior like a pair of human Ping-Pong balls, and Trevor cracked the crown of his head on the steering wheel. The excruciating pain made him cry out, and tiny lights danced behind his eyes.

Trevor pressed his eyes closed and begged silently: Please God, not again!

Then all was still.

The Brujo had to turn away from his struggle with The-Other to see what it was that so agitated the raven. Through the bird's eyes he saw the men coming. The Brujo's rage exploded at the men, and he called for the beasts.

At that instant The-Other struck him again. But the Brujo's fury had fueled his own strength, and he was able to seize The-Other.

The Brujo commanded him: *Look there*.

The-Other looked through the raven's eyes and saw the beasts who were attacking the men below them. He cried out in fear, *Dad* . . .

The Brujo sensed that The-Other was losing his power. The-Other was in pain. The Brujo struck him again, and The-Other spun away, dropping to his knees.

The-Other tried vainly to ward off the Brujo's blows.

Suddenly the raven was calling to the Brujo again, more urgently than before: *Brother, you must come.*

But the Brujo's full attention was on his fight with The-Other. He did not hear the bird.

The raven shrieked, *Brother!*

The Brujo still did not hear the bird. He was watching The-Other, who had fallen at last. The Brujo's pleasure increased.

As he raised himself above The-Other to strike one final, mortal blow . . .

Twenty-nine

Trevor Baldwin was fighting to retain consciousness when he heard the not-too-distant roar of a shotgun blast. The noise helped him to hold on. He opened his eyes. The Jeep was resting, miraculously right side up, at the bottom of a gully, thirty feet below the road.

Neither Trevor nor Alex was seriously hurt. Trevor had gotten wedged between the two front seats, and he was able to jerk himself free with a little effort. Alex had been tossed ass-over-teakettle and lay scrunched against the Jeep's rear hatch door. The librarian had managed to hold on to his papers, and none of them had fallen out of their folder as the Jeep had gone spinning down the hillside. Trevor extended a hand to pull Alex forward. They heard Brad Cusimano cry for help, and scrambled from the Jeep as quickly as they could. Trevor shouted at the top of his voice, "Brad!"

A cry floated back to them: "I'm here!"

Alex and Trevor jogged toward Brad, moving carefully over the rugged, slippery ground. They found him several hundred yards away from the Jeep. Brad was lying on his back, partway up the hill.

The still-smoking shotgun lay nearby. Brad was soaked, his skin and clothing slopped with mud. Though he seemed to be having difficulty moving, at first glance Brad didn't appear to be badly injured. But soon Trevor and Alex were close enough to make out the seeping stain that covered the upper part of Brad's left thigh.

Brad was pressing on the wound with both hands. Trevor knelt behind him to prop him up, and Brad let out a grunt of pain. Alex Doyle gingerly pulled at the bloody, shredded cloth of Brad's trousers to examine his leg.

Brad gritted his teeth and said, "Pretty goddamn stupid to fall down and shoot yourself." He looked over his shoulder at Trevor. "Course, another six inches to the right and it could've been a real *mortal* wound." Brad grimaced.

Alex looked up at Brad and Trevor. "I don't

think it's too bad, considering," he said. "It looks mostly superficial. Bleeding like hell, though."

Brad made a face. "Hurts like hell, too—"

Brad was cut off by a "Baaaaahhhh!" from somewhere above them. The sound startled all three of them. Almost immediately, more bleats came in answer to the first. Though it seemed as if the cries of the goats were growing fainter, the sound caused icy fingers to tickle Trevor's spine.

He positioned himself to hoist Brad by his shoulders. "Help me," Trevor commanded Alex.

Instead of moving to help, Alex held up a hand to motion for quiet and snapped, "Wait a minute."

The three of them waited quietly for several moments.

Then Brad said at last, "I don't hear anything."

Alex nodded, agreeing. "Don't you feel it?"

"Feel what?" Trevor asked.

"The Brujo," Alex said. "Something's happened to the Brujo."

Then Brad and Trevor could sense what Alex had felt, that the heavy malevolence that had hung in the air seemed to have faded. Alex reached for the shotgun, broke it open, and pulled out the shells in the chamber—only one of which had been fired. He snapped it shut and handed the unloaded weapon to Brad. Then Alex and Trevor cross-gripped their forearms and lifted Brad Cusimano in a two-man rescue carry and made their way back to the Jeep.

They placed Brad in the back of the vehicle, wrapping him in a blanket that Alex had found underneath the front seat. While the librarian treated Brad's gunshot wound as best he could with the Jeep's first-aid kit, Trevor examined the vehicle. To his surprise, he found that the engine had merely stalled out in the crash. The Jeep would still run.

Within minutes they were moving again. Trevor followed Alex's advice to stay off the main road, since they were less than two miles from the beach and the distance was shorter over the open terrain. Trevor engaged the Jeep's four-wheel drive, and off they went, bouncing through the muck.

They traveled in silence, though occasionally Brad Cusimano would let out a grunt—the only indication he gave that he was suffering. Brad was doing his best to hold it in, and Trevor drove as carefully as he could, to avoid jostling his injured friend. After a time, Brad fell silent, and Trevor glanced into the rearview mirror and saw that he had passed out from the pain.

While he was looking at Brad, Trevor heard Alex Doyle say, "He's better off."

Alex's voice seemed to break the gloomy spell of silence that enveloped them. The librarian was looking at Trevor with a peculiarly strained expression, as if what he was thinking caused him anguish. "What's the matter?" Trevor asked, keeping his voice low.

"I should tell you something," Alex said.

Trevor already had an idea of what the librarian wanted to say. He waited for Alex to go on.

"It's about your boy," Alex said. "When that

whatever-it-was touched us before, I got the feeling that . . ."

Alex paused as Trevor downshifted to roll over a log. The Jeep bounced hard, and Trevor shot a look back at Brad, who was still unconscious. Then he turned his attention back to Alex.

"We've got a little time to take care of this," Alex said. "How much, I don't know."

Trevor nodded.

Alex seemed to have to draw up his courage to tell Trevor: "Listen, Markie's not out here. He couldn't have got this far. The Brujo's got him, I'm sure of that, but I was wrong when I said that he was out here. I felt him, though, when that spirit touched us. Wherever Markie is, he's alive."

"I felt it, too," Trevor said.

Alex added, "I still think that when we find the Brujo, we'll find out where Markie is."

Trevor nodded again, though he wasn't really certain whether or not he believed what Alex had told him. He frowned.

"What's the matter?" Alex asked.

"There's still something else I don't understand," Trevor said. "I still don't know why Markie."

"What do you mean?"

"Why *my* kid?" Trevor asked. "Why not some other kid? Jesus, Markie can't be the only six-year-old boy on all of Catalina Island . . ."

"It's like I told your friend Cusimano," Alex said, nodding over his shoulder toward Brad. "Markie, with his imagination . . ."

Alex paused for a moment, thinking. Trevor

glanced over and saw that the librarian was looking out the windshield at the road ahead of them.

"When it came time for the shaman to take on an apprentice, so that there would be someone to replace him, he would always pick one particular boy who had special qualities," Alex went on. "Intelligence, spirituality . . . maybe some latent psychic power, I don't know for sure. But the shaman could always sense the special one. That was the one to whom he passed on his magic . . ."

Alex turned back to Trevor. "In a weird way, I guess you could call it an honor," Alex said. "Markie . . . he's a special kid."

The two men fell into silence again. Alex turned to watch the road once more, and Trevor returned his attention to his driving, working over in his mind what the other man had just said.

Thinking of his son distracted him, and Trevor had to spin the steering wheel to avoid a hole. He accelerated to climb a slight rise. He braked the Jeep to a halt when they came to the top of the rise.

They had reached the crest of a ridge overlooking a wide expanse of open beach. Trevor recognized the place instantly, though he had never been there before in his life. He had an unsettlingly strong feeling of *déjà vu*.

"This is it," Alex whispered. Trevor wasn't sure if Alex had spoken the words aloud or if they had only been in his mind.

There was a cleared space for vehicle parking at the base of the ridge, around which had been set several picnic tables. The ridge curved to the right, rising to a spot a good forty feet above the beach to a cliff, upon which rested a stone house. Trevor guessed that the house afforded a magnificent view on a beautiful day, but today the sky was a solid sheet of rain clouds, the ocean beneath the clouds several shades darker. The entire scene seemed to be bleached of color, devoid of life.

Trevor drove forward, sliding down the ridge toward the parking area. Once there, he swung the Jeep around so that its headlights pointed toward the crashing surf a hundred and fifty yards away. He shifted the vehicle into neutral and set the emergency brake, but left the engine running.

Alex picked up the shovel and the canvas bag and handed them to Trevor. Then he reached for the shotgun, which he had reloaded. The two men climbed out of the Jeep and started toward the beach.

They trudged along slowly in the wet sand, each step demanding an exhausting effort. Both men were bruised and aching and drenched to the skin, and Trevor could hear the overweight librarian beside him puffing heavily, out of breath.

They had taken a hundred paces—which had felt more like a hundred thousand—when suddenly both of them froze in their tracks. Trevor and Alex had felt the same chilling sensation at the same instant. Alex Doyle turned to the man beside him, and Trevor could see that beneath the flush of exertion the librarian's face had paled.

"It's here," Alex croaked.

They were startled by a vicious cry from overhead. They looked up to see a black winged shape circling high above them.

The bird cried out again.

Trevor set down the canvas bag, grabbed the shovel with both hands, and began to dig.

He worked quickly, oblivious to his body's pain. Occasionally Trevor paused to draw in a deep breath, ignoring the aching in his chest. He took one hand off the shovel and pushed back the damp hair from his forehead.

Trevor hoisted the shovel again and jammed it into the sand. Before long, he was standing up to his waist in the small pit that he had dug, forty yards up from where the gray waves crashed onto the shore. Beside the pit Alex Doyle silently watched Trevor, the shotgun clutched tight against him, as if the weapon would help him stay warm.

Trevor thought, What if it's not here? What if Doyle is wrong again, like he was wrong about Markie? What if all of this is for nothing?

His shovel struck something hard.

Trevor set the shovel aside, then bent down to use his fingers to brush away the wet sand that covered what he had found. Alex Doyle moved up to the edge of the pit, peered down, and whispered, "Christ."

Trevor had uncovered a human skull.

He stared at it for a moment, then reached down to touch the thing in the sand. Trevor's fingers brushed against the pitted, grainy surface of discolored bone.

And at the instant that his flesh made contact with the skull of the Brujo, Trevor *saw*.

The images kaleidoscoped in Trevor's mind. He was everywhere and nowhere.

He saw.

Trevor stood on a great dark plain. Before him was his son. Markie was struggling with a creature that was half man and half bird, a thing made of shadow. Another figure, that of a woman, lay nearby. She was whimpering in pain, could only watch helplessly as the nightmare-thing smothered Markie. Trevor could hear his son calling to him: "I'm trying, Dad . . . I'm trying . . ."

At the same time, Trevor was outside, floating above the streets of Avalon.

He saw.

It was as if he were looking at photographic negatives of the scene that was playing beneath him. All of the colors were reversed, and they shimmered surrealistically. Trevor saw hordes of beasts—dogs and birds and reptiles and insects—all of them savagely attacking the groups of men who had left their hiding place in the Casino. The men were fighting the beasts as best they could, shooting many of them, but the animals were too powerful and too numerous. Soon the animals would be inside . . .

"Let *go*!" Alex cried.

Alex reached down and jerked Trevor's hand from the skull, as if he were pulling him free of a live wire. Alex looked into Trevor's face and had to fight back an urge to scream.

Trevor's expression was insanely calm. His eyes were glowing yellow.

"I'm trying, Dad," Trevor said in a voice that was not his own, though it was one that Alex Doyle recognized. Markie Baldwin's voice.

Alex grabbed Trevor roughly by the shoulders and shoved him away from the skull. Trevor slammed against the side of the pit, and the jolt seemed to bring him out of his trance. Trevor shook himself and looked up at Alex Doyle, who was crouching beside the edge of the pit.

"Okay . . ." Trevor managed to grunt. "I'm okay . . ."

Alex hoped that he sounded calm. "I need you," he said.

"I saw Markie," Trevor told Alex. "He's fighting the Brujo. Grace was with him—"

Alex interrupted: "Grace . . . ?"

Trevor said, "Markie's the one who's been keeping it away from us—"

Alex cut him off: "Then let's get going."

The librarian helped Trevor boost himself out of the pit. Alex handed Trevor the canvas bag, then rolled himself into the pit. The librarian picked up the shovel and quickly dug the skeleton of the Brujo from the sand, taking care never to touch the ancient bones. Trevor held the bag open as Alex shoveled in the Brujo's remains.

Once the bag was filled, Trevor tied it shut. He helped Doyle climb from the pit, and the two of them trotted back to the Jeep.

BRUJO

Brad Cusimano was still unconscious when they got there. Alex clambered into the passenger seat and reached around to set the canvas bag in the back beside Brad. Trevor slid into the driver's seat, dropped the Jeep into gear, and they rolled away.

As he drove, Trevor tried to keep from thinking about the grisly contents of the bag that lay on the floor beneath Alex Doyle's seat, tried to keep from replaying the memory of what he had seen when he touched the skull of the Brujo.

Trevor forced himself to concentrate on what Alex was telling him about what they were going to do. Once they got to Brad's property, Alex would perform the *keruk* ceremony to release the Brujo's spirit. The ceremony required that they burn various goods belonging to the person who had died. Alex hoped that the relics he had stolen from the Casino's museum would do. There was also an incantation which was written down in Alex's papers and which had to be said over the remains of the dead.

Behind him, Trevor could hear Brad Cusimano moaning. He peered at him in the rearview mirror. It looked to Trevor as if Brad were in the throes of a bad dream, almost as if he were trying to pull himself away from the canvas bag that lay near him.

Trevor thought, A bad dream . . .

Alex picked up the bag and set it on the floor at his feet. Then he looked up at Trevor. "It won't be long now," he said. "Pretty soon it'll all be over."

"I hope to God you're right," Trevor said.

The Brujo prayed, Chinigchinich *help me* . . .

His power had suddenly fragmented, spread too thin between too many points of attack: the beasts, the men, The-Other. At that instant when he had raised himself to strike a death blow to The-Other, the Brujo had seen the sky open, had felt something *touch*, had felt the fabric of his spirit being ripped apart, and on the dream-plain had appeared yet another figure, the one whom The-Other called *Dad*. The appearance of *Dad* on the dream-plain seemed to renew The-Other's strength, and he seized the Brujo. "I'm trying, Dad," The-Other called.

But the Brujo broke free of The-Other's grasp, and he cried out to *Chinigchinich*.

There came no answer. There was only darkness.

The Brujo pleaded, *Help me*.

The-Other struck him once more, stunning him.

The Brujo heard the raven crying to him, *You must fight*.

The Brujo *reached* blindly, hoping against hope that his brothers could hear his desperate cry.

To his surprise, he could feel another spirit, one that was weak, one that he could bend to his will. He drew all of his power to him, then thrust it out at the one whom he had touched.

With all of his power, the Brujo *reached*.

Thirty

By the time the Jeep arrived at the condominium property, twenty minutes after the men had left Ben Weston Beach, the rain was coming down around them in sheets. A flash of lightning lit up the sky.

Trevor parked the Jeep and switched off the engine. Alex reached behind him to grab the gasoline can and a long, thin plastic tube, both of which he handed to Trevor. "I hope you know how to do this," Alex said. "We don't need much—less than half a can will do."

Trevor took the gasoline can and the plastic

William Relling Jr.

tube from Alex without a word, then stepped out of the Jeep. The rain was falling very hard. Trevor heard a distant clap of thunder.

He walked to the Jeep's gas tank and set the can on the ground beneath it. Then he unscrewed the cap, dipped the tube into the tank, and squatted down next to the can. Trevor sucked on the end of the tube until he drew foul-tasting gasoline into his mouth. He spat out the gas, then jabbed the tube into the spout of the gasoline can.

It took less than three minutes to fill the can halfway. Trevor pulled the tube from the tank and drained the last of the gasoline from the tube into the can, then replaced the gas cap.

Alex was waiting for him in front of the Jeep. The librarian held his folder, the canvas bag of bones, and a handful of flares. Trevor grabbed the shovel that Alex had set on the hood of the Jeep, and the two men stepped forward, walking toward the hills that rimmed the tiny piece of open land.

At the base of a rise, Alex instructed Trevor to find some rocks they could use to build a small bier for the remains of the Brujo. While Trevor gathered the chunks of stone, he could sense that his link with Markie—the link that had been formed by the spirit of the Brujo—was still there. In his mind Trevor imagined that he could see his son in the clutches of the shadow-thing—but Trevor also noted that his appearance in the other world had seemed to renew Markie's strength.

Trevor whispered aloud, "I'm here, Mark," and prayed that the boy could hear him.

Brujo

He returned to Alex Doyle to find that the librarian had dug a small hole in the rocky earth. Trevor piled up the stones he had found as Alex emptied much of what he had brought into the hole: the pipe and carvings and bits of pottery that he had taken from the museum. He picked up the pipe and held it as an offering to the dark sky as he uttered, "My gift. For you."

Alex took the can of gasoline and poured it into the hole, soaking the stuff he had tossed in there. He looked up at Trevor, then over to the canvas bag. Trevor hesitated for a moment, then reached over and picked up the bag and set it atop the pile of stones. He nodded to Alex Doyle, then backed away.

Alex reached into his jacket and pulled out one of the flares that he had brought with him. He knelt before the hole he had dug. The folder, wrapped in plastic, lay before him, spattered by the driving rain.

Alex struck the flare and tossed it into the hole.

There was a flash of fire, and Trevor instinctively took another step back. Alex quickly picked up the folder from the ground, unwrapped the plastic, and pulled out a sheaf of papers. He began to chant.

The wind grew fiercer, rising in pitch to a howl, bending the flames in the small hole. And from behind him Trevor could hear something else that chilled him, an inhuman voice. Screaming.

He turned around.

Trevor saw Brad Cusimano lurching from the

Jeep toward Alex Doyle, arms thrust forward, wailing in rage and agony. Brad's face was twisted into a mask of insane hatred. His eyes were glittering yellow, light dancing within them like the flames of the fire. Brad was screaming unintelligibly, though words seemed to form themselves in Trevor's mind: "My land . . . my land . . ."

Trevor thought to himself: The Brujo.

He cried out, raising his voice above the roar of the wind: "Brad! *No!!!*"

He leaped across the flaming pit just as Brad lunged at Alex Doyle. Trevor knocked Brad away, and the two of them crashed to the ground. They grappled on the slick, rocky earth, and Trevor hooked his arms around Brad, holding him as Brad struggled to pull himself free.

Trevor could hear Alex Doyle shouting, "Don't let him go!"

Brad flipped onto his back, pinning Trevor's arms beneath him. For a moment, both men were frozen in position. Trevor looked down into Brad's face, saw Brad's mouth bent in a hideous, repugnant grimace, saw Brad's shining yellow eyes glaring at him with sheer loathing. Their eyes locked, and Brad hissed.

Trevor Baldwin's vision returned.

Trevor was once more on the dark plain, locked in struggle with the shadow-thing, keeping it away from his son who lay unmoving on the black ground nearby.

Trevor felt his heart sink.

Then the thing was screaming at him, trying to

tear itself free of his grasp. Trevor held on to the thing as tightly as he could. He turned to look at his son and saw Markie's small chest heaving slightly. He cried out, "Mark, I'm here!"

The shadow-thing turned to look at Trevor with golden eyes.

Then it skrreeeked at Trevor, and with a sudden, violent twist, it jerked itself free of him momentarily. Before Trevor could react, the thing raked his back viciously with its claws, shredding his flesh. Trevor howled in pain, but managed to seize the creature once more, in spite of the fiery agony the thing's claws had inflicted.

Trevor forced himself to hold on with all of his strength, but he could feel himself weakening. He cried out, almost without thinking, "Help me."

And he heard a voice calling to him, from not far away, "I'm here!"

Trevor looked up and saw the other figure, the spirit manifestation of Grace Mitchum that he had seen before, coming toward them from the edge of the dark plain. Trevor watched as she gently lifted the boy in her arms. She carried Markie away, and Trevor saw the boy open his eyes and smile at her.

Suddenly Trevor heard another voice, a disembodied voice, singing:

> *"There above, there above*
> *Above shall go*
> *The spirit to the sun*
> *Long ago I wept for them*
> *But now I weep for you"*

The shadow-thing heard the song, and it began to cry.

Trevor let go, and the shadow-thing slumped to the ground.

Trevor moved away slowly to join the woman and the boy she was holding. The three of them watched as the shadow-thing raised its own voice to cry along with the song that repeated itself, over and over. Trevor stood with his son and the woman who held him. Markie reached out to take his father's hand.

The three of them stood on the dark plain, listening to the song and the voice of the shadow-creature. They listened for a hundred years.

The shadow-thing lifted itself into the air, rising higher and higher over the dark dream-plain, beating its great, black wings. All the while it cried out its pain, its fear, its loneliness . . .

Then there was a sun-bright burst of lightning and a deafening crack of thunder, and the shadow-creature burst into a ball of living flame.

And all at once Trevor was back in his own reality, back on the sacred land, holding Brad Cusimano in his arms. He could hear Alex Doyle singing above the whine of the wind.

And the earth exploded.

From the mound of rocks on which lay the remains of the Brujo there shot a pillar of orange fire, hurling the stones high into the air. The force of the blast knocked Trevor and Brad to the ground, and the incredible brightness of the explosion forced Trevor to shut his eyes tightly. His ears rang from

BRUJO

the sound of the blast, but he could also hear the voice that he had heard in his vision. The voice of the shadow-being.

The voice of the Brujo.

The voice sang to the heavens, a tremendous cry of release, of relief, of peace: Chinigchinich, *I come.*

Then it was gone.

Trevor lay on his side on the wet ground for a long time, afraid to move, dimly aware of the patter of rain as it fell on and around him. He felt cold. He heard a distant clap of thunder.

He opened his eyes.

Brad Cusimano lay beside him, eyes closed, his face scratched and bleeding, flecked with mud. Trevor pulled himself up painfully, feeling the burning of the skin on his back, then lifted Brad's head, resting it in his lap.

Brad's eyes blinked open, then he winced. It took him a few seconds to focus on the man cradling him and he croaked, "Trev . . . ?"

"Don't talk, buddy, okay?" Trevor said softly. "You'll be all right."

Brad nodded and closed his eyes once more.

A voice called to Trevor, "Is he okay?"

Trevor looked up.

There, a few yards away from him, was Alex Doyle. Alex was still kneeling before the small, charred hole in the earth. The fire in the pit had gone out.

Alex's portly face was blackened with soot that

had been smeared by droplets of rain, but beneath the grime was an expression of concern. Trevor said, "We've got to get him back to town—"

He was startled by a *skwaaaaaak* from above, and Trevor's heart leaped in his chest. From nowhere, a huge black raven suddenly appeared, landing on the ground near Alex.

The librarian turned to look at the bird, and it stared back at him curiously, for a long time.

Then, with another *skwaaaak*, the raven flew away.

Trevor eased Brad gently to the ground, then slowly rose to his knees. Alex crouched on Brad's other side, ready to help Trevor carry his injured friend back to the Jeep.

They paused, looking at each other.

Both knew what had happened, though neither of them could have put what they were feeling into words. The vision was gone. The shadow-thing was gone as well. It was over.

There was only the rain.

Trevor Baldwin smiled, because the rain felt very, very good.

Thirty-one

Late Sunday afternoon, Trevor and Markie Baldwin were taken back to the mainland aboard a Coast Guard cruiser. Brad Cusimano had been brought back a few hours earlier, via jet helicopter, to a hospital. Before Trevor and Markie left the island, Trevor learned that though Brad had lost a great deal of blood, he would arrive at the hospital in time to save his leg.

While on the Coast Guard cruiser, Trevor recalled how odd it had felt to return to Avalon and find Markie safe with Grace Mitchum. By the time he and Alex and Brad had gotten back to the city, a rescue ship had made a successful, uneventful crossing to Catalina, and the authorities were already supervising the safe exodus of the people who had hidden inside the Casino. Some of the rescuers and the Avalon policemen were shooting the dogs and cats and birds that seemed to be wandering aimlessly around Avalon. Trevor thought this was cruel and unnecessary, since the animals no longer seemed inclined to attack.

Markie remembered nothing of what had happened to him after leaving the airport Saturday afternoon and being frightened by the storm. While Markie spoke to him, Trevor looked into the boy's eyes to see if he could tell whether Markie was hiding something, keeping something inside. But Markie was sincere. He had no memory of anything that had happened until the moment when Grace Mitchum had led him from the dark storeroom.

Trevor had been questioned by the authorities. He gave them no explanations, just told them to ask Alex Doyle. After some deliberation, they decided to let Trevor go, though they informed him that he would very likely be called back to testify at an official inquiry into the weird events of the past three days.

Father and son didn't reach Trevor's house until well past dark. Trevor unlocked the gate, and Burt, the dog, came running up to them, barking happily. Trevor backed away from Burt, momentarily frightened, until Markie reached out to hug the animal. Then Trevor rubbed Burt's head and shut the gate behind them.

Markie was very sleepy, and Trevor put him straight to bed. He tucked the boy in and promised to return to look in on Markie before he himself went to bed.

Trevor left Markie's bedroom and went into another part of his house to use the telephone. He called the hospital to ask about Brad and was told that he could have visitors as early as the next day. Then Trevor called his ex-wife, who had been waiting anxiously to hear from him. Claudia had been listening to news reports of the terrible things that had happened on Catalina Island, and she had been worried about both him and Markie. We're fine, Trevor told her. I'll bring Markie home tomorrow.

Then he hung up the phone and sat quietly, thinking.

He sat for some time.

Then Trevor got up and switched off the lights in the house. He checked on Markie once more, then went to bed.

He had been lying in the dark for a few minutes when he heard his bedroom door opening. Trevor waited, not speaking. Then he heard Markie's voice ask, "Is it okay if I sleep in here, Dad?"

"Sure, sport," Trevor answered.

The boy crawled into bed next to his father, pressing himself into Trevor's side. Trevor put his arm around him.

It wasn't long before Trevor could feel Markie breathing deeply and regularly. He closed his eyes and soon, like his son, Trevor was fast asleep.

They slept, and they dreamed no dreams.

THE BEST IN HORROR

☐ 58270-5	WILDWOOD by John Farris		$4.50
58271-3		Canada	$5.95
☐ 52760-7	THE WAITING ROOM		$3.95
52761-5	by T. M. Wright	Canada	$4.95
☐ 51762-8	MASTERS OF DARKNESS edited		3.95
51763-6	by Dennis Etchinson	Canada	$4.95
☐ 52623-6	BLOOD HERITAGE		$3.50
52624-4	by Sheri S. Tepper	Canada	$4.50
☐ 50070-9	THE NIGHT OF THE RIPPER		$3.50
50071-7	by Robert Bloch	Canada	$4.50
☐ 52558-2	TOTENTANZ by Al Sarrantonio		$3.50
52559-0		Canada	$4.50
☐ 58226-8	WHEN DARKNESS LOVES US		$3.50
58227-6	by Elizabeth Engstrom	Canada	$4.50
☐ 51656-7	OBSESSION by Ramsey Campbell		$3.95
51657-5		Canada	$4.95
☐ 51850-0	MIDNIGHT edited by		$2.95
51851-9	Charles L. Grant	Canada	$3.50
☐ 52445-4	KACHINA by Kathryn Ptacek		$3.95
52446-2		Canada	$4.95
☐ 52541-8	DEAD WHITE by Alan Ryan		$3.50
52542-6		Canada	$3.95

Buy them at your local bookstore or use this handy coupon:
Clip and mail this page with your order

TOR BOOKS—Reader Service Dept.
49 W. 24 Street, 9th Floor, New York, NY 10010

Please send me the book(s) I have checked above. I am enclosing $_____ (please add $1.00 to cover postage and handling). Send check or money order only—no cash or C.O.D.'s.

Mr./Mrs./Miss _____
Address _____
City _____ State/Zip _____

Please allow six weeks for delivery. Prices subject to change without notice.

JOHN FARRIS

"America's premier novelist of terror. When he turns it on, nobody does it better." —Stephen King

"Farris is a giant of contemporary horror!"
—Peter Straub

☐	58264-0	ALL HEADS TURN WHEN	$3.50
	58265-9	THE HUNT GOES BY	Canada $4.50
☐	58260-8	THE CAPTORS	$3.50
	58261-6		Canada $3.95
☐	58262-4	THE FURY	$3.50
	58263-2		Canada $4.50
☐	58258-6	MINOTAUR	$3.95
	58259-4		Canada $4.95
☐	58266-7	SON OF THE ENDLESS NIGHT	$4.50
	58267-5		Canada $5.50
☐	58268-3	SHATTER	$3.50
	58269-1		Canada $4.50
☐	58270-5	WILDWOOD	$4.50
	58271-3		Canada $5.95

AVAILABLE IN JANUARY
☐	58272-1	CATACOMBS	$3.95
	58273-X		Canada $4.95

Buy them at your local bookstore or use this handy coupon:
Clip and mail this page with your order

TOR BOOKS—Reader Service Dept.
49 West 24 Street, 9th Floor, New York, N.Y. 10010

Please send me the book(s) I have checked above. I am enclosing $_____ (please add $1.00 to cover postage and handling). Send check or money order only—no cash or C.O.D.'s.

Mr./Mrs./Miss _____
Address _____
City _____ State/Zip _____
Please allow six weeks for delivery. Prices subject to change without notice.

Ramsey Campbell

☐ 51652-4	DARK COMPANIONS		$3.50
51653-2		Canada	$3.95
☐ 51654-0	THE DOLL WHO ATE HIS		$3.50
51655-9	MOTHER	Canada	$3.95
☐ 51658-3	THE FACE THAT MUST DIE		$3.95
51659-1		Canada	$4.95
☐ 51650-8	INCARNATE		$3.95
51651-6		Canada	$4.50
☐ 58125-3	THE NAMELESS		$3.50
58126-1		Canada	$3.95
☐ 51656-7	OBSESSION		$3.95
51657-5		Canada	$4.95

Buy them at your local bookstore or use this handy coupon:
Clip and mail this page with your order

TOR BOOKS—Reader Service Dept.
49 W. 24 Street, 9th Floor, New York, NY 10010

Please send me the book(s) I have checked above. I am enclosing
$_____ (please add $1.00 to cover postage and handling).
Send check or money order only—no cash or C.O.D.'s.

Mr./Mrs./Miss _____
Address _____
City _____ State/Zip _____
Please allow six weeks for delivery. Prices subject to change without notice.

GRAHAM MASTERTON

- [ ] 52195-1 CONDOR $3.50
  52196-X Canada $3.95

- [ ] 52191-9 IKON $3.95
  52192-7 Canada $4.50

- [ ] 52193-5 THE PARIAH $3.50
  52194-3 Canada $3.95

- [ ] 52189-7 SOLITAIRE $3.95
  52190-0 Canada $4.50

- [ ] 48067-9 THE SPHINX $2.95

- [ ] 48061-X TENGU $3.50

- [ ] 48042-3 THE WELLS OF HELL $2.95

- [ ] 52199-4 PICTURE OF EVIL $3.95
  52200-1 Canada $4.95

Buy them at your local bookstore or use this handy coupon:
Clip and mail this page with your order

TOR BOOKS—Reader Service Dept.
49 W. 24 Street, 9th Floor, New York, NY 10010

Please send me the book(s) I have checked above. I am enclosing $_____ (please add $1.00 to cover postage and handling). Send check or money order only—no cash or C.O.D.'s.

Mr./Mrs./Miss _____
Address _____
City _____ State/Zip _____
Please allow six weeks for delivery. Prices subject to change without notice.